CW00543750

The Dead Bed

Robert Edsall

Published by Clifftop Publishing, 2022.

This is a work of fiction. Similarities to real people, places, or events are entirely coincidental.

THE DEAD BED

First edition. November 23, 2022.

Copyright © 2022 Robert Edsall.

ISBN: 979-8215273173

Written by Robert Edsall.

For Robinson,

and all my good teachers.

Thanks to the Book Club: Wendy Robinson, Lisa Jansz, Krista Simon, Thorin Beowulf, and to those who kindly read earlier versions of this story. Thanks also Dennis Leung, Gina Flaxman, and Michael in the Clare Hotel.

IN THE BEGINNING. ANNIE.

H*e was surprised when he saw her.*
    He'd grabbed a sandwich for a late lunch and recognised her as she approached along the busy footpath. She'd put on a little weight – who hadn't? – but she carried it well and was prettier for it.

Maybe she noticed him looking at her. As they were alongside one another she stopped and said his name out loud as a question.

'Annie?' he said hers back, and they both grinned and nodded.

What were the chances of this in a big city? They hadn't seen each other since uni.

She said now wasn't the right time, but she'd love to catch up.

'Really?' he asked, before he could stop himself. They were never friends at university. She was a bit up herself, he always thought. 'Of course! That'd be great.'

She typed his number into her phone. An old phone, he noticed. He wondered what she was up to these days.

He was about to find out.

EIGHTY PERCENT OFF!

P atrick opened the cardboard box of Christmas decorations. He lifted a tube of silver balls from the box, light as a feather, and gave it a shake. He was hoping for jingle bells but got nothing.

He had bought all this festivity a year ago in the New Year sales. Eighty percent off! He had missed last Christmas in the shambles of Claire leaving him. Or had he left her? She was still in the house in Balmain, so he had left her.

Today was her birthday. The family joke at her birthday parties was that she was born a month before Jesus. November twenty-fifth.

Way back in that life, their Christmas decorations had been handmade and smelled like home. Their curly-haired son, Ben, had sat on the floor mending things, refusing to throw stuff away. The more mangled the angel, the more marvellous it was.

Patrick's phone rang loud as a party. He'd tried filling his rented terrace house with music but it only half worked. It didn't get rid of the emptiness. He guessed the call would be an editor reminding him of a deadline on a piece for the summer section of the *Sydney Morning Herald*. No number appeared on the screen.

'Hello,' he said. There was a slight delay and instinct let him know the caller was Ben. It was the first time he'd heard from him in ages.

'It's Mum's birthday,' Ben said.

'Hi Ben! Thanks for calling. Great to hear from you! Yes, happy birthday, Mum! Well done for remembering. Where are you?' It was too much, too fast, Patrick knew, but Ben ignored it all anyway.

'Are we going out for dinner?'

'Who?'

'You and me and Mum.'

'Remember that I'm not with Mum anymore?'

'That's alright.'

'It's not alright. It makes me sad. I miss you all. Where are you calling from?'

'My phone.' Ben chuckled weirdly at his joke.

He had a phone. That was good. He often lost them or had them stolen. He knew what day it was too. Mum's birthday.

'Are you in Sydney?' Silence. Getting a straight answer out of Ben was like charades.

'Yeah.'

'*We* can go out for dinner. Just you and me. My shout.'

He grunted. 'What about Annie?'

'Annie who? You want to bring someone?!' This was a nice surprise.

'Yeah, but she's dead. That's what I want to ask you about.'

Patrick was jolted but he'd been jolted before, many times. Experience kicked in without thinking. All those books on schizophrenia, doctors and family counselling sessions.

'She's probably not real, Ben,' he said as calmly as he could. Silence. He knew Ben would be trying to sort out what might be real. 'Hallucinations, remember,' Patrick said. He had no idea what state Ben was in, whether he was on or off his medication, but he sounded calm. And strange.

'Hell,' Ben said. 'Lucinations.'

Patrick smiled. They used to play these mad word games all the time. When Ben had left home, he had taken his precious dictionary but left behind most of his clothes. Patrick loved his boy. His mangled angel.

'Are you with Annie now, Ben?'

'Yeah.'

'Is she OK now?'

'Well. No, obviously.'

'Why is that obvious to you?'

'Yeah, well she hasn't drunk her tea and she's dead and she's got a dart in her arm.'

An overdose. Since his illness was diagnosed Ben had been both a drug user and a ranting puritan, depending on the moon or his medication. It was the 'magical mystery tour'. It was all or nothing. Patrick – and Claire – were either treading quicksand trying to manage Ben's problems or else had no idea where he was, or how he was. Patrick no longer knew which was worse.

Now Ben was back with a bang.

'Ben, we'll sort it out,' Patrick said, hoping it was true. 'Where are you?'

'Yeah, it's where we live.'

'You live with Annie?' Silence. 'In a house or...' or a halfway house, or a ward, locked or unlocked, he'd been in them all, lost and found like a ball.

'Yeah, no, a white house. There's a brick in the front yard.' Ben coughed loudly into the phone and kept coughing. He didn't sound good.

When he finished, Patrick asked, 'What's the address?'

'Forest Street, Forest Lodge. That's how I remember it. Not *Farest* Street. That would be too far away. You wouldn't live there!' He chuckled again.

Patrick was stunned. He also lived in Forest Lodge. They might have bumped into each other in the street or the library!

'What's the number?'

'One oh two. There's a brick in the front yard.'

Patrick wrote numbers on the flap of the Christmas box and drew a brick.

'A white house, you said?'

'Yeah.'

'I'm going to come there, Ben, and I'll be there in ten minutes. Really soon. OK? You stay there.'

'Yeah. Should I phone Mum and wish her happy birthday?'

'No, don't phone Mum! And don't touch Annie. Wait until I get there, OK? Don't phone Mum. OK?'

'OK.'

'Actually, what's your phone number? It didn't come up when you called.'

Patrick wrote the number on his cardboard Christmas box.

'I love you, Ben. Thanks for calling me. Stay put. I'll be there very soon.'

Here we go again. He felt his pockets for keys. Felt his head for a brain. He remembered to type Ben's number into his phone. It didn't sound like Ben was on his medication but he didn't sound paranoid either. Just stressed. A conga line of GPs and specialists had treated him since he had undressed and walked out of his final school exam without writing a word. That was two years ago. It felt like a decade.

• • • •

He was at Ben's place within minutes. Most of the street was renovated but 102 was a dumpy single-storey white terrace with a rusting iron roof. There *was* a brick in the bare front yard. A wheelie bin lay on its side next to the front door like a shot animal.

He knocked on the door and took a deep breath. It was early afternoon with the sun shining. Just another day.

The thump of footsteps inside the house. The door opened and there was Ben. Sort of. The curly hair was gone and the blonde sheen of a crew cut made him look skeletal. His green eyes bulged. He was wearing a brown T-shirt with 'Carnival' written on it and faded denim jeans that almost slid off his hips. Dirty bare feet.

'Hello, Ben!' Patrick said and spread his arms for a hug.

'Yeah, I don't do hugs any more,' he said dismissively. 'I'm allergic to the twenty-first century, you know.'

'Actually, I didn't know that,' Patrick admitted, dropping his hands to his sides. 'And anyway, you're safe with me because I'm from the twentieth century.'

'Is Mum here?' he asked.

'Nope.'

Ben's bones blocked the door space. He shared Patrick's lanky build.

'Can I come in?' He didn't mention Annie in case she was just a thing. Like Mum not being here. Like the family in bits.

'Yeah,' Ben said, turning back into the first room off the hallway.

Patrick followed with a sense of dread. The room smelled bad. There was Annie, naked on her back on a double bed, the sheet carelessly down around her waist. Her skin had begun to mottle against the mattress. This was all real, and surreal. He looked across at Ben, who shoved his hands into his pockets and stared down at Annie with big eyes like he was staring into a bonfire. Annie was in her late twenties, pretty and pale, short hair. Dead.

There was a red dart – a dartboard dart not a syringe – askew from a bruise in the joint of her left arm. A bullseye in a small stain of blood.

'Can you shut the front door, Ben?' he said.

It felt like the world could just walk in and that felt wrong. Everything felt wrong. Ben shuffled away and Patrick looked around the dismal room. There was a dartboard on the wall, a half-filled bookcase by the sash window, an orange beanbag, a mug of tea on the floor and clothes strewn about. A plastic milk crate held a few vinyl records.

Annie lay with her palms turned up like a drowned Ophelia. It was like someone had arranged her.

Ben reappeared. 'Yeah, she's dead, hey?'

'She is, Ben. She is.' He wanted to put his arms around Ben and walk him out of the room and out of this life. It wasn't the first time he'd wanted to do this.

'I made her a cup of tea,' Ben said and nodded towards a blue mug. The milk was scum on top now. Everything suggested she had been like this for hours.

'We have to call the police,' Patrick said.

'No way!' Ben broke his own rule and hugged himself. 'She's so still. She's like a plant.'

He was beginning to sound psychotic. Little wonder.

Likely to cause harm to self or others was the clause cops and carers used to coerce and manage the mentally ill, often with force. 'The police force' Ben called it. Word nerd. Smart arse. Living on the streets, Ben had been on the wrong end of this force. Patrick knew some of the history but, like everything with Ben, there were gaps and loops and wrong turns.

'Is Annie your girlfriend?'

'Yeah. Not now. Nothing's very good. That's what I wanted to ask you about. What do we do?'

It was a good question and Patrick had no answer. He hadn't seen Ben in months and didn't want to confront him straight away with the police.

Gently. 'Ben, do you know what happened to her? Do you know why she's dead?'

'Yeah. No,' Ben said, and shook his head. His bulging eyes stared down at her.

'When did you find her like this?'

'When we woke up.'

'This is your bed? Together?'

Ben nodded.

'So, you went to bed together last night and when you woke up, she was like this?'

'I think so but that doesn't make sense, does it?' He stared at Patrick now. 'Does it?'

Patrick had seen this look before. Help me. Save me. Nail me down. 'Well. Do you know how the dart got into her arm?'

'No.'

'Think hard. Did you put it in there? Maybe you thought it was some kind of medicine to make her better. To make her breathe again.'

'Maybe.'

'Maybe.' Patrick sighed and ached all over.

'Maybe she did it herself,' Ben said simply.

He was right! Maybe she did. He felt relief wash over him for discovering an option that didn't accuse Ben. Maybe Annie was a user, delusional, maybe *she* thought it was medicine or drugs she was administering.

But a dart wouldn't *kill* her.

'Does anyone else live here?'

'Yeah, Mick.'

He felt more relief.

'Where's Mick now?'

'Work. He works. He wrecks things.'

'What do you mean?'

'He smashes things up with a hammer.' Ben flailed his arms around in imitation like a mad marionette.

Let Mick find Annie when he gets home from work, Patrick decided. *He* could call the police.

'I think we should get out of here, hey? Let's go back to my place where we can think straight.'

'Cool.'

Cool? For fuck's sake.

'Don't touch anything, Ben.' Though he lived and slept here. Ben nodded. 'Do you need to grab anything? Have you got your medication?' Ben left the room and stomped down the hall. 'Shoes! Please get some shoes,' he called after him. Ben reappeared with a canvas bag slung over his shoulder and a pair of battered runners dangling from his fingers.

When he pulled the front door closed behind them it made a hollow sound.

'Have you got your keys?' Patrick asked, too late.

'To the kingdom. To the kingdom,' Ben replied. 'Have you got any marijuana at your place?'

· · · ·

B ack at Patrick's place they walked through to the sunroom. 'I was going to decorate the tree,' he said, nodding at the cardboard box spilling decorations onto the table. Ben looked around the room. 'I haven't got a tree,' Patrick confessed.

'Well, Christmas is crap anyway.'

'That's the spirit,' he said. 'Would you like a juice?'

'Yeah.'

'Take a seat.'

There was a red leather couch under the window and Ben slumped down on it. Patrick had bought the couch second-hand from a lesbian couple in Newtown when he had moved in a year ago. After they had delivered it, they had all sat drinking tequila on it until midnight. It was typical of his coincidental, new single life. His actual life.

When he returned with the juice Ben was already snoring softly. His legs took up half the room. He was a good sleeper, particularly on medication. Sleep would do him good, before the trauma of what happened next. Police. Interviews. Sadness.

Patrick breathed for what felt like the first time since he had gotten the call.

He drank the juice and looked at Ben. He had pink cheeks. He didn't look unwell even though he was skin and bone. The afternoon sun revealed a wispy blond beard. He always was a good-looking boy. He and Claire each claimed credit.

Claire.

He grabbed his phone, then hesitated. He knew he should call her. He wanted to. But unless he was two steps ahead of her, he would soon be five steps behind. *And* it was her birthday. She would be going out with Fuckface or whatever his name was. He decided to let Ben get some sleep and *then* get her involved. She'd know what to do, of course.

He texted Claire instead: *Happy birthday!* Then he opened a bottle of shiraz. He needed to drink a little and think a lot. He texted her again: *Ben also wishes you happy birthday.*

That would get her attention, so he turned his phone off, and thought while Ben snored.

C laire played tennis on Thursday afternoons and usually won. She had met Denise through Philip, her new man. It was strange for Claire – new people, new restaurants, tennis again after years. Denise had three kids and her husband's trucking business was making them rich. Philip was their accountant.

They played for an hour. Six-three, two-six, six-four. Claire won. They were sitting in front of the weatherboard clubrooms. Two council workers mowed the surrounding park, ear muffs over shaggy blond hair. The air smelled of cut grass.

Both women swigged from plastic water bottles and cooled down.

'Can I ask you something personal?' Denise asked. They were friends but not best friends, by a long shot. 'You don't have to answer if you don't want to.'

'It's OK,' Claire said.

'When you broke up with your husband, was one of you having an affair?'

This was new. They had talked about work, house prices, but never the grunt of things. She decided to see where it led.

'We weren't having affairs.' She waited on Denise. They both drank water. The lawnmowers buzzed. 'Are you asking because you're wondering about me or wondering about you?' Claire asked.

Denise looked into the distance. She was pretty in a bland way, her brown hair tied back in a ponytail for tennis, big eyes, perfect teeth that Claire guessed were bought some time later in life, after the trucks started paying.

'You and I can talk, right?' Denise said, fixing Claire in a stare.

'We can talk.'

'I've met someone,' Denise said. 'I can't even believe it when I hear myself say that. I'm married to Andy. We've got three kids! I'm me. I don't "meet someone".' She looked exhausted.

'I was the same, even though Patrick and I had separated when I met Philip. It just felt weird. Who have you met?'

'The greengrocer.'

Claire grinned and Denise laughed.

'I know it's ridiculous,' Denise said.

'I'm not saying that. Life can get *way* more ridiculous than that.'

Denise put her water bottle down and leaned her head forward into her hands.

'He's married too. It's mad.'

'Has he got kids?'

Women talking.

'No. I couldn't do that. Well! Listen to me. What about my kids? My kids don't come into it because I know I'd never do anything to hurt them. So I say.'

She rubbed Denise on the shoulder.

'I'm forty-seven! He's thirty-two. There's something wrong with his wife. They can't have kids. "The mother is everything," he says. He finds me sexy because I'm a mother! I'm some sort of Madonna, apparently.'

One of the lawnmowers stopped in the park and suddenly the world sounded mono, tinny. Denise sat upright and pulled herself together.

'Sorry. I needed to tell someone.'

'Thanks for telling me,' Claire said. They weren't best friends and never would be. Philip's was a world of different people and she often felt like a fish out of water. Or a little bit bored, if she was honest.

'I'm tempted to make a joke about fresh vegetables,' Claire said. They both laughed.

'I've shopped there for ages but suddenly it all changed. He loaded a box into my car and we smiled at each other and then it was like in the movies. We kissed.' She shook her head. 'That should have been it but next time, we made sure to kiss where no-one could see us.'

It sounded romantic and Claire pictured him, slim, unshaven, sad-eyed, good with his hands and lips.

'Maybe it's just something that you need to get out of your system. He makes you feel good, says the right things. He's young. It doesn't mean your marriage is over.'

'It makes me *feel* like my marriage is over.'

'Funny, I've never felt like my marriage is over,' Claire said. 'It just isn't happening.' Her mobile phone beeped in her bag.

'You can get that,' Denise said. 'I'm OK.'

'Don't worry.'

The other lawnmower stopped and there was a quiet lump in the conversation.

'How did you know when your marriage stopped happening, then?' Denise asked.

Claire sighed. 'Now it's my turn for a confession. We weren't having affairs, but Patrick had a "meaningless" one-night stand. He was away at some writers' weekend. Well. It wasn't meaningless to me. I was working really hard, and he wasn't, and we had the pressures of Ben being ill.'

Now Denise rubbed her shoulder.

'He was drunk, of course, and she was much younger. Bliss in the Blue Mountains.'

'Oh boy,' Denise said. 'I'm sorry, honey.'

'I called for a break – more out of anger than anything – and for both of us to decide what we wanted. Before he'd properly moved out I find out he's spent another weekend with her!' She shook her head. 'It didn't last beyond that weekend, apparently. But our separation has.'

Their sympathies had become complicated. Somehow, they weren't telling the same story any more. Claire's mobile phone beeped in her bag again.

'Get it,' Denise said, removing her ponytail scrunchy and reaching for her racquet and water bottle.

She checked the message: *Ben also wishes you happy birthday.*

She scanned up to the previous message: *Happy birthday!*

'All OK?' Denise asked.

'Yep,' she said and packed her things away too.

Back at their cars, Claire farewelled Denise to her Range Rover and her new complicated life. She phoned Patrick but got his voicemail.

'Thanks for the texts,' she said. 'Have you heard from Ben or did you make that up?'

Patrick was hopeless. In the early days she had liked his flakiness. He was her tall and dreamy other half. She was organised and he was not. She had to get to work but he wanted to stay in bed, mapping her body. She wanted that too back then.

ANNIE

They were in his car, though it felt as big as a room to her. A BMW four-wheel drive with black leather seats. The car had been his idea. She'd suggested a cafe again but he'd said he'd like a view, as if there were no cafes in Sydney with a view.

He parked in an empty car park on the cliffs facing the Pacific Ocean. There was a small fishing boat about a kilometre offshore, bobbing about on the mesmerising blue. She wondered who was on board and what their lives were like.

With no explanation, he rattled a couple of pills into his hand and silently offered them to her. She looked – Xanax, she guessed – and shook her head.

'You used to,' he said, and she smiled. His smile back was full of very white teeth. An advertisement to his customers, no doubt.

He grabbed a metal flask from between the seats and swigged the tablets down.

This was their third meeting, including her 'accidental' meeting with him on New South Head Road. In fact, she'd been watching him off and on for a week, unsure of her plan, alert to the places she might choose to go with him. Could she do it?

She hadn't asked about his family when they met in the cafe; she didn't want to know, but he had told her anyway. A wife and two little kids. He had spared her the rigmarole of opening his wallet to display a picture but she guessed the wife was blonde. She guessed they had a dog, too, but didn't ask. Probably a Labrador. Big and stupid.

She had her own back story half-true and ready to tell. Not married. Not particularly focused. She'd spent some time overseas working for aid agencies. Didn't see much of her father.

She was tossing out lost-soul bait. A life different to his. A life he might in some way long for. Tablets in a car park felt like he was on the line. They made small talk; the ocean huge before them.

15

'Everything I said about my wife and kids the other day is true,' he said suddenly, the Xanax kicking in, his head leaned back on the headrest. 'But I got married too young.'

She vaguely remembered he'd got married during uni. He supplied tablets back then too. His dad used to run a pharmacy. Now he ran it.

She put her hand on his knee. He looked down at her hand and gave her another of those big, white smiles. She moved her hand away and tucked her hair behind her ear.

'What the fuck's going on, Annie?' he asked happily. 'Because I've got a feeling this isn't friends reunited dot com.'

She said she would take one of those tablets now.

ANNIE'S MIX

Patrick drank more of the bottle of wine than he had planned. He drank all of it. He sat at the dining table in the sunroom, watching Ben sleep. It was absurdly serene given what had happened and what might happen next. Sunlight and shade flickered through the trees in the garden. Hours passed. No police arrived at his door.

He was worried about the dart in Annie's arm. He was worried about everything, but the dart was manic behaviour. Ben behaviour, when he wasn't well. He tried to think things through but found himself endlessly concocting alibis for Ben. It couldn't have been Ben. He'd negotiated his illness for years. If anyone was going to die, it was Ben.

But whatever had happened in that room, Annie was dead.

He started concocting alibis for himself. Was it a crime to leave a crime scene? Was it even a crime scene? Annie might have died of a heart attack. There was no sign of trauma. That's what he decided had happened. She had died of natural causes.

With a dartboard in her arm.

Part of him wanted to get in the car and escape with Ben and the contents of the fridge. Some getaway. He had a friend with a farm up the Putty Road.

He'd phone Claire instead. Ben needed all the support they could muster.

Eve, his shiny black cat, appeared in the sunroom with a meow and wanted to jump on Ben – new bodies were always interesting. Patrick took her food bowl out onto the small deck and fed her there. The backyard looked out over a valley filled with big old trees in a park. On the other side of the valley the spire of the Hunter-Baillee Memorial Church poked at the sky.

Ben's eyelids fluttered. His body twitched. Now and then he muttered. He was dreaming. There was a long time when Ben never dreamed. His medication zonked him out. Patrick wondered what medication he was on now, who prescribed it, where he had his prescriptions filled. He was glad that Ben was still trying to be well.

He went into the kitchen and clattered the coffee machine and put it onto the stovetop. When he went back to the sunroom, Ben hadn't moved but was wide awake.

'Oh. Hi, Ben.'

'We'd been arguing, Dad.'

Bash. Crash. 'Who had?'

'Me and Annie. She's dead, isn't she?' Patrick nodded. Ben closed his eyes. 'I'd smoked some dope out the back with Mick and she got all aggro. "It makes you crazy and it'll kill you," he said, mimicking her voice. '"What you're on, blah, blah".'

The confession was dreadful. Patrick and Claire knew from experience that dope wasn't good for Ben. So did Ben. Poor Annie.

'So, what happened next?'

'Can I have a glass of water?'

Patrick went and got it and Ben gulped it down greedily. Appetite. Hunger. Patrick realised they should eat something. 'Can I have another one, please?'

He gulped that one down too. 'We were in bed and she took some of her pills to calm down but it didn't work.'

'What kind of pills?'

'Sleeping pills, I think. She's got all kinds of pills. I wanted one too but she wouldn't give it to me.'

The coffee hissed and spat in the kitchen and Patrick went to get it. He leaned on the bench for balance. 'Milk in your coffee still?' he called out.

'Yeah.'

'I've got no sugar.'

'Two sugars!'

'Not today.' They were talking from different rooms and different lives. He took the coffees and sat next to Ben on the couch.

'Can you not sit there, please?' Ben asked. Patrick moved back to the wooden chair at the table with the box of Christmas decorations. They both sipped in silence.

'And then she kneed me in the back really hard,' Ben said. He put his coffee on the floor and stood up and lifted his T-shirt and turned his back to Patrick. 'Is there a bruise?'

There was. The colour of eggplant. None of this was a hell lucination. That made everything worse.

'Yes.'

'I knew it!' Ben dropped his T-shirt and sat back down. He picked up his coffee, cradling the mug with both hands.

'Did you fight often?'

'A bit. She hit me more than I hit her.'

He didn't want to believe that Ben would hit a woman, hit anyone, but he had seen it in their own house in Balmain as they had all adjusted to his illness and struggled to get the medication right.

'She really hurt me, and the room just kind of went wild. I thought there was fire coming out of her. I thought the house might burn down.'

'Jesus, Ben!'

'I know. I was high, Dad!' He paused. 'I put my pillow over her, but not hard. I don't think I hurt her. I just stopped her.'

'Stopped her hurting you?' Ben nodded. 'She was still breathing?'

'I think so.'

But in that state, he wouldn't know. It was late afternoon now, with the worn-out cries of currawongs in the valley. This day was ending, but where would it end? In what lost world?

'How did the dart get into her arm? When did that happen?'

Ben shook his head. 'I don't remember doing that.'

Not much of a surprise. He was high and in bed with a violent, burning girlfriend. Shit was bound to happen.

'I can see an evil clown's face up there,' Ben said.

He followed Ben's gaze up to the ceiling rose and after a while he could sort of see it too, multiplied in the pattern. 'You're lucky, because I can see six of them,' he said.

'But the meanest one's looking at me,' Ben said. He felt things, saw things, heard things that others didn't. Once in Balmain he had asked Patrick if the moon was real. Life was a constant rattling terror and joy. A ride on the ghost train.

'I think it's time we called Mum.'

'It's still her birthday, isn't it?' he asked, brightening.

'Yep. Do you want to take a shower? Or you can have a bath. It won't be long enough for you but I'm sure you'll figure it out. I'll grab you a towel.'

'I don't piss in the bath, I piss in the shower. It saves flushing the toilet.'

'Right,' Patrick said. 'I think you've probably got that the right way around.'

'If it's yellow let it mellow, if it's brown flush it down,' he recited.

'Great,' Patrick said, faintly repulsed. 'A nursery rhyme for the ages. Save water.'

'I learned that down in Tassie. We were saving the old-growth forests.'

Tasmania? Maybe it wasn't a ghost train. Maybe it was a roller-coaster.

'And you had toilets in the old-growth forests?'

'No. We crapped in the bush.'

'That's one way to enrich the wilderness.'

Ben laughed. 'Yeah, the loggers wouldn't go near it. We used to crap all around their camp and they'd step in it and "fuckin' greenies" we'd hear them say. We'd crap around the giant old trees to protect them.'

'Terrific,' Patrick said supportively. Where had Ben gotten the money to travel to Tasmania?

'Yeah. I shat in the seat of one of their bulldozers.'

'Sat?'

'Shat. Shitted.'

'Right. Was that a good idea?'

'Not really. They saw it there.'

Patrick really wanted hours of having this talk and more like it but now wasn't the time. It was wonderful and strange to be given a glimpse into Ben's world.

'OK. I want you in the shower before Mum gets here. And do you have any other clothes in that bag? It would be nice for you to be looking handsome for her birthday.'

'Yeah, righto.'

'And what about your meds? Do you need to take some? It's been a mixed-up day.'

'Eight o'clock,' Ben said. 'I take them at night now.'

He checked his watch. Six twenty. 'So which doctor are you seeing?'

'No doctors. Doctors can't fix you, she says. I'm on Annie's mix.'

'*Annie's* medicating you?' Patrick asked, incredulous. Ben nodded. 'Is she a doctor?'

'She's kind of a chemist.'

Patrick sighed. He didn't feel like hugging Ben anymore; he felt like shaking him.

'How long have you been with Annie?'

Ben shrugged. 'A couple of months.'

'And she's been medicating you all that time?'

'Yeah. Once she'd figured me out in her little red book. We do yoga too.'

Patrick laughed in spite of everything, remembering the years of effort family and specialists had put into diagnosing and helping Ben. 'She figured you out in a couple of months?'

Ben grinned. Some of the pressure in the room popped.

'Well! At least you're still alive,' he said. There was a lot to find out. He felt sorry for Annie. 'Now I'll grab you that towel,' he said.

He turned his phone back on and listened to Claire's voicemail. They didn't talk much these days and it was good to hear her voice again. When they had first got together, just hearing her voice on the phone sometimes gave him an erection.

He felt like another glass of red but forced himself to wait. He took a towel in to Ben, who was already under the shower. Then he phoned Claire.

'Hello, Patrick.'

'First things first – happy birthday.'

'Thanks. And what was that about Ben wishing me happy birthday? Have you heard from him?'

'I have. In fact, he's here now at my place.' He heard her intake of air. 'He's been asleep and now he's having a shower. And he *did* wish you a happy birthday.' He wondered suddenly whether Ben had remembered to bring his phone. He hadn't seen it.

'How is he?'

It was his turn to breathe in. 'He's been living in a share house five minutes from here, believe it or not – typical Ben – but he's had some really bad news. His girlfriend died this morning.'

'Oh, poor Ben! I'm coming over. I want to see him.'

'Good. There's more to the story, of course. I'll tell you when you get here. Do you remember my address?'

'Of course.' It was in her phone.

She'd been there to drop him off, early on, with a camp bed and a cardboard box. She hadn't been inside, determined not to help him too much. His old friend Stuart had found the house – someone Stuart knew, and he knew everyone – otherwise she was convinced Patrick would have finished up in a youth hostel on Glebe Point Road. He probably would have enjoyed that.

She'd arranged counselling before they split up, ever functional. Their lives were worth saving. He had agreed. They had sat in a calm room in a mansion in Hunters Hill and answered gentle questions from a woman with a deep voice and green glasses. The harbour had sparkled outside and made Patrick think about drowning.

'I've just got to make a couple of calls about tonight. I was going out, but I should be there in half an hour,' she said.

'OK. Don't leave it too long.'

'I'm not going to leave it any time at all,' she said, annoyed. 'Unlike you. And by the way, did you know all this when you texted me earlier today?'

'Not all of it. No.' That was *sort* of true.

'Just as well. See you soon.'

HACK

Patrick had fallen into journalism many years ago and only ever freelanced. When he saw those busy newsrooms in movies, he doubted he could ever work that way. Better to write in your board-shorts in the front room.

After completing an arts degree at Sydney University, he had worked in the public service. It was his job to write letters to legal firms about invalid pension payments. There was one letter with an error that he took back to Leslie in the typing pool for correction. *Your client is receiving invalid pension for a cute back pain* it read.

'*You're* cute,' he said to Leslie. 'Their client's back pain is *a*cute.' She grinned. He wanted to ask her out for a drink but was too shy. He was tall and a bit gangly, and Leslie *was* cute.

But he could write. He submitted an unsolicited humorous piece about Australia's bicentenary and it was published in the *Sydney Morning Herald*. He was paid what he regarded to be a fortune. He wasn't even a journalist. The day editor phoned. He was delighted with the level of response and wondered if there was 'anything else' in him.

'Wry stuff. I don't want anything too subversive. You can't shit on our readers every week.'

'No. Of course not,' he said, unaware that he'd already shat on them once.

'And I don't want anything that is critical of the Queen. She's out here to open the new Parliament House in May and we want to keep our options open.'

Patrick agreed because it seemed like the professional thing to do. He would submit another piece and if that 'hit the mark' they would talk about a regular column.

He felt summer's slow pulse and the next piece he wrote was about the carcass Christmas trees put out with the rubbish, turning brown in the sun. The seasons and ceremonies retreating. He phoned Sydney

City Council and confirmed his suspicions that much more money was thrown into fountains at this time of the year. New year and all that.

In 750 words he nailed the end of the season.

We all wish harder when a new year begins. We hope this holiday lightness will go on forever. It never does.

Australia Day arrives just too late to save us, like the cavalry in a black and white movie, and we head back to work.

The editor liked it and Patrick's career as a freelancer was underway. He was offered a weekly column and by the end of 1988 he was a minor celebrity in his early twenties. He soon learned that the media feeds off itself. Radio stations started to contact him, wanting interviews. The music press wanted to know his favourite records. He started getting invitations to film premieres and bar openings.

No-one ever asked if he was a public servant and he never told them.

Towards the end of the year, he was invited by the University of Technology to speak to their journalism students. He felt like a fraud. The students almost certainly knew more about journalism than he did.

He said yes to the offer. He was in the habit of saying yes to everything. The bar openings, in particular, had resulted in more drunken sex than he had ever had at university.

He took a sickie from work and spent the morning nervously re-working a kind of lecture on his experiences of breaking into the media as a freelancer. He tried to make it sound harder than it was. He wore blue jeans and a white open-necked shirt, brown belt and brown shoes. He took a neat vodka alone at the hotel on the corner before he went on campus.

There were a lot of females in the journalism class, he noticed.

Claire – it turned out – was one of them, sitting in the third row, wearing a pale pink singlet. He noticed her more than once. She spent most of the class leaned back, blonde hair, her stomach flat as a surfboard, her breasts a promise.

She took notes, which astonished and aroused him.

An hour later he was back in the hotel on the corner, drinking beer at the bar, when Claire and a girlfriend walked in.

'Hello, professor,' she beamed, lovely teeth. A battered black day-pack full of books pulled her shoulders back, displaying her breasts. Her friend was shorter and a little overweight. He couldn't recall seeing her in class.

'Hi there!' he said. 'Can I buy you a drink?' The Pet Shop Boys were bopping in the background. The bar was empty. Claire looked at her friend.

'Thanks! I'll have a beer,' she said.

'Bundy and Coke,' her friend said. 'No ice. No straw.'

'Did you get that?' Patrick asked the bartender, who was leaning, bored, at the bar. He nodded. 'So, two Tooheys, thanks.'

'Why don't we sit over there?' she said, pointing to a round table halfway across the room.

'I'll bring them over,' he said. He glanced at them as the barman poured the drinks. She had a nice arse in her faded blue jeans. After the vodka and a beer, he was already dangerously cocky about his importance. And now he was a university lecturer.

THE PIZZA POLICE

When Ben reappeared from the bathroom, he was wearing the same clothes. He looked skinny, but pink from the hot water, and healthy. *Claire will be happy*, Patrick thought. *Until she finds out what happened.*

'Have you got a change of clothes? Or a different shirt at least?' he asked.

'This is OK.'

'No, it's not. I've phoned Mum and she'll be here soon. I'll get you one of my shirts.'

'Is this your place?' Ben asked as Patrick turned to leave.

'Yes.'

'Where'd you get the money for that?' It was an odd question, Patrick thought.

'I'm renting,' he said. Ben laughed. 'What's so funny?'

'I didn't think old people rented,' he said.

That was the strange brat in him. The boy from Balmain. Before his illness, Ben had always had a social conscience and they had both encouraged and admired that. On the Magical Mystery Tour he sometimes came out with the most jaundiced remarks that baffled everyone.

'Well, a lot of us do. If we can afford it. Which I barely can.'

In fact, there was no way he could afford it except that the house belonged to a friend of a friend. Patrick didn't know why the rent was reduced, and didn't ask. It was semi-furnished when he moved in. The dark wooden wardrobe in his bedroom was like a coffin stood on its end. The oval mirror in the door was already cracked.

Someone else's bad luck, he figured, and got on with making his own.

He didn't have many shirts to choose from. Working from home and having no money kept him off-trend. He had one half-decent suit and a couple of ties for those occasions where he had to dress up. He

27

wore clothes well – he was tall and broad shouldered – but these days he settled for the casual, unironed look. His homeless look, he told friends.

Now that he was about to see Claire he changed into a blue-and-white check shirt she had bought him a couple of years ago. They had both agreed, back then, that he looked handsome in it. He chose a plain pale blue shirt for Ben.

His guts heaved suddenly. This all seemed so ordinary when he knew it was not. By now – he hoped – Mick would have found Annie, and the police would be in Forest Street. Not *Farest* Street. Not far away. Hurry up, Claire. Know what to do.

Ben looked good in a fresh shirt. He'd tossed his T-shirt onto the couch and Patrick cleared it away. It stank of stale sweat.

'Hey, have you got your mobile phone with you?' Patrick asked.

Ben's brow creased in thought. He felt the back pocket of his jeans. 'I think I left it at my place. Should I go and get it?'

'No. Mum's about to arrive. I guess Annie's phone is back at the house too?'

Ben nodded. 'I don't use my phone much. It's only a cheap one. It's OK.'

He wondered how long it would take the police to put together the pieces of their broken family and find them all here. You watch the police dramas on TV but they're edited. You have no sense of how much time has passed. An hour? A day? As if in answer, there was a knock on the door. Bang. Bang. Bang.

'Stay here, Ben.'

Patrick walked down the corridor.

It was Claire.

Black jeans. Black Converse shoes. An untucked white shirt. She had a small bag hooked over her shoulder. Her hair was cut shorter than the last time he had seen her and was dyed with blonde tints.

'Hello, Patrick.'

He leaned down and hugged her, too tightly. She waited for the embrace to end, he could tell, with only one hand on his shoulder.

'It's good to see you!' He was whispering now. 'I didn't want to say much on the phone but Ben's girlfriend, Annie, died in their bed this morning, or last night. Ben can't remember exactly what happened.'

'What!?'

'He'd smoked some dope. It's all hazy. I thought maybe you could talk to him and see what he tells you, see if it's what he told me. I'll hang back.'

She nodded. Processed. 'Maybe he's delusional. God, I hope so.'

'He's not. I picked him up from the house. Annie's there and she's dead.'

He saw the anger and disbelief in Claire's green eyes. She was furious at him for not calling sooner. 'When did all this happen? Have you been drinking?'

Patrick shrugged. 'There was one glass left in the bottle from last night.'

'That'd be a first. Unless it was the second bottle.' She shook her head. 'Where is he?'

'He's straight through and out the back.'

He followed her. Ben let Claire hug him, Patrick noticed. He longed for their old lives, not the lives they had or what he felt was coming their way.

'Happy birthday, Mum!' Ben said. She hugged him again.

Patrick wanted more wine, but didn't dare. When their marriage was under stress he drank more and Claire drank less. It had been more than a year since they'd sat together.

Under Claire's careful questioning, Ben explained that Annie had found him in a warehouse share house in Newtown. He wasn't well. He'd gone off his medication and was couch surfing. She had made him meet her the next day in a cafe. She wanted to know what he knew about his diagnosis and medication. She asked him if he wanted to get fixed up.

'When I said yes, she leaned across and kissed me,' Ben said. 'On the lips,' he smiled. Patrick wondered how many girlfriends Ben had had. Ben's recollection of last night and this morning remained the same when he told Claire. Girl on fire. Everything terrible.

'I'm starving,' Ben said. 'Dad said we could go out for dinner for your birthday.'

'No, I didn't!'

'We can't, Ben, not after what's happened,' she said, and put her hand on his knee.

'Well, let's get pizza,' Ben said, dazzled by his idea.

Claire and Patrick looked at each other. They went to the kitchen. 'We have to call the police,' she said.

'Agreed. But he also needs to eat. I don't think he's eaten all day.'

'Well, that's your fault.'

'Probably. I think we get a pizza and help Ben prepare. Then call the police. Ask him not to tell his 'girl on fire' story.'

'Are you serious?'

'Yes! We don't know what happened. He doesn't know what happened. She was taking pills. Ben smoked some weed. He didn't know up from down. We confess all that. He went to bed, woke up and Annie was dead. Let *them* figure out what happened. That's their job.'

'But what if he's responsible?' Claire hissed. 'And we're lying to the police. *I* want to know what happened.'

'Me too. If he's guilty, we'll find out. They'll be all over that room. And Annie. But don't let Ben offer himself up on a plate. We know what his experience with the police is like.'

Claire seemed to be considering this.

The sun was down on the day now. Patrick felt strangely that the past had been erased. They were all in a house together again, his house.

He didn't want to think about why. He wanted to grab Claire and kiss her and then get pizza and the police.

'Order a pizza,' she said, invading his thoughts. 'I agree with you. He needs to eat. Then we'll call the police.'

They'd almost finished eating when he remembered Ben had to take his meds. Annie's mix. From what Ben had told them, it seemed she was actually helping him. She had a "drugs degree", he said. They did yoga together. Simple.

Ben was in the front room, finding his canvas bag and meds, when Patrick's phone rang.

The screen showed it was Ben calling, but he didn't have the phone. It was the police.

A DECEASED PERSON

'I'm Detective Senior Constable Harrison. Who am I speaking to, please?'

'Patrick Hyland.'

'You received a call from this phone this morning. Can you tell me who that call was from?'

'My son.'

'What's your son's name?'

'Ben.'

'And where's your son now, Mr Hyland?'

'He's here with me.'

'Thank you. And what's your address?' Patrick paused. His instincts made him want to fight back. 'The address, please.' He was dumbstruck. It was all happening, after a long day of pretending and hoping that it might not. 'You don't seem surprised by my call, Mr Hyland. Most people are surprised by a call from the police.'

'I know what this all about,' he said. 'I was about to call you.'

'Good. Just the address, then.'

He gave the address. He could hear through the phone a police siren starting up in Forest Street. 'Do not to leave the premises,' Detective Senior Constable Harrison said, and hung up.

'I'll get Ben,' Claire said. The box of Christmas decorations was still on one end of the dining table, now alongside a pizza box. He doubted he would get the decorations out this Christmas after all. Doubted he would buy a tree. He was in a kind of daze now.

Claire called out in panic from down the corridor, 'Patrick! He's gone!'

Patrick tore through the small house and its rooms. The canvas bag was gone and so was Ben. He ran into the street. He could hear the police siren for real now, closing in, close. No sign of Ben.

32

'Ben!' he called. 'It's going to be OK!' The police car turned into his street, red and blue lights flashing, catching Patrick in the headlights. 'Fuck.'

He stepped back onto the footpath and signalled to the approaching car. A big guy, late thirties, dark hair and sideburns, stepped out of the car. He held open his police identity.

'Patrick Hyland?'

'Yes.' He lifted his hands and let them fall to his sides. 'He's gone.'

'Your son?'

'Yes, my son.'

'How long ago?'

'A few minutes. Since you called me.'

'I told you not to leave the house. Have you any idea where he might go?'

'No.'

Harrison thought about this and looked up and down the street as if Ben might reappear. It could happen. With Ben, anything could happen.

'Let's go inside,' Patrick said and pointed to the flashing lights. 'Can you turn all that shit off? The neighbours will think I've killed someone.'

Their eyes met and Patrick regretted his choice of words.

Harrison seemed even bigger in the small sunroom. He wore a well-cut suit and one of those huge, fuck-off metal watches. A young, uniformed policeman had joined them and opened a digital notebook. Introductions were made and IDs were flashed again. Claire wondered if she'd seen Harrison on TV. He had that sort of face.

'It looks like we interrupted dinner,' he said, nodding to the table, the pizza box. It was incongruous, given all that had happened, and Claire winced.

'Would you like a seat?' she offered.

'No thanks,' Harrison said but the young constable sat down on the red couch. Patrick and Claire sat down on wooden chairs. 'You said you were about to phone me, Mr Hyland. Why was that?'

They looked at each other with grim resignation. Claire spoke.

'Our son Ben suffers from schizophrenia. Long periods come and go where neither of us hear from him or know of his whereabouts.'

'But he's been here today?'

'That's right. Patrick got a call from him this morning, out of the blue.'

'Today's Claire's birthday,' he jumped in. 'I invited him over to help us all celebrate as a family. It was over dinner that he told us about... Annie, is it?'

'And what did he tell you?'

Patrick heaved a sigh. 'He told us his girlfriend was dead. We didn't even know that he had a girlfriend and we were just trying to get a sense of how real any of this was when you called.'

'Did he seem delusional to you, as parents? Was he agitated?' Harrison looked to each of them for a reply.

'He seemed... disconnected,' Claire said. 'Unsure of things. That's not a surprise.'

'Is Annie dead?' Patrick asked. Claire looked at him. She knew he'd seen her.

Harrison considered. 'There is a deceased person. What did Ben say happened?'

Patrick grabbed Claire's hand, husband and wife. 'Look, I don't want to speak for Ben or give a second-hand version of things. I'd rather be out there to see if I can find him. He told us they went to bed and, when he woke up this morning, she was... "a deceased person". He has no idea how that happened.'

'Do you believe him?'

'Of course!'

'Why do you think he left here?'

'He doesn't like the police. His illness has put him in harm's way before.'

'You've no idea where he might have gone?'

'No.'

'You don't have a holiday house...?'

Patrick laughed. Harrison looked at Claire. She shook her head. 'I know this must seem suspicious to you but it's what Ben does. He disappears,' she said.

Harrison reached into his suit pocket and produced a business card. He handed it to Claire. 'Please give me a call if you find or hear from Ben. We need to speak with him and I give you my word that we'll be sensitive to his health issues. And we'll need to speak to both of you again as well. I'm sorry this has spoiled your birthday.'

It was only after they'd gone that Patrick noticed the smell of aftershave. Harrison's, he guessed. Something with cypress in it. They sat in glum silence.

'I'm going to check one more time,' he said. 'Maybe he's hiding under the bed.'

The lights of Annandale were glimpses of other lives in the darkness across the valley. Claire looked around the room for the first time. There was a bowl of water on the floor in the corner. Patrick must have a pet.

They had only had one family pet when they all lived in Balmain. Ben had got a guinea pig for his tenth birthday. He named it Cuddles and he literally cuddled it to death within weeks. He 'squeezed it too tight', he said. It rattled them as parents. Ben had wanted to get another one but it had never happened.

Patrick reappeared with a piece of paper and handed it to Claire. I DON'T WANT TO GET YOU INTO TROUBLE. BEN.

'Shit.'

'The cops have his phone, so we can't call him,' he said.

She stood up suddenly. 'He might go to Balmain!' She grabbed her bag from the back of the chair. Patrick was hoping she might stay. They could go looking for Ben together. Find him. Live happily ever after. A fugitive family.

'How long since he's been there?' he asked.

'Oh, a strange evening where he appeared with no warning and I played Scrabble with him, months ago.'

'Did he win?'

'He won. Then left the next morning. Even if he doesn't know it, he's going to want somewhere

'He's good at hiding.'

'Yes, he is.' She stretched up and kissed him on the lips. A peck. 'Why did you lie about going to the house?'

'I didn't lie. I misguided. I thought it would be better for Ben and our story.'

'Our story!' She shook her head. 'You don't have to fuck this up, Patrick. It's bad enough already.' She stopped halfway down the corridor and turned back to face him. 'Don't try any heroics with Ben. If you see or hear from him, call me. Agreed?'

'OK. Ditto.'

'In fact, call me anyway. Every day.'

He stayed out the front and watched the taillights of her car disappear around the corner.

B en wasn't at Balmain. Blame Man. Blame Me. All the stupid mangled names he had given it.

Claire followed Patrick's lead and went from room to room, turning on lights. She looked in the garden shed. She called out. Ben still had a key but she never really expected to find him. It saddened her that after he had left home, it was never Ben's refuge. It had been a happy home.

She had inherited the big house after her mother died. The swing she had swung on as a girl, she had then lifted Ben onto as a boy. Pushed him high. 'Higher! Higher!'

He squealed like a girl, Patrick used to say.

'Nothing wrong with being a girl,' she replied.

Over the years they replaced the swing ropes and the seat, built a cubby house, bought a trampoline, knocked a wall through to extend the kitchen. Family life. Neither of them wanted many children. They only wanted one. When Ben's illness was diagnosed, they were all sure they could handle it. They talked and hugged and found specialists and loved each other.

It bared its teeth and grabbed them by their throats.

She thought about phoning around the old networks they had set up when Ben first started disappearing. But one by one they'd all gone cold and now she couldn't face the prospect of explaining what had happened this time. She phoned Philip instead.

'Hello, love.'

'Hi. How are you?'

'I've had better birthdays.'

'I'm sorry. Is Ben OK?'

'I hope so. The police came around and he disappeared.'

'The police?'

'Yes. There's an investigation, to see what happened.'

'Of course. He's gone again?'

'Yes. He left when he heard Patrick talking to them on the phone.'

'Do you know where he's gone?'

'No. That's Ben. I'm back home. He's not here. He left his phone back at his house and the police have it. As usual there's no way we can contact him.'

There was a silence. 'How's Patrick coping?' Philip asked, politely.

'He's OK. He went over to the house and picked Ben up this morning. He saw the girlfriend. It wasn't gory or anything.'

A silence descended.

'I'm sorry we missed that booking tonight.'

'Me too. Did you sell it on eBay?'

'I wish I'd thought of that! I just cancelled. And lost my deposit. Not that I'm complaining.'

'Of course not. How's your mob?'

'All well, thanks. It looks like Grace has found work with a law firm down in Hobart, so she won't have to come up after all.'

'But you wanted her up here.'

'I do. But it might not be a bad thing for her to get some experience down there, live at home a bit longer, help Mum out.'

She could hear the sadness in his voice.

Not for the first time, she wondered if she and Philip were really just a lonely-hearts-club band. A kind of confessional where they told each other how hard it was to not be with their families, and to be understood. He had three kids. She hadn't met his family and he hadn't met hers. She'd seen photos on his phone and there were albums and frames in her house where he sometimes stayed over.

'I'd like to come over,' he said, as if he'd read her meandering thoughts.

She thought about it. 'I'm really exhausted. We've both got work tomorrow.'

'I'll bring a shirt and tie. You've never seen me iron a shirt, have you? I've become quite an expert.'

Philip was a dapper, smallish man. Smaller than Patrick. They'd been seeing each other for six months now. He wore red-rimmed glasses and had a buzz cut of salt and pepper hair. He wasn't a pens-in-a-pocket kind of accountant.

'Seriously, I think it'd be good to be there. And if anything happens with Ben, I can stay, or go. I'll do whatever you want.'

'OK. Sounds good. See you soon.'

'Half an hour.' He hung up.

Ha! Fan hour. Ben and his bloody word games were back inside her head.

IS THAT ALL THERE IS?

P atrick went searching the night.

He was looking for Ben but didn't fancy his chances. He couldn't stop thinking about Claire in his house.

There was a cold wind blowing and he wished he'd put on a coat. He walked to Forest Street very late in the night of the long day. Who knew what Ben might do? Maybe he went back to get his phone after all.

There was police tape blocking the entrance. It wasn't a front garden. It wasn't anything.

The blind was drawn in the front room but a bright light sliced out from the edges and into the universe. Forensics searching for his son. Poor Ben. Poor Annie. There was a police car parked in the street. There was noise from the pub down on the corner. The world carrying on.

He walked home.

He didn't sleep well. Red darts and bruises and red and blue lights. When he woke, Eve was six inches from his face, staring at him with her green eyes. She meowed. She talked to him. He talked to her too. She knew all about his financial troubles.

He groaned. What do you do after a day like yesterday? He cuddled Eve.

At least Ben knows where Patrick lives now. He wouldn't know the address but he'd be able to find his way back here. And he knows Balmain. Patrick thought it unlikely he'd show up at either place. Not after that note he left. Self-harm or suicide had mercifully never been Ben's thing, so far, in spite of the voices. The clear and present danger was risky behaviour, running out of meds – even Annie's mystery cocktail – getting back on the drugs, not eating well, not caring, sleeping rough.

He phoned Claire from his bed.

'Hello, Patrick. It's Philip here. Claire's in the shower. I only picked up because I thought it might be something urgent about Ben.'

Patrick hung up. So much for his fantasies about family. It seems there'd be an accountant in bed with them as well.

Eve wanted more cuddles but he was mad and sad now, so he shoved her aside and got under a shower too. His phone rang. That would be Claire.

He was going to find Ben, he decided. That would show her. He'd win her back, like in some crappy movie that he knew he wouldn't watch.

Who *was* Annie? Maybe the best way to find Ben was through her networks. Maybe he had somewhere to go after all. He cursed himself for not asking Ben what Annie's surname was.

He put on coffee and searched for news online, eventually finding a couple of pars about a death in the inner west. Police had established a crime scene. That old Peggy Lee song waltzed into his head. Is that all there is?

He phoned handsome Harrison and, while he waited for an answer, he realised Harrison wouldn't know that he and Claire were no longer a couple, and didn't live where he thought they did. What a shit detective.

'Cooper. Hello.'

'I was after Something-or-other Harrison, please.'

'What's it about?'

'An incident in Forest Street in Forest Lodge yesterday.' Incident? Where did that come from?

'I know it. What's your query?'

'I wanted to know how things are progressing. An update, I guess.'

'What's your interest?'

'My son lives there. It was his girlfriend who died.' Patrick could hear some papers shuffled.

'Ben Hyland,' Cooper said 'Have you found him?'

'No. Have you?'

'No.'

'We're anxious about Ben, obviously, but also want to know what you think happened. Can you tell me more?'

'We're making enquiries. Forensics have been on site. There's nothing more I can tell you at this stage. I'll give you my number. It looks like I'll be taking over this case.'

'Already?'

'There was a murder in a motel on Glebe Point Road. Detective Senior Constable Harrison has taken that investigation.'

Annie's squalid death had already been bumped down the order, it seemed.

• • • •

The cold wind from last night was gone and the sky was vivid Sydney blue. The small front gardens were full of summer already, the seasons out of whack, the planet spinning wrong. At least the world was warmer for Ben if he was sleeping rough. Earth Destroyed. Son Safe. Patrick couldn't help daydreaming headlines.

He walked back to Forest Street and was surprised to see the police tape gone. The house was its dilapidated self again. The front blind was still down. If it was no longer a crime scene, there was nothing stopping him. He'd done some investigations over the years, trying to make a living writing as a freelancer. He knew some tricks.

He stepped over the low metal gate and checked the letterbox. It was stuffed with pizza flyers and a single letter from a local car dealer. The envelope was crisscrossed with slug trails and the corner had been eaten away.

He cupped his eyes and blinked through the gap in the blinds. In the gloom inside, he thought he saw someone step away from the window. Someone had been looking out at him.

He knocked on the front door, his heart racing. He felt he was trespassing.

No answer. He knocked again and waited. It must be the house-mate, Mick. The wrecker. He hoped so. Mick could tell him a lot. If he answered the door. Why wouldn't he answer the door? He knocked again and this time he heard footsteps approaching from the back of the house. The door swung open.

A man, maybe fifty, greying hair and neat beard, blue overalls and very blue eyes, stood there. He looked fit for his age. Not a clapped-out tradie.

'Hello,' Patrick said eventually. 'Are you Mick?'

'No. Who are you?'

'I'm Patrick Hyland. I'm Ben's father.'

The man nodded. 'Who's Ben?'

'My son. He lives here.'

The man nodded again. 'He's not home.'

'Do you live here?'

'No.' He gestured with his thumb to the corridor behind him. Patrick noticed now that he was wearing latex gloves. 'I was here to fix one or two things up, after the police left. I'm about finished now.'

'Oh. Do you know much about what happened here?'

'No, mate. Do you?' Patrick shook his head. 'Young girl dead, apparently,' the man said.

'Apparently. Look, would it be OK if I came in and had a quick look around? My son may have left some medications here that he needs. It'll just take a minute.'

The man stepped aside. 'No worries. Do you mind if I stick with you?'

'That's fine.'

He entered and turned into the room. It smelled of chemicals. The bed had been moved. The mattress was stripped and leaned against a wall, mottled with human stains. The wooden base leaned against another wall. The cup of tea was gone, and the dartboard. And Annie. The bookcase had been moved nearer to the corner, he thought, still half-filled with books, as if an earthquake had rearranged the room slightly. The man stood by the door and watched him

'Nothing in here,' Patrick said. He turned and walked down the corridor as if he knew where he was going and what he was looking for. The layout of the house was almost identical to his own.

He guessed the next bedroom was Mick's. There was a mess surrounding an unmade double bed. There were bright orange and green hi-vis vests on the floor and draped over furniture. There were empty beer bottles and a bong still filled with dirty water.

'Is this your son's room?' the man asked from the door, where he stood watching Patrick take it all in.

'No. This is Mick's room.' This was a weird tour. He looked around once more as if he was hunting those missing meds.

The small lounge room was a similar mess. Too many chairs and couches, none of which matched, one with an armrest missing. The tiny square TV looked as if it might produce a black and white picture. A thin orange curtain on the only window cast a sickened colour over everything.

Patrick wanted to get out but he stepped past his chaperone and walked through to the crappy kitchen and then to the cold bathroom out the back. The medicine cupboard had no door and he looked across the shelves. There were a couple of plastic bottles of tablets that he lifted and inspected. Phenergan. Ibuprofen. Aspirin. A green tube of Berocca. Eye drops. Band-Aids, including a bloodied, used one on the side of the sink. Why didn't forensics take that, he wondered.

Patrick was familiar with many of the drugs Ben had been prescribed and there were none of them here. Nor was there a Vegemite jar with 'Annie's Mix' written on a handmade label.

'Nothing doing,' he declared. 'Thanks for your help.'

'What kind of medication is he on?'

'Psychotropics.'

The man nodded, as if he knew what that meant. Patrick nodded.

THE DEAD BED

• • • •

Two hours later Patrick was in The Nag's Head hotel, waiting for his mate Stuart Brand to show. The pub was on the corner of Forest Street, just down from Ben's house. After one beer, everything was starting to feel surreal. How close Ben had been and how far away.

Stuart bowled in, round and brown as a wine barrel with a shock of white hair and a white moustache. He slapped Patrick hard on the shoulder and then extended his hand in a single movement. 'How are you?' he beamed.

Patrick shook the meaty hand. 'Been better.'

'What are you drinking?'

'Coopers this time.'

'Doesn't anyone drink the local beer?' He met the eye of a blonde barmaid. 'Another Coopers, thanks, love, and a schooner of Old.'

'Been out today?' Patrick asked.

'Bloody oath. Ten knots. Beautiful. Except I took Nancy. She had a hangover and moaned the whole time. I should have thrown her overboard.'

Stuart was a keen sailor and had been a mentor to Patrick during his journalism career, such as it was. He was a journo's editor back then, a robust writer who knew the ropes, disliked management, and brought a kind of tabloid enthusiasm to the venerable *SMH* masthead. He wouldn't get a look-in as editor these days. Newspapers were doomed anyway. Patrick still read the *Herald*, trying to keep up, but he did so in the local library to save money. He trawled the magazines up there too and had written for everything from surfing and music magazines to men's health. He also wrote quite a lot about wine. He'd tried blogs. He'd tried everything over the years.

'What have you been up to?' Stuart asked and sipped his Old and waited for an answer with foam in his white moustache. Women – smart women – told Patrick they thought Stuart was like a washed-up pirate. Many wanted to dislike him, but couldn't. Many also did.

Patrick sculled the last half of his beer to get on even terms with Stuart, then he sipped the next one. 'I'm in a bit of strife, actually.'

'Bitches or banks?' Stuart asked. It was like talking to a page three headline but Patrick didn't mind.

'Worse!' he declared and held his palm in the air to stop Stuart before he could say anything. Generally, it was a split-second thing. 'A detective in a good suit.'

'Christ!' Stuart said. He actually looked startled. 'What's happened?'

He told the story yet again. It was like an accident happening in slow motion. Stuart just listened, alert. On the high-mounted television in the corner, Patrick could see golfers in Singapore silently hitting balls.

Patrick felt pissed already. 'I'll get the next round,' he said.

'I know you will.'

'Actually...' he said, knowing that he was low on cash. He never took his cards to the pub because he didn't trust himself not to spend money he probably didn't have.

'Oh, for fuck's sake. Here's fifty,' Stuart said happily, smacking it on the counter. 'Owe me.'

When the barmaid put the change back on the bar, Stuart picked it up and stuffed it into his pocket. He picked up his beer and drank, leaving another scum on his moustache. It didn't seem to bother him. He's a walrus, Patrick thought, looking at him, not a pirate.

'So, *I'm* going to find Ben,' Patrick declared 'before the cops do, and I'm going to sort all this shit out.'

'Yeah, well, good luck with that.'

'I need your help. Find out who Annie is – was – her surname, and also what the cops think happened. No-one will tell me anything.'

'OK, mate. My networks aren't what they used to be, but I'll try.'

'Thank you.'

'Right.' Stuart drank his beer. 'You been getting any pussy?'

They were moving on, apparently. 'No,' Patrick confessed.

'I think Claire still loves you,' Stuart said. 'And she'll need you more than ever to get through this. Fuck Phyllis or whatever his name is. You be the man.'

'That's what I'm being. That's why we're here drinking beer and planning! And being.'

'You used to get a bit way back when,' Stuart said, keen as always to talk about sex. 'In fact, a hell of a lot, as I recall. I was jealous.'

'You had Nancy,' Patrick pointed out.

'Jesus, don't remind me!'

'Here's me: celibate, lonely, son wanted by the police, me not wanted by wife, half pissed. And *you've* been out sailing.'

Stuart roared with laughter. 'You could always rattle a tale. I'm going for a piss.'

The bar was filling up again with a relaxed afternoon crowd. There was silent soccer on the TV now, played in driving English rain. Outside the pub, the light was almost gone but there was a yellow hue on things.

He now missed Ben with a maudlin, physical ache. Stuart returned from the toilet and Patrick told him that he was heading home.

'Be the man!' Stuart urged in reply, finishing his beer and glancing up at the soccer in the rain. Patrick suddenly couldn't remember what man he was meant to be.

T*he arrangement worked.*

She got her pills – 'You're not swallowing all these, are you?' his white teeth asked, but he didn't seem to care – and he got to plug into a life looser and more dangerous than his own. For him, it was like going back to university and getting the girl he had never got.

One day he told her he was uncomfortable dealing with feeling in his car.

'I have a room,' he said. 'Very private. I have the only key.'

'That sounds dangerous.'

'Only if you want it to be,' he said.

'Why would you have such a room?' she wondered aloud.

'It's a registered premises with the Pharmacy Board of Australia,' he said. 'Secure.'

That could kick things to a whole new level, she realised. And it would compromise him if things went wrong. In her experience, things usually did go wrong. The world was ruled by entitled fuckwits and she was doing her best in her own small way to change that.

THE ONLY CHILD

P atrick had done his best way back on that day after his university 'lecture' to snare Claire with his charms. It hadn't worked.

Her friend was charmed and drank like the sponge she resembled. 'Bundy and Coke. No ice. No straw,' she recited every time he went to the bar. Claire agreed to a second beer but sat on it and kept herself tidy. He convinced himself that he liked that in a woman, even though it gave him the shits.

After four beers and Bundy and Cokes with no ice and no straws and no sign of relenting from Claire, and no more money, he decided to call it quits. With all this beer and nervous adrenaline, he was pissed anyway. He didn't even try to get a phone number from Claire. He thought she was hot but she had this way of reminding him that he wasn't hot himself.

He went home and wanked.

The end-of-year corporate party season was just cranking up. From Fridays through to Sundays Patrick woke up with hangovers, occasionally in other people's houses and sometimes in other people's beds. None of it meant much to him other than the miracle that it was happening.

When he met Sue, it was like the world slowed down. She was Chinese- Australian with a broad, happy face and a gold complexion. Her hair was as black as his was blond. She was smarter than him to the power of ten, he guessed. They met at the Sydney Opera House over glasses of sparkling wine. It was another early Christmas gig – he couldn't remember who had invited him, maybe no-one – and, when he had told her his by-line (it was never just 'Patrick' at these events), she had swayed back a little and grinned.

'Is that you?' she asked.

'Who?'

'You! From the paper?'

What it was to be in Sydney on a warm night at the Opera House, the loud hum of voices filling the foyer, free grog. He leaned forward and bent to her ear. 'That depends whether you like it or not,' he whispered. He could smell her perfume.

'Yeah, mostly I like it. It's very clever. I like the word play.'

He bowed slightly, like a visiting conductor from Europe. They talked about him and how he came up with ideas, about deadlines, and he took two more glasses of sparkling wine from a tray as it passed. He wasn't sure how much later it was when he finally asked what she did.

'I play principal violin with the SSO,' she said.

'Wow!' he blurted. He looked at her slender hand holding the glass. It looked naked and skilled and suddenly pornographic. He didn't know a violin from a viola. 'And what's the SSO?' he asked, to say something and regain his balance. She assumed he was being clever and laughed.

She had an apartment in an old art deco block in Rushcutters Bay and they went back there in a taxi before the night was worn out. It had high ceilings and polished wooden floors and not much furniture. There were two bedrooms. One was furnished with a music stand and an upright chair and two violin cases on the floor. There were neat piles of music scores stacked like totems against one wall. A sash window was wide open to the night and he could hear the clinking of sailboat rigging.

Was he out of his depth? Yes. He had never slept with a Chinese woman. Lurid teenage myths of horizontal fannies mingled with the fragrant perfume of frangipani wafting in from outside. She frightened and aroused him. They sat on a shabby club lounge and drank gin and tonics, listening to Jackson Browne's *The Pretender* on vinyl through large speakers.

'Why do you like this record?' he asked, his head tilted sideways on the back of the lounge, looking at her dark eyes. She was slumped back too, looking at the high ceiling, her face a dish, her small breasts upright in a silk top. Her legs drifted open and closed.

'He was born in Germany,' she said. 'It has some of that displaced sadness.'

'He's American!' he said.

'Of course. But actually not. That's the secret.'

Patrick absorbed this. His legs swayed open and closed too now, a kind of sexual semaphore. 'Were you born here?'

'Yes, I was. But culturally, sometimes, I feel displaced too.'

'And the 'displaced sadness'?' he wondered. She nodded. 'Are you The Only Child?' he asked.

She smiled. 'Track five. You know the record. Yes. What about you?'

'Yes, as well. My dad died in an accident at work when I was ten and when I left home, my mum moved into a small flat in Ashfield.'

He didn't know why he was saying all this. Maybe it was the music. Maybe it was the serene atmosphere of her apartment. All he knew was that this felt different to the noisy other places that he had been. She was different as well.

'I bet you miss your father,' she said.

He thought about it but said nothing. He did miss him. His long absence when Patrick was learning how to be a teenager and a man. The melancholy record played. She put her hand on his thigh. Normally that would stop him thinking about sadness. Instead, this time, he began to cry. She put her arms around him and curled against him, small and warm as a cat.

They went to her bedroom. It was filled with a four-poster wooden bed with mosquito netting. The effect reminded him of those complicated sailing ships built inside a glass bottle. The only other thing in the room was a standing clothes rack with a few dresses on hangers. As he undressed in the light from the window, the gossamer dresses wafted like coloured skeletons in a breeze.

Their sex was tender and real. He felt huge. Lying afterwards in her arms, her small breasts softly against him, the masts in the bay clinking, the sweet air, the pale light through the gauze, a siren wailing somewhere up in the Cross, he was as happy as he could ever recall being.

The next day, Claire phoned. How did she even have his number?

She called him Professor Patrick again, which he knew was a joke, but he liked it. Apparently he had given her his number that day in the pub, written on a beer coaster. They agreed to meet on Friday in the same bar. He wondered if this was a mistake because he'd arranged to meet Sue again on Saturday and was looking forward to it. Everything with Sue had a kind of delicacy to it, a fineness and finesse. She was a vase of light.

But there was nothing wrong with meeting up with one of his old students, he told himself. He asked her whether Miss Bundy would be there as well and was pleased to hear that it would just be the two of them. It was almost a date.

When he got there, she was already sitting at a table against the wall, reading a street newspaper, a half glass of white wine on the corner of the table. The bar was crowded and noisy with Friday night. The jukebox was blasting a Queen song.

'Hello!' he shouted.

She looked up and smiled. 'I didn't think you were coming.'

'Am I late?' He was always late, even when he tried not to be.

She looked across at her wine. 'By about half a glass.' She wasn't wearing a watch. In fact, she was unadorned. She was tanned skin in a tight blue T-shirt.

'I'm sorry. Do you want another?'

'I want to ask you something.' He dragged a wooden chair and sat down. 'Is that glass half full or half empty?' she asked, pointing to her wine. He looked at the glass and then looked at her. She had green eyes and full pink lips and he looked at both and then back into her eyes.

'I thought you were studying journalism, not philosophy,' he said. 'Or is that physics?' She didn't say anything but her gaze was friendly and interested.

'Half empty,' he said. 'My fault, because I wasn't here to drink it with you. And if I said half full you wouldn't let me buy you another one, so what are you drinking?'

She leaned into his ear to counter the noise. 'Riesling.' He could smell it on her sweet breath.

The night went well. They drank in the pub until it was dark and then went to a cheap Lebanese restaurant that she liked near the uni. They drank more riesling out of tumbler glasses and ate bread and dips with their hands. She announced that her course had finished and she was no longer a student. They clattered tumblers. He felt like saying her life was ahead of her but realised that would make him sound old.

'My results aren't all in but I think I'll do well,' she beamed.

'Such confidence! That'll be the riesling,' he joked. 'Or the visiting professor. Why aren't you out drinking with your mates?' he asked.

'I am,' she said. It was a line too but it was a good one. He put his arm around her shoulder and dragged her towards him and kissed her lightly on the lips.

She wouldn't go home with him. After much pleading, while she waited for a taxi, she agreed to see him again tomorrow. That was going to clash with Sue but now wasn't the time to finesse.

In the morning he wandered around his small flat, feeling lousy and wondering what to do. He didn't have Sue's number. He seriously considered making his way across to Sue's place – he remembered where it was – knocking on her door and apologising that he wouldn't be able to meet as they had planned.

He would do that.

He didn't do that.

He met Claire on Saturday night at a more fashionable bar than the pub on the corner near the uni. It went well. They agreed to meet again. And again. Good sex started.

He never met Sue again, although he remembered her well and once saw her on TV playing principal violin at the Sydney Opera House. Seeing her inside the TV was like the time she was in that sailing boat bed in a room in Rushcutters Bay.

H e was woken with another hangover. Or was it the same one? He felt like he'd given whatever happened to Annie two days head start.

There was someone knocking on his front door. The bedside clock displayed 8:10am. Eve was wide awake to the commotion and, when the next knock banged, she jumped off the bed and headed for the back of the house. Scaredy cat.

Patrick slept naked and hopeful. He tossed the doona back and sat for a moment on the edge of the bed, his reliable morning erection more upright than his brain. He took a moment. He grabbed his jeans off the floor, pulled them on carefully.

Another knock. Who knocks that hard this early, he wondered? Badly dressed God botherers? A twenty-year-old with a clipboard on behalf of an African nation? One of those food-box companies?

He opened the door. Police. Again.

A man in a light brown suit – you didn't see them much anymore – was holding ID up to Patrick's bleary gaze.

'Detective Cooper. I think we spoke on the phone. Mr Hyland?'

He nodded. Cooper was mid-forties, overweight, he looked like someone had pumped him up past what was safe and the brown suit might not hold. He had a buzz-cut ginger skull. He was the identikit opposite of Detective Senior Constable Harrison and Patrick already liked him for it.

'Have you got news?' he asked. Cooper shrugged his shoulders. Maybe. 'Come in.'

He led them out to the sunroom. The room where things happened. The small lounge room in the middle of the house was too gloomy during the day.

The cardboard box of Christmas decorations was *still* on the wooden table. For fuck's sake, put that back in a cupboard, he told himself.

He put the Christmas decorations on the floor as a way of starting things and they both sat down at chairs around the table.

'Actually, I'm going to go and put a shirt on,' Patrick said.

'Nice view,' Cooper said when Patrick returned. It was another bright morning. The distant church spire, the old Kodak factory, now a block of flats. The valley was full of huge treetops from a park that ran along Orphan School Creek down into Blackwattle Bay.

'Have you heard from Ben?' Cooper asked.

'No, and I know we've done this routine before, but have you?'

'No. Is Mrs Hyland at home?' he asked, looking around as if that might make her appear.

Patrick wished it was that easy. 'She doesn't live here. We've been separated for a year now.'

'I'm sorry.'

'Me too.'

The room went quiet. Cooper laced his fingers together and put his hands gently on the table. He met Patrick's gaze. 'Anne Benson. Twenty-eight years old. Good family. Semi-estranged. Complicated, like most families. University education. In fact, her father's still a professor there at Sydney Uni.'

Patrick maintained eye contact. He was being the man. A man. What man? Did Stuart set this up? He closed his eyes. He was surprised how sad he felt for Annie's parents. Ben was missing. She was dead.

'Thank you,' he said.

'You never met her?' Cooper asked.

'No,' he sort of lied. It was too late to go back and start again. He felt dizzy, so he opened his eyes again.

'Her parents also didn't know she was living with your son.' Cooper grimaced a smile. 'Two strays. Is Ben a drug user?'

Where was this coming from? Where was it going? 'Prescription drugs, of course. Dope now and then. Bad for his schizophrenia.'

Cooper nodded. 'He knows it's bad for him and mostly he's actually an anti-drugs campaigner.'

'Harder drugs? Heroin?'

'No.'

'Are you sure of that?'

'Of course not. But I'd guess not.'

'You'd probably know,' Cooper said, apparently convinced that parents know their children. That was nice. Patrick felt like reaching over and touching those kind, clasped hands. 'How long had they been together?'

'A couple of months, I think. But until Ben showed up here, we didn't know that he even had a girlfriend. We told Harrison. Ben disappearing like this is not unusual. In fact, it's usual.'

'Has he had other girlfriends?'

'One or two, I think. Nothing serious.'

'Have you ever known him to be violent – on or off prescription drugs?'

There were no marks on Annie. Pillows don't leave marks.

'No,' he lied, hoping his voice was steady. 'Shouty. Moody. Slamming doors. For the most part, even with his illness, he's been a good kid.'

Cooper seemed to think about this. 'My daughter, Polly, she's thirteen, she has mild autism.'

Patrick was flummoxed. 'I bet she's beautiful,' he said.

'We think so. Not all her classmates do.'

'Kids, hey? It's not all beer and Skittles.'

'No.'

'I went to the house yesterday. Forest Street.' Cooper seemed interested. 'I thought Ben might be there. You can't tell what Ben might do, and he *does* live there.'

'No luck?'

'No, but I met the cleaner you'd sent in.'

Cooper leaned back in the chair. 'A cleaner?'

'I didn't get his name.'

'Describe him.'

'Blue overalls. Blue eyes. Beard. Fifties. Latex gloves.'

'That's interesting,' Cooper said. 'I don't think he's one of ours.'

'Really?'

'Cleaners go in if it's been a violent crime scene. This one wasn't. The housemate agreed that we didn't need to send in the cleaners.'

'Actually, I don't think he said he was a cleaner. He said he was there to "fix things".'

'What time was this?' Cooper produced a tiny notebook from his pocket and wrote in it.

'Eleven-ish? He let me walk through the house with him. I wanted to see where Ben lived. What happens next? If Ben walks through the door there, are you going to arrest him?'

'I'd start by interviewing him. He woke up and she didn't. You can put two and two together.'

Patrick remembered an idea from his walk home. 'I had a drink with a mate at The Nag's Head yesterday. Maybe there's CCTV of 102 Forest Street. It's not far down the street...'

Fuck. It would show *him*! Arriving, and leaving with Ben.

'Not operational,' Cooper said. 'We checked. A lot of venues would rather let their bouncers resolve a situation with no help from cameras or police.'

Patrick promised himself to be good for the rest of his life. 'Just a thought,' he said. He wanted to ask about the dart in Annie's arm, but of course he wasn't supposed to have seen it.

'Keep up the good work,' Cooper said, grinning and standing and offering his hand.

Patrick stood and shook it. 'Can we get Ben's phone back? It might help me track down where he's staying.'

'Have you got a number? That would help us too.' Cooper got out his tiny notepad again.

'No.' Yes. It's written on the cardboard flap of that box of Christmas decorations on the floor there. 'I don't understand. Harrison phoned me with it.'

'That was a burner phone. It showed your number because Ben didn't hang up after calling you. Otherwise, it's untraceable.'

'Right,' he said, as if pieces were falling into place, except they weren't. 'I was surprised he had a phone. He's always losing them.'

'These phones are popular now, with all these dating sites. Who wants to give out their real number to someone who might kill you?'

'Right,' Patrick said again, baffled.

'Do you think Ben might have met Annie through a dating site?'

'No. Ben's never really cared much for modern technology. I think they met the old-fashioned way – in a share house somewhere. Germs and lentils.'

· · · ·

WHY would Ben have a phone like that? Where the hell would he get it? He wondered again about Ben's guile. He phoned Claire.

'Any news?' she asked straight up.

'Some. Not much.' He wanted to see her. He wanted the family back together in Balmain. It was typical of Ben that he might make that possible and impossible all at once.

'And?' she asked impatiently.

'Can we meet for lunch? I don't want us to do all this over the phone.'

'I'm at work.'

'So am I,' he said, knowing that would irritate her. Him a lazy free-lancer, though half the ABC ran on freelancers now. He could never get over how snobby Claire was about it all. It seemed to be part of the ABC Charter.

She was an executive producer in News and Current Affairs. News-caff, to the in-crowd. She'd worked her way through producing a slate of factual shows, documentaries, natural history. It was a slow tilt, but by the time Ben was a boy she was spending much of her time at weekend picnics on her mobile phone. Patrick and Ben would throw a frisbee while she walked away in circles, one hand at her ear. Mobile phones got better and devoured her. Phone calls during dinner, early morning flights out of their lives.

'Are you free now, or flat out?' she asked sarcastically.

'I can probably make some time.' They were arguing like a married couple. 'Where will we meet?'

They met in the food hall of Central Park. It was a modern jungle-tower of apartments on the site of the old Carlton and United Brewery on Broadway, just around the corner from the ABC.

'So. What "not much" news is there?' she asked.

'I had a visit from Detective Cooper this morning. He's now work-ing the case. I got Annie's surname from him and did a bit of research on her. When Ben said Annie was a kind of chemist, he wasn't far off. She graduated and then did a master of pharmacy at Sydney Uni. Her old man's still a professor there.'

'Well, that's a relief. So, she's a chemist?'

'This is just me and Google but she never seems to have registered with the Pharmacy Board after graduating.'

'So, where's she getting Ben's meds from?'

'No idea. Ben wasn't seeing a doctor. Not for months. "Doctors can't fix you." Annie was fixing him.'

Claire hunched and sighed. She worked her chopsticks and took a mouthful of noodles. He forked his beef rendang. The food hall was filling up with students, construction workers in fluoro jackets, occa-sional suits and ties.

'Why do you study for a masters for all those years and then do nothing with it?' she asked.

'She's not doing nothing. She's fixing Ben. Was.'

'Do you believe that?'

'I want to. *He* seemed to believe it. And under the circumstances, don't you think he looked at least OK?'

'Well. Yes. But by the end of the week, wherever he is, he'll be out of even her medication.' She picked up her bowl and drank from it like it was a French coffee cup. She plunked it down. 'Maybe after killing her. What else did Cooper tell you?'

'Not much...'

'Can you stop with the "not much" bullshit, please, even if it's true. Tell me everything you find out. OK?'

He told her the scant details. She looked at her sports watch. 'I'm worried sick. I have to go.' She reached across and put her hand on his. 'Really. Thanks for the update. What do you plan to do next?'

He was in charge, apparently. He felt good about that, at least.

'Go to her funeral.'

Claire did a double take but kept her hand on his. 'Why? When is it?'

'Not sure. Out of respect. To meet her parents. To give Ben a lift home.'

'Do you think he'll go?'

'I doubt it, but who'd know whether he's paying attention?'

'Do you want me to come?'

'It's up to you. But yes.'

She smiled grimly and let go his hand. 'I'm really busy. End-of-year special. I'll think about it.'

'How often does Phil stay over in Balmain?'

'Seriously?' she asked. She grabbed her wallet and phone off the table and left.

On her way back she was waiting at the lights on the corner of Broadway and Harris Street. A throng of hungry students jostled around her, keen for lunch between lectures. Cars and trucks rattled by and made it feel like she was standing on the Hume Highway.

She hadn't told anyone at work about Ben. She had smart and caring friends she normally confided in. Most of them had children with troubles of their own. They covered for each other. When deadlines allowed, they drank wine and beer at an office table covered with yesterday's newspapers. All sorts of confidences were exchanged about husbands, kids, colleagues, lovers, the ABC, turmoil.

Not this time.

She'd never been ashamed of Ben in her life. Instead she was proud of the way he battled and survived. He was beautiful. Now there was a thing she couldn't nail down. Or maybe she could. Did he kill Annie? Her son.

Walking back into the cavernous atrium of the ABC, she decided to activate the old networks to search for him. They were social workers, Salvos, refuge miracle workers. Unlike with friends, she could keep these enquiries clinical and confidential. She would contact her solicitor friend for legal advice, in case they found him.

She had to do something because she was beginning to feel unreal. The prospect of going to Annie's funeral scared her. Something deep inside her had shifted and that scared her too.

ANNIE

Within a month she was mixing up medicines in that dangerous room, the noise of the street a muffled soundtrack from the world she kept fighting. She worked at a long white workbench. There was an APF24 handbook, pharmacy scales, a mortar and pestle, a hand-operated pill press, latex gloves, pipettes, powders, pills.

She wasn't registered but she knew what she was doing.

So did he, though he never really asked. He let her get on with things in private. He supplied the room and the components and looked the other way.

The room was an old apartment above the chemist, professionally secured. There was a bedroom where they fucked and sweated and took tablets to get them where they wanted to be. Which was often not the same place. Sometimes it was. He turned out to be an OK guy, in a hounded and hopeless kind of way.

She reminded him often that he could say no to her. He never did. Their deal remained haphazard because that's what she wanted. It was never as predictable as sex for access, though he tried that on now and then.

And all the while she modified her pill batches, meticulously recording the details in her little green book, and then took them back out into the world to do good. She thought herself an alchemist.

He thought she was a little unhinged but didn't care. His life was better now. More ragged. Now he had it all. A family to adore and a mistress to suck his cock and take away some of his pain.

P atrick was sitting on the low brick wall in front of 102 Forest
Street. Sad Central. He'd called into the supermarket on the way
home from lunch with Claire and there was a plastic bag of shopping at
his feet. Cat food. Orange juice. Cut-price steak. He got what he needed and couldn't afford anything more.

He felt guilty about the plastic bag. Colostomy bags, Ben used to
call them, and as a family they used recycled bags for years. Now look
at him.

He was waiting speculatively for Mick but also just having a rest.
The day was warm. His long legs stretched out across the footpath and
crossed at his ankles. He wore striped socks and red New Balance shoes
like a dandy. He'd thought several times over the lean years of surviv-
ing on writing that he might become an investigator. Insurance claims
preferably. He wasn't interested in spying on couples falling apart. He
knew how much that hurt and would never take money to facilitate it.

Unless it was really good money.

He'd gone so far as to search 'private investigator + Sydney'. Most of
the websites were an embarrassment, trumpeting that they'd appeared
on breakfast TV or some shit commercial radio station as evidence of
their credentials. One site promised they would charge less per hour
than a plumber. So they should. At least a plumber could unblock your
toilet, instead of sitting in a car watching a house and listening to the
cricket. Other firms had 'specialist' fidelity testers who would, for a fee,
probably more than a plumber's fee, try to crack on to your partner in
the gym or at a bar after work. They didn't reveal whether they'd go so
far as to fuck someone for a fee. It was a miserable business.

A woman across the street appeared in her front yard to water her
garden. She wore a floral dress and was slim and in her forties. Her haircut confused him about her sexuality, for some reason. She looked at

him boldly as she hosed the garden. He picked up his shopping and walked across the road.

Patrick enjoyed tending his small back garden. He knew a thing or two. 'Nice garden,' he said. 'Plenty of afternoon sun.'

'Thanks.'

'Some trouble across the road there,' he said.

'Yes. Terrible.'

'My son lived there.'

'Is he OK?'

'I think so. What were they like as neighbours?'

She shrugged. Nice shoulders, muscular and brown. 'All the things people say on TV. That sort of shit doesn't happen around here.'

'Did the police interview the street?'

'Yes.'

'Anything to report?'

'It wasn't a party house.'

He heard a metal gate clatter behind him and turned to see a man in a high-vis jacket putting a key up to the lock of 102. 'I better go and talk to Mick,' he said. 'Thanks for chatting.' She nodded.

The door was closed by the time he got there and he knocked loudly. He could hear work boots clomping back towards him down the corridor. There was no waiting this time. The door opened.

'Hi there. Are you Mick?'

'Who's askin'?' An Irish accent.

'I'm Patrick Hyland. I'm Ben's dad.'

'Who's Ben?'

Patrick swayed like a gust had hit him. Mick was bearded, broad, young. He'd be good at demolition. 'Ben,' he said as calmly as he could. 'The boy who lived in that front room with Annie.'

'Fish.'

'What?'

'Fish had that room.'

'With Annie?'

'Aye. Do you know about Annie, do you?'

'Yes. At least I know she's dead. I don't know about Fish, though.'

'I thought you said he was your son.'

For a wild instant Patrick hoped everything was mere confusion, there was someone else, an alibi, a third man. As if. 'Tall. Skinny. Buzz cut. Big green eyes.'

'Aye, that's him. I'm Mick.' He offered and they shook hands, a grip that nearly broke Patrick's fingers. 'Is he OK?'

'I think so. He's gone missing.'

'Yeah, he hasn't been here. The cops keep checking. You wanna come in?'

Patrick almost suggested the pub on the corner but then he wanted to be in the house, as though its ghosts might talk. They walked through to the pitiful lounge room with the orange curtain. He was beginning to lose track of who knew he'd been here and who didn't.

'I misheard at the door and thought you said your name was Patrick Ireland! That'd be hard core. Do you want a beer? I'm just home from work and I'm parched.'

'A beer would be great. Thanks.' He put his colostomy bag on the floor and sat in a broken armchair. His phone beeped a message in his pocket. Mick returned with two stubbies of Resch's beer.

'Old man's beer,' Patrick said, taking the bottle.

'The beer here's piss. This ain't so bad.' He watched as Mick sculled his. 'Sorry,' he said. 'I gotta move out of here. There's a bad vibe. Do you want another?'

Patrick grinned. 'I haven't started yet!' Mick went and got another for himself.

They talked. Fish was always Fish in this house, apparently. Mick had arrived home from work and found Annie in the front room. 'Bloody terrible. They were arguing, them two, the night before. I could hear them,' Mick said.

More evidence of the truth. 'Did you tell the cops?'

'Yep.'

So much for Patrick's grand plan. 'Did they argue often?'

'Not that I heard.'

'Ben said you two smoked a joint out the back.'

'Aye.'

'Did he smoke much dope?'

'No. Hardly ever. More likely to come out the back and lecture me. I dunno why he decided to join me this time.'

'Other drugs?'

'I don't reckon. Annie had some gear.'

'What's that mean?'

'Prescription drugs. LSD. All sorts.'

It was beginning to seem Annie rattled like a jar. He wondered whether Ben was on harder drugs, and followed Cooper's lead. 'Heroin?'

'Never. Look, we didn't see all that much of each other. *She* never lectured me.'

Patrick drank some beer. 'That's what they were arguing about. Ben smoking dope with you that night.'

Mick rubbed the side of his face, then looked back at him. 'How do you know that?'

'I'm just telling you. I'm not lecturing you either. None of this is your fault.'

Mick nodded. 'But how'd you know about the argument? And us takin' a joint?'

Patrick had stuffed up, again. 'Ben – Fish – showed up at my place out of the blue a couple of days ago. He told me.'

Mick thought this through. 'So was Annie OK when he left her?' He was angry now. Patrick shrugged his shoulders, as if he didn't know. 'Fuckin' hell! This place,' Mick said in despair.

'I'm sorry. Ben is unpredictable. He's gone again. He's unwell.'

'Aye. Did he tell you she was dead?'

'I don't think he believed it. He can't remember what happened.'

'She had a dart in her fuckin' arm! I don't think she died in her sleep!'

'No. He told me about that, but...' He hunched his shoulders.

'Can't remember?' Mick said bitterly. He swigged his beer and a deep silence fell over the room. Patrick wanted to open the curtain, or tear it down.

'How long have you all been living here?'

'I've been here six months. They moved in maybe a couple of months ago.'

'How did you all meet?'

'It were just a website. I'd advertised a room. Annie got back to me.'

'And how did you all sort the rent? Were they working?'

'Not sure. I leave early. They were in and out. I hardly saw them. Annie paid me cash for the rent.'

'Seriously?' he asked.

Mick nodded. 'They were fuckin' weird, man. Weirder than I thought, apparently.'

'Do you know what work Annie did?' Mick shook his head. 'Did Fish work?'

'Dunno, man.' He was shutting this thing down.

'Do you guys have a cleaner?'

Mick laughed in spite of things and looked around. 'What do you reckon?'

'It's just... I came round here yesterday hoping to catch you and a bloke opened the door. He said he was the cleaner. He had latex gloves on.'

'He was *inside* this house?' Mick asked, incredulous.

'Yeah.'

Mick thought about it. 'Maybe he was with the cops. They've been all over the place.'

'I mentioned it to the police and they said he wasn't one of theirs.'

'I've no idea who that was! Jesus Christ! I've gotta get out of this fuckin' place.'

Patrick didn't blame him.

SATURDAY MORNING, HIS PLACE.

In 1990, Claire had a journalism degree and couldn't get a job in Sydney. She couldn't believe it, and neither could he. He kissed his way down her belly. She had the *Herald* wide open in bed. Saturday morning, his place.

'I could write better than that!' she complained.

He kissed her blonde bush. He was in the white sheet tent while she rattled the pages up above.

'Chloe-fucking-Daniels gets a by-line,' she complained. 'She's shit!'

Her tang on his tongue. After a while he felt the featherweight of the newspaper lowered down onto the sheet above him. Her legs relaxed apart. Later, he stood naked in the small kitchen and made Vesuvius coffee and stared at the hypnotic gas ring. The machine gasped and squirted like sex. He took two red cups filled with coffee back to bed.

'I can't believe you're a public servant with your own column and I can't even get to rewrite press releases for page seven.' She held the cup in both hands between her beautiful breasts, pillow up against the wall, the newspaper rubbish at the end of the bed now, and on the floor.

'Neither can I,' he agreed, propped beside her. Now and then he tasted her sourness on his lips, depending on how he sipped the coffee.

She wouldn't move in with him even though her parents sort of approved of him. They read his columns. 'Most amusing,' her father declared drily. He had a banking background but was now someone senior at the Wheat Board, whatever that was. He smoked a pipe and went to church and when Patrick was over with Claire, he felt like he'd walked through a secret door to the 1950s. Even her father's conservative views seemed scripted. He took to calling Patrick 'young man.' If Patrick was looking for a father figure, Colin was not it. He drove Claire mad too. On the bright side, Patrick really liked her mother, Cassie.

Claire wouldn't move in but she stayed over. She was unemployed and it was a hard ask for him to go to work while she was there, tanned and naked. She teased him shamelessly. He was late often.

Soon after they had gotten together, his freelance party circuit had slowed down. That suited him. He took her along to events so she could network but she got sick of telling people she was unemployed, having drinks spilled over her, and Party Patrick getting pissed. They stayed in more often and went out for dinner, just the two of them, like a young married couple.

'Have you got any actual friends?' she asked him one night over French food in Surry Hills. The red wine was good. He was becoming an expert, he thought.

'What's an "actual friend"? Does that mean they have moving parts?'

'Friends, then.'

'Not really,' he said. She looked at him from the future and he wilted. 'I never really did have.'

'Why's that? You're a social guy.'

He shrugged. 'To be honest I never really felt like I needed close friends. I'd rather read a book.' He lowered his voice. 'Or fuck you.'

'I was going to say I hadn't noticed you reading books.' He smiled at her. 'But I've noticed the fucking,' she whispered back.

He was now writing feature articles for different supplements of the newspaper as well, throwing sickies at work so he could interview girl apprentices in non-traditional trades or winemakers up in the Hunter Valley.

'Do you think you'll stay as a public servant?'

'Forever?' he joked.

'It does happen, you know.'

Candles flickered on each table. Edith Piaf was warbling, in case it didn't already feel French enough. He rubbed his leg against hers under the table. Her eyes drifted up to his hair.

'What?' he asked, self-consciously flattening his wild blond locks. She reached across and ruffled them back up again.

'Don't listen to me,' she said. 'Don't change.'

He poured more wine for them both. That was the end of it. 'You'll get a job,' he said. She looked young and suddenly sad.

In February she did get a job, with the ABC at Gore Hill as a production assistant in TV. It was dogsbody work that should have gone to a 17-year-old – delivering VHS tapes, getting coffee, fielding phone calls, paperwork – but it was in the media. She was good at it. She had an instinct for organisation and got on well with people.

A new show called *Media Watch* had launched the previous year and in June she got a temporary gig. Suddenly her media studies and organisational skills came together. The program was a success, she was noticed, and her media career was underway.

Their sex got even better, he thought. She always had energy but now she exerted it more confidently. The power was shifting and he liked it. He took to rubbishing TV. She threatened to feature his 'dud' column on her program. Lying in bed, they agreed it was for the best that their media careers were in different fields after all.

For the rest of the year Claire worked her arse off and socialised heavily with the ABC crowd. Patrick felt comfortable with them too. The politics and red wine and an arrogant sense of influence made them all feel like gods.

ABC Gore Hill was a rambling old campus of buildings and once, when he went to pick her up late after work, they fucked on a green swathe of lawn heading back down to the car park. She squealed when she felt the wet grass beneath her and he held a hand over her mouth like a mugger.

Her pay wasn't great but her prospects were. Patrick pressed her to move into his flat properly. 'You can't work for the ABC and live at home with your parents in the 1950s,' he argued. 'We've got a fourth-term Labor government. We rule the world!'

THE DEAD BED

Neither of them had travelled overseas and when *Media Watch* wrapped at the end of the year, they spent Christmas lunch with his mother, Christmas dinner with her parents (better food) and New Year's Eve stoned on the terrace house roof of one of her friends from university, while the midnight fireworks popped and smeared across the darkness.

In January 1991 they flew to India. He'd thrown in his job and she had two months leave from the ABC. The day he quit his job he got drunk as a skunk and vomited all night. He was terrified at the prospect of getting back to Australia and having to survive entirely on his wits.

'You've got me now,' she consoled, and he gorged on her promise.

India astonished them both: the grinding rural poverty, the caste divisions, the overwhelming population, the flex of failure and history, bulging public transport, beggars and beasts in the streets, bodies on fire on the Ghats.

They spent a month going nowhere in particular in northern India. In a small village with no shade, they bought hunting scenes hand painted on silk, unframed. Tigers with spears in them, surrounded by hunters. The seller shook them in the dry air and dust puffed out before he rolled them up in sheets of newspaper.

Years later these paintings hung on the walls in Balmain and quietly terrified their one and only child, Ben.

THE MEANING OF STARS

P atrick wasn't sure how long he had been with Mick at Forest Street but when he got outside it was like another day. Dark clouds had appeared and, during the ten-minute walk back to his place, thunder rumbled and a southerly bluster blew his shopping bag against his knees. He seemed to stand waiting at the lights by the Forest Lodge primary school forever. It began to spit rain like bullets.

He tried to remember if Eve was inside or out in the garden. She didn't like thunderstorms. Not even the house or his lap were enough protection for her when lightning bolted. She hid under the bed or the couch.

He was still amazed at Mick's version of that disconnected household. They were on top of each other but came and went like ghosts. He could understand Ben living that way – he'd seen it in Balmain – but surely it was weird in a house where you all chose to live together?

It gave him an idea. Maybe he could rent out a room in *his* house. His rented house. If he could find someone he never saw to pay $200 a week, it would actually change his life.

CHANGE YOUR LIFE FOR $200! He typed in his head. A head line.

His house was close to the city and the uni. There were bound to be people interested in sharing it. It would have to be someone who was never there because he was there almost all the time.

He wondered for a moment whether he should run the idea past Stuart, who might run it past the owner, but decided against it. He didn't want to jeopardise the current arrangement, where he deposited his rent directly into a mystery bank account every fortnight. There was no lease, no prohibition on pets (or permission), no clauses to prevent subletting, no problems.

He got home just as the rain really hit. Eve was on the bed, wide-eyed awake and ready to hide. He rubbed between her ears and told her he loved her.

The downpipe out the back overflowed when there was anything more than drizzle and now it was flooding across the brick terrace and onto the azaleas. There were rectangular dead patches on the small back lawn where he'd left the sunbed too long in the same place. They looked like fresh graves.

He stood at the window and wondered about Annie's funeral and where Ben was. Was he in this storm or sheltered from it? The police investigation seemed lackadaisical at best. He was grateful for Cooper's update and empathy, but there was no sense of urgency. On the bright side, at this rate the police would never find Ben.

The drift of rain across the treetops in the valley was beautiful.

The Christmas cardboard box was still on the floor. Finally, days that felt like weeks later, he took it through to the front room and dropped it in a corner. This was his writing room, his office, his morning sunroom, the room that faced the street, the room Ben had left. He tried to imagine someone else living here. Where would they put their bed? In his house. How would they look nude? In his house. He'd have to move all his stuff to the lounge room. Could he write out there, with his ghost guest coming and going?

He remembered the message that had beeped in his pocket in Forest Street. It was from Claire. *Where's Ben's dictionary?* It was amazing they hadn't thought of this before.

Ben had asked for the dictionary for his fifteenth birthday. He loved words, learning them, knowing them, then deconstructing and mangling them. He and Claire both took credit for this love and loved him for it. He was the only fifteen-year-old boy they knew who wanted a dictionary for his birthday.

The *Concise Oxford Dictionary* soon became his strange diary. He scribbled in it to redefine words so they fitted his life, or found words that found him and put gold star stickers alongside their meanings. He drew pictures in the margins and made mad cross-references. He pressed flowers from the back garden, or colourful chocolate foil wrappers, between its white wordy pages.

He had taken the dictionary with him when he left Balmain. They both knew he carried it as a precious item into his unknown worlds.

His phone rang. It was Lloyd. He'd done some work for him over the years. 'Lloyd, hello!'

'Hey, Patrick. Merry Christmas.'

'You too. Long time, no hear. How's business?'

'Flat chat. You know we got taken over by Sphere?'

'No, but then I don't know what Sphere is.'

'International. American originally but they've got offices all over now and we're one of them.'

'Congratulations. If they bought you out you must be rich.'

'Well. Still working like a bastard.'

'Rich and stupid generally do go together.'

Lloyd laughed. 'That's not much of a way to apply for a job, Patrick.'

'Is that what I'm doing?'

'Do you want one?'

'No, but I need one. Actually, I've just been thinking about getting a tenant in to help pay the rent.'

'In that case, the job's yours.'

'Right! This is going well. When do I start?'

'You start and finish on Wednesday. All day. Taxation department, I'm sorry to say. You've probably heard that they've cocked everything up with some new computer system.'

'I read something. Made me think I needn't worry about getting in last year's return.'

'That might be a bit optimistic. Anyway, they've shat themselves and want to recruit before Christmas to sort things before everyone realises.'

'So, where's the job?'

'Our office in the city. Same office, different letterhead. I'll text you all the details. You're up for this? You don't need to check your diary or anything?'

'I'm looking at it now.' He wasn't. He didn't really have one. 'Wednesday's good.'

'That's great. Early start. 8am. We should finish about five. Your tax and bank details all the same?'

'I think so. Can you text through what you've got and I'll confirm?'

'Will do. Should I ask how things are going?'

'Probably not.'

'Ha! Maybe we can catch up for a drink before Christmas. We'll be having some sort of party.' Those were the days, Patrick thought to himself. 'I'll give you the details on Wednesday.'

'That's great. Thanks a lot, Lloyd. I appreciate it.'

'Cheers, mate.'

He dropped the phone back onto the desk. Wow! He was tempted to think he'd conjured all that himself with his magical thinking on how to make ends meet. It was a busy time, what with Ben and all, but he could spare a day. For money.

He'd worked for Lloyd as a scribe a number of times over the lean years – which were most years. It sounded good but actually all he did as a scribe was sit in on job interviews, take notes and prepare reports on candidates. Some of the jobs were interesting, on naval bases on the harbour foreshore, and once they flew him to Brisbane in mid-winter.

He would have to get his suit out and give it an airing.

CRYING IN THE CHAPEL

I t turned out he needed his suit for a funeral, too.

Patrick didn't often travel over the bridge these days. They did things differently over there. They had money, for one thing. And lots of them wore those awful boating shoes on the weekends, for another. They probably had boats. Someone must own all those millions bobbing in the coves.

He was going to Annie's funeral at the Northern Suburbs Crematorium. Claire was unable to make it.

The crematorium grounds were vast. He drove along sweeping drives through topiary gardens. The weather had improved on yesterday's but in the distance, over North Sydney, a rainbow struggled to appear. It was just a shimmer.

There were various chapels and, as he drove, he saw different groups of mourners, young and old, dressed in dark clothes. Even babies in prams were part of the big rhythm of death out here.

The chapel car park was less than half full. He was twenty minutes early and sat in the car watching who arrived. He doubted Ben would show and wasn't sure he wanted him to although it would be good to see him alive, and hug him into the twenty-first century.

One or two cars of young people arrived and he peered to see who got out. They might be friends of Ben now for all he knew. With ten minutes to go, he wandered down to the chapel, an annex to larger chapels that faced off discreetly to other car parks.

He saw who must have been Annie's parents, being consoled by everyone who arrived, her father tall and fleshy and fiercely composed, her mother distraught. She lifted her large sunglasses and dabbed her eyes with a handkerchief. Women he guessed were her sisters comforted her. He dreaded the prospect of talking with them.

He was the last to head inside and sat a few rows behind the mourners. Exposed beams loomed over the half-empty pews. Annie's coffin sat square to the chapel, covered in red roses.

The eulogy was brief. The funeral guy professionally lamented the tragic early loss of this gifted student, a troubled soul capable of great kindness, a free spirit and wanderer, loved by her friends and her family. Her father walked to the podium and started firmly and with angry grace, but then wept and finished before he had intended to.

A female university friend said Annie was the one to party with, who loved life, who challenged orthodoxy and then sometimes just disappeared from the scene without notice. Now she had disappeared again. He wept with the rest of them, at last. He couldn't help it. Grief is contagious and life is such a sweet, complicated thing to lose. He wanted Ben to appear now.

Recorded piano music played as family and friends filed out into the windy sunshine.

Outside, the mourners stood around in small huddles. Annie's friend from university was now jigging a baby on her hip. Annie's parents were surrounded by others. Patrick approached the woman with the baby. 'You spoke well,' he said. 'I'm sorry Annie's not around to party anymore.'

She smiled weakly, her baby struggling in her arms. 'Thanks.'

'My name's Patrick. Annie was my son's girlfriend.'

She smiled. 'That's good,' she said, looking around. 'Is your son here?'

'He couldn't make it. It's complicated.'

The woman's red hair blew across her face in the wind. 'That sounds about right for Annie,' she said kindly.

'Do you know why Annie sometimes "just disappeared"?'

'Not really. She got kind of intense and then she stopped coming out with us all. She wasn't on Facebook. No mobile. Didn't see her around at parties anymore.'

'No mobile! Wow!'

'I know, right?'

'Did she have a boyfriend then?'

'Adrian? Adrian Blair, that's right.' The baby squirmed. 'Nice guy. A bit schizo.'

'What's that mean?' he asked.

'Sorry. He *was* schizophrenic. I'm not just being flippant,' she said, looking at him. 'He had mood swings and, now that I look back, I think Annie swung with him. It was scary sometimes. Annie said the cure was worse than the disease.'

'Do you mean his medication?'

The woman nodded. Annie's parents were shaking hands and accepting kisses and looked set to move away. 'I want to pay my respects to Annie's parents. Thanks again.'

Her parents were walking up a path to the car park, holding hands. Rather than ambush them on the narrow path, Patrick waited until they walked across the car park. The blinkers flashed and beeped on a black Audi.

'Excuse me,' he said.

They both turned to face him. In her large sunglasses, her mother looked like an extra from a 1960s Italian film.

He extended his hand towards the father. 'I'm Patrick Hyland. I'm very sorry for your loss.' They shook hands, her father's grip furiously strong.

'Thank you,' he said, tilting his head back and looking down his nose at Patrick as though he might ordinarily wear reading glasses to see up close. 'I'm sorry, I don't think we've met. How did you know Anne?' His voice was deep and round.

'I didn't. I have a son, Ben, and Annie was his girlfriend.'

The father swung a right hook with surprising speed for such a big bloke and hit Patrick perfectly on the jaw. He collapsed onto the bitumen like a sack of shit.

'Stephen!' his wife cried. Patrick sat upright, leaning on one arm to steady himself. 'Are you alright?' she asked him. He was light-headed.

'Leave him, Alice! He's not in a coffin.'

Patrick wiped his lip with the back of his hand and saw blood. He could feel it warm and metallic in his mouth. 'I'm OK.'

'And Anne's dead, thanks to your bloody hopeless son. Where is he?' Stephen loomed over Patrick as if he might lay into him again.

'I don't know,' he said, adrenaline kicking in now. 'He's missing. But if I have to put him in a coffin soon I'll send you an invitation.'

'Don't bother,' Stephen said, retreating into the driver's seat of the car, slamming the door closed so that Patrick felt a puff of wind.

'Let me help you up,' Alice said, but he waved her back.

'No. Thank you. It's OK.' He kneeled for a moment and got his balance.

'Can you move your jaw?'

He did, and nodded. He stood and Alice half helped him up anyway, her black bag slipping down her arm and hitting him on the thigh. Stephen started the Audi.

'Thank you,' Patrick said again. 'Actually, I understand. I'm sorry for approaching you like that. I'm sorry about Annie.' Stephen tooted the horn. 'Ben loved her.'

'The police say he's in hiding.'

'Is that what they said?' That didn't sound like Cooper. Maybe they tailored the message according to who they were talking to. 'My son has an illness. And he's prone to disappearing.'

'Schizophrenia?' Alice asked, world weary.

'How did you know?' Patrick asked.

'She has form. She was a great one for lost causes, our Anne.' She put a hand on Patrick's forearm. 'Not that I'm saying your son is a lost cause. And neither were most of the others. I never met him but I'm glad Ben loved Anne. I'm glad she didn't die alone.'

Most of the others? The more Patrick knew, the less he felt he knew. Stephen tooted the horn again and leaned on it this time.

'If you want to sue us, we're in the phone book. Benson. Montague Road.' She walked around the back of the car and was gone. The black Audi revved and was gone too. Patrick spat out a gob of blood.

• • • •

He met Claire at a small sandstone café in Balmain an hour later. She could make time for this but not the funeral, he noted bitterly. Not that she was a shirker. She was brave and bold, he knew, but seemed off kilter with all this.

'What happened?' she asked, looking at his split lip.

'I got punched by Annie's father, Stephen, at her funeral.'

They were sitting on metal chairs on the footpath and a young waiter appeared. Patrick ordered a strong flat white. He wanted wine but there was none on the menu. Claire ordered a skinny latte and water.

'Why did he punch you?'

'I told them Ben was her boyfriend and I was his father.'

She leaned back. She was wearing a red short-sleeved shirt with a green string pendant and she looked gorgeous. She put her hand flat, facing up on the table and he took hold of it.

'Oh, Ben!' she said.

'Ben boy. All I have to do now is mention his name and someone punches me in the face. I think our work here is done.'

She clenched his hand. 'I've never seen you punched up before.'

'I've never been punched up before.'

'It kind of suits you.'

'You just wish you had thought of doing it.' There were times back when they separated when he had thought she might hit him. She never did.

The waiter brought coffees, then a bottle of water and glasses. Nothing matched, not even the cups and saucers. Discord was the new chic.

'Her father was distressed, obviously. Maybe he just wanted to punch someone, and I was nearest to him'

'Isn't he the uni professor?'

'He is. I've been assaulted by an ageing academic! Aside from that, it was worth going. I spoke to her mum and an old uni friend of Annie's and I think Ben had found someone good.'

'And dangerous! It sounds like she was illegally experimenting on Ben.'

'That doesn't make her bad.'

'Doesn't it?'

'Everything I heard today suggests her medicating Ben wasn't just junkie stuff. She's qualified, but freelancing. And it sounds like she's done it before Ben. Her mother implied there'd been others. I don't think it was all hapless and hopeless.'

They drank coffee. She looked into his eyes. 'Good on you,' she said with love. 'For going to the funeral and being angry and smart like this.' They were still holding hands. They hadn't done that for a long time. He felt the stirrings of an erection. Probably best not to mention it.

She leaned forward and ran her finger gently over his swollen split lip. Definite erection now. 'Thanks, Patrick. Don't keep any secrets. I have to get back home to work.'

'So soon? I might have concussion. You probably should sit by my bed and watch me sleep. Or stop me from sleeping would be the medical advice, I think.'

'Don't tempt me.' She stood and walked away and took her nice arse with her and he got the sense she was teasing him. He hoped so.

He walked to Dick's Hotel and had a beer in the garden out the back under canvas sails. It was the first of December, mid-week and not yet crowded. He used to drink here a bit when he still lived in the family home, with the family wife and family son. He was lonely now. He'd enjoyed holding Claire's hand.

Scotty in the corner recognised him when he was ordering his beer. 'I thought you were dead, you bastard,' he said by way of greeting.

'Not yet, Scotty,' Patrick said. 'I'm too old to be dead.' That would confuse him. Young people die, Patrick thought. Not me.

After a couple of beers, he drove home to Forest Lodge. An endless procession of jets rumbled down to land under the clouds at Sydney Airport only a few kilometres away. Eve demanded cuddles even before food, which was unusual. She'd been neglected. He sat on the red couch and roughed her up behind the ears, tickled under her chin.

Frozen sliced pork was thawing in the microwave. He planned to make a stir-fry with chillies and basil from the back garden. His nice back garden. Before he got up to open a bottle of red, he let Eve know that he was going to get back together with Claire.

THE FIZZ. 2000.

B en was born in April 2000, a week and a half overdue. He was a good weight at 7lb 3oz. Under all that slime he was kind of blue. His head wasn't the right shape either, Patrick realised in a kind of daze, and wondered why none of the hospital staff seemed alarmed.

Claire was pale and torn and beautiful. Seeing her function like an animal had overwhelmed him. Even before Ben wailed his first breath Patrick had been wailing with Claire and he was worn out. Just hours after the birth, after time spent in a room with his wife and their miracle tiny boy wrapped in a white rug between them, he went home.

It was almost 10pm and he should have gone to bed but he was too tired and too wired to sleep. They were living in a narrow terrace house in Summer Hill, near the train lines into the city. It was a warm, airless night. He could have gone to the local pub but he wanted to walk and breathe. He crossed the railway tracks on a footbridge, lingered to watch a couple of trains, tubes of light and noise, hurtle towards the city or out into the universe. What a universe!

The territory over here was strange. He found a pub on a corner, old and suburban with an L-shaped bar, mostly empty. The barman was overweight with an overweight moustache that kept him in some kind of weird proportion, like a giant. Patrick ordered a glass of champagne.

'We've only got Seaview sparkling.'

'A glass of that, then!' he said.

It was only available by the bottle and so he ordered that. He could walk home with the leftovers if the bar closed. The giant removed the cork from the bottle without a sound, no pop or celebration, and poured a glass for Patrick. He put the bottle into a plastic cooler with some blocks of ice and set it on the bar.

Patrick lifted his glass and tilted it to watch the bubbles sway to Claire and Ben and him. He held it up to the light, then poured the cold fizz down his throat. The first glass didn't last long. He poured a second.

A young woman appeared at the bar beside him and waited for service. The barman was loading the dishwasher with a rack of glasses.

'You look like you're enjoying that,' she said. Black wavy hair, soft red lips, wearing a pinafore, high-waisted, pleated below, a bit like a school uniform.

'Indeed, I am,' he said. 'I've just become a father.'

'Today?' she asked. He nodded. 'Congratulations. That's wonderful. A boy or a girl?'

'A boy. Ben. Would you like a glass to celebrate with me?' Patrick asked. 'Please. It's not right to be doing this by myself.'

'Are you sure?'

'Mr Barman, may we have another glass?'

They moved to a wooden table by the window. Her name was Ineka. She smoked and he said he didn't mind even though he did. Everything seemed strange and trivial to him. He wanted to tell her about the astonishing sight of his son's head appearing but that seemed too intimate and he wasn't sure that he wouldn't start wailing again.

Ineka did the right thing and asked obvious questions, whether they had a baby room ready at home, did they know it was going to be a boy. He was drunk with happiness. Her questions made him feel special, as if he was new in the world like Ben. In a way he was. She smiled a lot and when she drank most of her fingers flared away and didn't touch the glass. Her fingernails were painted black.

'Do you have children?' he asked when the bubble of conversation hit some dead air.

She shook her head and blew cigarette smoke out the window. 'Some day I'd like to but I'm only twenty-four and my career is just taking off.'

'What do you do?'

'I'm in communications.'

He had no idea what that meant, even though he suspected he was in communications too. 'Good choice,' he said enthusiastically. He liked her hair and her square face.

They finished the Seaview and he offered to buy another bottle. She declined, there was work tomorrow, communicating. She was going to walk home and he offered to be a chaperone. Her shoes weren't sensible or maybe it was the wine but at some point, she stumbled and he took her hand to steady her. Her hand was warm. They steadied each other under the green street lights until they got to her place, another narrow terrace house lined up in another street, like dominoes. As she fumbled for the key, Patrick leaned back and looked up at the night sky. There were pale stars. His heart was belting.

'Do you want to come in?' she asked. 'Your choice.'

She flicked on a light in the hallway. She kicked off her shoes and left them there. He walked in. One more drink, he told himself. She went into a bedroom and he stood at the door there and watched her. She leaned over a double bed and turned on a bedside lamp with a golden shade, then rolled over and propped on her elbows. They looked at one another.

Patrick wasn't sure if things were getting more, or less, complicated. More. Much more, but the world was strange tonight. It was unleashed and sudden and tomorrow it would settle down. 'Maybe I should close the front door,' he said, glancing back down the corridor and seeing her red shoes there like spots of blood on the wooden floor.

'Maybe you should,' Ineka said.

When he got to the front door, he could feel the warm outside air and see the dark. He thought about things again. He stepped outside and closed the door quietly behind him, and walked home.

C laire was in the third tier of audience seats. There was no audience. It was mid-morning and they were rehearsing that night's episode of *Last Week's News*. It was a show she had pitched and created and this was the second series. That made it a success, though success didn't mean anything anymore. You could still be cancelled without notice.

LWN was an antidote to the twenty-four-hour news cycle. Instead of trying to keep up – the ABC had an entire digital channel devoted to that – they had slowed down. A couple of researchers and a host kept tabs on stories as they blurred past and then revisited them to check on the changed lives of those involved.

The news didn't have to come from the previous week. Sometimes they picked up threads from a month or a decade ago. Viewer posts to the website mostly said, '*I'd forgotten all about this. Thank you!*'

She was reading the latest version of the script but she was tired. She hadn't slept well after speaking to her solicitor friend yesterday. This was one way back to Ben, she hoped. Legal. Technical. Tick a box.

'Ben may have killed his girlfriend,' she had said over the phone, after pleasantries.

'Oh!'

'Indeed.'

Silence. 'And is she dead?'

'Yes.'

Claire admired the question. Sonya's daughter had gone through school with Ben. They had dated for a while, cute and clumsy. Sonya knew about Ben's mental health issues and delusions. Claire wondered if she was thanking her lucky stars on the other end of the line; her daughter was safe.

Ben was facing up to twenty-five years in prison, apparently. 'But that won't happen,' Sonya said, matter of fact, supportive.

Involuntary manslaughter, with Ben's established mental health issues, as well as his drug use on the night, might result in a sentence of ten years or less. It was still a death sentence, Claire thought, the script in front of her blurring. Ben was young and good looking. He was a smart arse. He couldn't fight. He needed medication.

Claire's phone beeped. It was Denise. The forecast looked terrible for tennis on Thursday, apparently. She was about to go grocery shopping. Exclamation mark. Smiley face.

Claire smiley-faced back. She felt bad for Denise. A good marriage is a gift. Life pours in its daily magic. She had had many years of that. But a bad marriage? With kids? There was pain ahead for Denise. For everyone.

Claire had never felt her marriage was bad. Annoying, yes. Patrick lacked motivation, drank too much, hadn't coped well with Ben's illness. Who had? He hadn't gotten fat, like Denise's husband. He had never got boring. She could see why some poetess in the Blue Mountains might fall for him. And why he might reciprocate, even. But it had hurt her in a way that still surprised her. Even after she had started her relationship with Philip, it had never felt to her that Patrick was gone from her life. Now he felt more in her life than ever.

Her phone beeped again. It was from Patrick. Of course it was. *CALL ME* in capitals. There was so much electrical equipment and insulation in the studio, most phones would not operate for a call. She dumped the script onto the seat beside her and stepped down and out of the studio. The vast foyer was busy and she found a quiet couch over by the glass wall looking onto Harris Street. Her phone usually worked here.

Patrick answered in an excited rush. 'Annie died of respiratory failure!'

'Wait! What?' Her own heart was racing.

'I've heard back from Stuart. She died of respiratory failure after a heroin overdose.'

'They were taking heroin?'

'Well, *she* was, apparently. Christ knows, but according to Stuart, Ben's no longer in the frame. He didn't do it!'

Claire breathed deeply. 'I hope not.'

'What's that mean?'

'He put a pillow over her head. That could...'

'Oh, Jesus, Claire! It was a heroin overdose! Not a fucking pillow.'

'We need that confirmed by the police, Patrick,' she said, still executive producer in spite of her rush. 'Will you follow up on that?'

'I will. I will. It rings true. I felt the sting had gone out of Cooper's investigation already. This is why.'

'Where are you now?'

'I'm in my back garden.'

'I'll be there in ten minutes. Let's talk and have a drink.'

Music to his ears. He had the gin, and was surprised to find there was tonic in the fridge as well. A precautionary, prehistoric purchase. Alcoholic instinct. He changed into a white cotton shirt just as there was a knock on the door. Not a police knock, this time.

Claire stepped inside and put her arms around him. He hugged her back and she started crying. Soon she was sobbing. He held her tighter and breathed in her smell, relived her size and shape in his arms.

'Most of my visitors cry when they leave,' he said eventually, 'not when they get here.'

She peeled back and smiled. Her eyeliner was a mess. 'Oh my God! I've been so wound up. Have you got a tissue?'

'Come through.'

She went to the bathroom while he prepared two strong gin and tonics with ice and lemon. He went and grabbed sprigs of thyme from the garden and tossed one into each glass as well. Showing off. It was a mild afternoon and he took the drinks out into the dappled sunlight on the deck.

She reappeared and they touched glasses. 'There's no way Stuart will have got this wrong, is there?'

'It's Stuart! What do you think?'

'No. But why hasn't Cooper told you?'

It was a good question. He didn't want to think about the answer. 'He did ask me a while back whether Ben was a heroin user. I wondered what that was all about.'

'Do you think he is? It sounds like Annie's not the angel you think she is.'

'Oh, cheer up.'

They both sipped, still standing, then dragged the metal chairs out from under the table and sat down.

'I'm trying not to be too happy,' she said. 'Here's to poor Annie and her parents.'

'Even the one who punched me?' Patrick asked.

'Even him.'

'Well, here's to Ben, too.'

They sat on the deck and drank gin together.

After a few months, she told him she wanted a break. She was exhausted.

'How long for?' he asked, surprised at his own panic. He needed a chill pill.

She didn't know. Not long.

And that was Annie, and she was gone.

BODY AND SOUL AND CHARDONNAY

When Patrick called him, Cooper confirmed Stuart's scoop. Toxicology had recorded heroin and Valium in Anne Benson's bloodstream. A deadly cocktail.

'The heart rate drops,' he said, 'blood pressure falls. In a worst-case scenario, the body just forgets to breathe. Accidental. Stupid. Death by misadventure.'

Patrick wondered if he could parlay that term into an article. Would you rather die in an adventure or a misadventure? He drew question marks on a notepad so he would remember later.

But it didn't make sense.

What he'd heard from Ben and Mick didn't tally with the idea of Annie as a heroin addict, not that he planned to argue with the finding. Fish was off the hook. Ben had told him Annie had taken sleeping pills that night, after their argument. He just hadn't mentioned the heroin. Who would tell a dad that?

Officially, the police still wanted to interview Ben. Unofficially, based on evidence and resources, Cooper said they were 'reprioritising' the investigation. It was close to closed.

Now all they had to do was find Ben and tell him.

They divided up the search. Claire was going back to their networks: social workers, refuges, one-time school friends. At the very least she could get the message out to Ben that he wasn't in trouble. Patrick would find out if Ben had new friends, and where he might be. They hadn't been focusing full throttle on finding him until now. They were used to him being gone, and finding him might have meant prison and despair. Not anymore.

Patrick grabbed an old phone book that had been in the house when he moved in. The print seemed very small and he wondered if he might need glasses soon.

Benson. Montague Street. A woman answered. 'Hello, Mrs Benson. This is Patrick Hyland. We met at your daughter's funeral. Your husband punched me.'

'Yes.' She was hesitant. 'How are you?'

'On the mend, thanks for asking. My jaw's OK. I won't be pressing charges. I wonder if we could meet to talk about our kids?' There was a long delay where time poured into a grave. He waited. He could hear soft piano music playing in the background in her house.

'Yes,' she said eventually.

They met in a cafe on Military Road – comfortable chairs, shit coffee. Without her sunglasses on, Alice had beautiful pale blue eyes. Her hair was softer. She was air-conditioned, middle-aged, North Shore. Patrick liked her anyway. When it was obvious they were going to outlast a coffee, he offered to buy her a glass of wine. She suggested a bottle of chardonnay. He conceded.

'People find it hard,' she said, relaxing at last. All that rigid self-control, the funeral, the family, was behind her now. Patrick guessed she'd decided he was an ally, of sorts. 'They want to be kind but they don't know what to say.'

'What can you say? I think grief accumulates. Everyone brings their own grief to yours and it's a great big lead balloon. But happiness blows through you like a breeze.'

The corners of her mouth bent down. 'Stephen's wretched because he and Anne had been arguing.'

'When?'

She scoffed. 'Always. That's all they ever did since she finished uni. She was very bright. I was a nurse for twenty years. We both knew Anne knew her stuff. She flew through honours.'

'And what was her stuff?'

94

'Pharmacology. Or people, in Anne's case. It wasn't all science for her. There was the "soul".'

He remembered Alice's remarks after the funeral about Annie falling for schizophrenics. Annie's old uni friend had said the same thing. And then there were 'most of the others'.

'You said Annie had a history of helping people with schizophrenia?'

'She did.'

'How did she find them?'

'I'm tempted to say in the gutter. I don't know. How did she find Ben?'

'In a share house in Newtown.'

She sipped her chardonnay.

'What did they argue about? Her and her dad?'

'After uni she refused to register or go into practice. The more Stephen argued, the more she defied him. She lurched from one "case study" to the next, sleeping with them – I'm her mother, she told me – turning all she'd learned into some kind of sordid pilgrimage. It drove Stephen mad. It drove me mad too, but in the end I relented because otherwise we'd have lost her completely. Well...' she waved her hand in mid-air, dust to dust.

'Was Annie schizophrenic too?'

'No! No, she was just empathetic and, what...? "Revolutionary", she used to say.'

'How did you stay in touch with her?'

'She'd phone me. We met up now and then, like this.'

'So she had a mobile phone?'

'Of course. Doesn't everyone?'

'Not Ben. Well, he's had them but then loses them. He called me after Annie died. The police said he used a "burner" phone. Do you know what that is?'

'I've no idea.' She looked suddenly exhausted.

'Me neither. Are you OK?' She nodded. 'Thanks for talking with me.'

'I'm sort of enjoying it,' she said. 'I'm glad she didn't die alone. It could easily have happened.'

She asked about Ben and he told her the little he knew about their relationship. That Ben had loved her. He wasn't just a "case study", though Patrick thought now that he might have been. He told her he'd visited the house and spoken with the housemate. He confessed the place was a little sordid and, under the circumstances, obviously sad.

'I didn't go,' she said. 'Stephen went there with the police and said the place was a disgrace.'

'Ben said Annie was supplying his medication.'

Alice nodded. 'That'd be right. That's what she did.'

'Where would she get the medication from?'

'She didn't trust the drug companies, or indeed the medical profession. It was all this cloak and dagger stuff, in her head, because she said she was treading on their turf.'

'But she was getting drugs from somewhere. Ben was on them.'

'I think she used whatever prescribed medications these boys were on – they were always boys – but modified them on the basis of her own "diagnosis". She'd know how to do that. And then her "body and soul" treatment. Different drugs and doses. Diet. She was no fool but it's so dangerous. Illegal. According to her she had cured people. Got them off their medication. She thought the big drug companies were after her because she was going to ruin their business model. Their pills were full of rubbish, she said. Fillers and flavours. And just wrong, usually.'

'You think she was paranoid?'

Alice shook her head. 'Delusional.'

'But where did she get the non-prescribed drugs?'

'I've no idea,' Alice said plainly. 'She wouldn't tell me. I'm telling you what I know.'

'Thank you.' He paused. 'Sorry. I have more questions.' Alice waved her hand, inviting him on. 'Were you surprised by the autopsy results?'

'We were! Annie's taken drugs over the years but she knows what she's taking, and how to take it, and heroin was never her thing, as far as I knew. And that dart in her arm.' She shook her head and took a slug of wine. 'But I was numb by then and nothing surprised me. The whole thing comes from another world but it's a world she chose to live in.'

'Ben smoked dope that night too. That surprised us because he knows how bad it is for his state of mind.' Two lost souls swimming in a fish bowl. Pink Floyd played in his head.

'We couldn't believe it. Didn't want to believe it. But they had the syringe.'

Patrick did a double take. He hadn't seen a syringe, or gear for that matter. Not that he was ever supposed to have been there. 'Where was that found?'

'In the bedding.'

'And did forensics check the syringe?' he asked, like a lawyer setting Ben free.

She nodded. 'Her fingerprints. Until they told us that, Stephen blamed Ben. In spite of that evidence, I think he still does. Now that she's gone he wants to blame anyone but Anne. He'd probably punch you again if he saw you. He used to box, you know.'

'It felt like it. Quite the renaissance man. Brains and brawn.'

'In his day. His world's closed in.'

He could feel himself relaxing. Maybe it was the chardonnay, but more likely it was the distance increasing between Ben and trouble. 'I'm sorry to ask this, but I'm sure you've asked yourself. Is it possible that Annie meant this to happen?'

She poured the last of the wine. More of it in her glass, he noticed.

'Suicide? I think Anne would be the last person to kill herself. She was ferociously sure of herself.'

Patrick nodded and gave Alice a gentle smile. As a parent, that would be a consolation. He changed the subject. 'As far as I can tell, neither Ben nor Annie were working. What were they living on? She paid the rent in cash apparently.'

'Don't tell Stephen. I'd arranged an account a while back that I put some money in each month. Not much. Not enough, whatever that is, but I'm glad to hear she was paying rent. I didn't want her homeless or selling herself to fund her revolution. How does your Ben fund himself?'

'No idea! He's been on sickness benefits and was on a pension for five minutes before yet another review sent him back to Centrelink, or whatever it's called now. He never had the patience to jump through their hoops. He was going to start his own business ironing shirts: IRONY, he was going to call it.'

Alice laughed. 'That's good. Has he ever ironed a shirt?'

'He has. He was weirdly interested for a while there, and good at it. In spite of his problems, he's a great kid.' He was about to eulogise Ben and Annie's time together but remembered Ben's confession about their fighting and hitting. He'd seen their bruises. He drank the last of his wine instead.

'Do you know if Annie had any close friends?' He finally asked the question he had come here to ask, the question that could be a map back to Ben. 'Someone who might know where Ben is or even be offering him a couch?'

'I think the only friends she had were those she was sleeping with and "treating".' She drew air quotes. That included Ben. Her bitterness was painful to watch.

The chardonnay was empty. They agreed to stay in touch. The North Shore fancied itself as the Left Bank and Patrick kissed her farewell lightly on both the cheeks she offered. He left with the name and address of one of Annie's ex-boyfriends, or patients, or whatever they were. This boy didn't have a mobile phone either, it seemed. A pattern was emerging.

Less than half a bottle of chardonnay wasn't going to put him over the limit he reasoned as he got int his car. At a set of lights not far from the cafe, Patrick saw the cleaner from Forest Street walk across Military Road. He grabbed his phone and snapped a couple of pictures before the lights changed and he had to move forward with the traffic. The chance to confront him was gone.

But something bigger was going on, Patrick decided.

DEAD DRUNK

B en came home one day when he was fifteen and found both of his parents dead on the back lawn.

He'd been at tennis with his friend, Sid. They had poured glasses of chocolate milk in the kitchen and wandered out into the garden. His mum was on her back, her feet facing him so that all he noticed were her shoes and then her chest, all poking up. His dad was nearby, face down on the lawn. They were side by side like sardines.

'Holy shit!' Sid said and Ben was glad because that meant he wasn't imagining it all. Recently he'd been having weird flashes where things that couldn't possibly be real happened right around him. He'd grind his teeth and before long the world sorted itself back to boring reality. He didn't tell anyone.

But his parents dead on the back lawn was too much, and even Sid could see it.

Ben could feel his eyebrows stabbing into his forehead. 'Mum?' he said. His voice was weird too, sort of high pitched inside his head. He felt like he was ten years old.

'Let's call my parents,' Sid said from somewhere.

Ben stepped out onto the lawn. His mum's mouth was open.

'Don't touch them!' Sid shouted.

Ben leaned over his mother and saw her tits were moving. She was alive. 'Mum!' he said, dropping his glass of milk onto the grass and bending to her. She jerked and coughed and rolled to her side. 'Mum, are you alright?'

She leaned up onto an elbow and rubbed Ben on his arm. 'Yes, honey, I'm fine. You're home! Sorry. I must have fallen asleep.'

Now he saw an empty wine glass on the grass beside his dad.

'You're both pissed, aren't you?' Ben said standing up again. At least they both still had their clothes on. Sid was grinning and looking stupid. 'Why can't you fall asleep in chairs like normal drunks?'

Claire rubbed her hair. 'Are you back from tennis?' She was trying to sound all mum-like and normal. She smiled at Sid. 'Hello, Sid!'

'Hello, Mrs Hyland.'

Ben's heart was still racing and he was embarrassed. He walked across and sat down firmly on his dad's arse. 'Hey, Dad! We're ready to be picked up now.'

Patrick bucked him off and rolled over onto his back, covered his eyes against the sun. 'Right. Yep.' He farted.

Claire joined in, trying to be mother sensible. 'Would you put the kettle on, please, Sid? Ben, can you make us all a pot of tea?'

Sid wandered back into the house. Ben rolled onto his back on the soft lawn and looked up at the sky. There were clouds that didn't look real. The world was really getting more difficult. He felt like he was losing control. He didn't tell anyone.

The whole world was strange and not all bad.

G o early. A cop had told him that when he was researching an article on 'dob-ins' and Australian culture. No-one liked a dobber
but the police got a surprising number of arrests and convictions from
information supplied by the public. Sometimes it was random information from neighbours who'd seen something suspicious. More often it
was rivals wanting to assist the police in locking up the competition.

The trick to successful arrests was to doorknock early, the cop had
said. 'The criminal element stays out late and sleeps in,' he had explained earnestly.

'So do musicians and waiters and shift workers, even journalists,'
Patrick had said.

'Exactly.'

Patrick was in a smelly lift in a housing commission high rise in
Camperdown. It was just after 8am and he was hoping to catch Evan at
home.

The lift doors opened onto a narrow concrete walkway on level
eight with a chest-high concrete safety wall. The view of the morning
stunned him. City buildings rose like steam in the warm air. He took a
moment to look at it all. It was the weekend but the city was beginning
to hum and growl. The weekend hardly meant anything anymore, especially this close to Christmas.

He walked past identical green doors until he came to 815. He
knocked, too gently. Part of him, most of him, was guilty at this out-
rageous intrusion. He waited and listened. Somewhere a yappy little
dog barked. Someone coughed a death rattle and hacked phlegm. There
were smells of stale cooking and cigarette smoke. Down in the streets a
siren sounded.

He knocked again, loud and insistent this time, like the cops who
knocked on his door these days. There was noise from inside 815 and
the door opened.

A thin young man with black-rimmed glasses and wild black hair winced at the light and seemed to take a while to focus on Patrick. Grey tracksuit pants hung low on his hips and emphasised his penis. He was bare-chested and sinewed, healthy, a triangle of chest hair matched the thin triangle beard on his chin.

'What is it, man?' he asked, still blinking.

'My name's Patrick. Are you Evan?'

He scratched his wild hair. 'That depends.'

'I'm a friend of someone you knew.' He suddenly realised that Evan might not know Annie was dead. He felt like a complete bastard.

'Who's this friend?'

'Look...'

Evan stepped backwards and closed the door in one quick movement. The safety chain slotted into place before Patrick knew what had happened.

'Annie!' he said to the green lacquered door. The yappy dog started barking again somewhere overhead. Reggae music began its percussion on mid-air. 'She gave me your address,' he said loudly, joining the din, lying. Bringing Annie back to life.

'She doesn't know my address,' Evan called from inside.

'Well, how come I'm here?' he asked. Nothing. 'We should talk.' He waited for a response that didn't come. 'I have some bad news.' He waited again.

The rest of the tower block played its stale tunes but Evan's door was quiet. After a minute of waiting Patrick turned away and leaned on the safety wall and looked out. The air was still and a morning haze made the view as unreal as a canvas backdrop on a stage.

The safety chain rattled behind him and he heard the door open. 'Who told you where I live?' Evan asked.

Patrick turned around. 'Annie's mother, Alice.' Evan's jaw muscles flexed. He looked Patrick up and down like he was seeing him for the first time.

'And the bad news?'

'I'm really sorry to tell you. Annie's dead.'

Evan breathed in and leaned back. Adjusted slowly. 'What happened?'

'A heroin overdose.'

'Bullshit! Annie! No fucking way.'

'I agree with you.'

'You a copper?'

'No. I'm a friend of a friend. Look, can we talk over breakfast? I'll shout. It doesn't look like you'll eat too much.'

'You'd be surprised.' He shook his head, still digesting the news. 'Fuck! I'll take breakfast. I'm vego, so you're vego too or we don't do it.'

'Eggs are vego, right?'

'Right.' Evan turned back into the room. He emerged wearing a black T-shirt and slammed the door behind him. He walked away towards the lifts without saying a word. The dog started barking again, or maybe it had never stopped.

The cafe was small and nearby. Evan was barefoot and they sat on chairs at a wooden table on the street. At least they weren't on milk crates.

They ordered coffee and eggs on toast. Evan ordered a side of spinach. The blonde waitress brought a bottle of water and Patrick gulped a glass down. Evan fingered his little beard so vigorously as he listened that Patrick thought he might rub it off. He had a watch drawn with a biro on his right wrist.

Evan convinced him that Annie was not a heroin user, not when he knew her. 'She took some pills. Early on we did some LSD – I had to find my centre, she said – and once we found it, she kept me off that too. She was no junkie and she worked her arse off to get me off it.'

He looked at Evan. There was an intensity, a kind of static that came off him, like Ben, and long periods where neither of them said anything. Patrick knew enough to let those spaces happen if he wanted Evan to open up.

'Annie's amazing, hey,' Evan said, his tenses still mixed up.

'It seems so,' Patrick agreed.

'She got me right. Maybe Ben will be OK. How long were they together?'

'A couple of months, I think.'

'Not long enough.' This frank assessment left Patrick taken aback. 'Six months, she reckoned. "Six months and you're fixed or you're fucked". She was boot camp with a big stick. Did she move in with Ben?'

'She did. Well, they both moved in somewhere.'

Evan nodded. 'You couldn't piss about or she'd leave, and you didn't want her to leave because she made you feel better, body and soul. And the sex.' He sipped his coffee. Patrick expected him to keep talking but he didn't.

'What about the sex?'

'It's sweet to have such sex when you've got your senses back. Not wiped out on the meds, you know? It's one of the drugs she uses, for sure, and better than the shit you get in a pop packet. It's one that kept me going.'

Patrick grinned. He hoped Ben had been having remedial sex with Annie. It seemed to be part of her regime.

'We used breathing, in sex. And yoga. Breathing is a drug if you know how to use it. Do you breathe when you have sex?' Black glasses and eyebrows looked at him.

'I think so. I haven't passed out,' Patrick joked.

'You're wasting it, man.'

He wasted a lot. Not just breath. He felt old and ordinary. Sex had never made him unconscious, though he'd had times when he was pretty close. 'How did you two come to live together?'

'I'd been in prison – dumb shit – and then found a space above a warehouse in Erskineville. It wasn't for rent; I just found the metal staircase out the back of an old factory and an open door and moved in. I met Annie in The Rose hotel.'

'Were you on medication?'

'Yes, sir.' He nodded and pushed his glasses back up on his nose. It was already humid. The waitress came and took their plates away. Patrick ordered more coffee. Evan ordered an orange juice. 'Most chicks ask me when I last combed my hair but Annie and I chatted a while and then she asked me what medication I was on. I thought she was a witch. How did she know that?'

Woman on fire. 'She's got a pharmacy degree. A masters.'

'I know that now, but we were in a bar. She had a hot body.'

Patrick remembered when he had wild hair and girls in bars had talked to him. Why did the world always spin one way? 'So, what happened next? How did she save you?'

'She came home with me. Looked at my medicines on the floor. Moved in. Well... I mean, she didn't leave. She seemed to have no other life.'

'She didn't bring any stuff?'

'She had this bag on a long strap on her shoulder.' He lowered one hand down beside his chair and put his other on his shoulder to illustrate. 'That was it.'

Was Ben fixed or fucked, Patrick wondered. He'd seen him, briefly, and he was starting to feel more optimistic.

'"Keep taking this stuff for now", she said, rattling my Medoxil. "You need it. But not this." Some other drug I was on for my schizophrenia. I can't even remember. She kept a little blue book and we talked about what I ate and what exercise I did and what other stuff I took and then she started supplying the pills for me.'

'Annie's mix!'

Evan nodded. 'Yep. Capital A dot M dot. She said pharmacy tablets were full of shit and not made for the bodies that swallowed them. She got me off the piss and the drugs, got me doing yoga. *She* knew my body. Taught me how to breathe. Teased me with her pussy. "The universe", she called it. Suddenly the universe worked for me. I took her mix and started to feel better. The meds fog lifted. I ate better and did yoga. When everything was right again, she set me free into *this* universe.'

'Are you serious?' Patrick asked, impressed and nonplussed and a little bit jealous. 'I'm a journalist. Some of this sounds like shit.'

'I'm just telling it like it is. It wasn't just sex, it was health and mind and balance. She's amazing.'

'What do you mean, "she set me free into this universe"?' he asked. 'Where did she go?'

'She moved out.'

'Why?'

He ran his hand through his mane of black hair. 'It was that thing. I was fixed. She said she loved me and we fucked one last time – several last times, but one last night – and she left in the morning.'

'But what about your medication? Her mix?'

'I was off it by then. Balance. Exercise. Food. Control. A way of living.'

'You're off medication?'

'Yes, sir.'

There was a massive story in all this. Patrick shook his head in disbelief. 'So, she just took her bag and left?'

'She'd lost the bag somewhere by then. She just left.'

Annie was the patron saint of pharmacology, travelling light. Body and soul treatment that she probably hadn't learned at Sydney University. He wished more than ever that Ben had had more time with her.

Why would she die of a heroin overdose? But she had.

'Annie did all this for you and you let her leave just like that?' Patrick asked.

'You can't stop Annie.'

'Do you know where she got the meds you took?'

'Nope.'

'You never asked?'

'Nope.'

Patrick leaned back. 'It was dangerous.'

'No, it wasn't.'

'Illegal.'

'Who gives a shit! So is half the crap our so-called government does.'

Patrick didn't disagree with that. Part of him wanted to give a lecture on the dangers of meddling with mental health and part of him wanted to cheer.

'She never mentioned anyone? Or rang someone?'

'Mister Infinity.'

'Who's that?'

'Dunno. She was gone now and then. She mentioned his name, that's all.'

'Mr Infinity? That's what she called him?'

'Yep.'

'How often did she meet him?'

'Dunno, man. She wouldn't let you keep tabs on her. She came and went her own way.'

Another household of ghosts, by the sound of it.

'I'm trying to find Ben. Is there anyone you can think of I could talk to? Annie's friends, any squats, street people you know who might be able to help me?'

'I never met any of her friends. I don't think she had any.'

'Didn't you think that was unusual?'

'She's unusual all right.' Evan put his hands together on top of his wild black hair. 'Sorry. Really. I left that life behind when she set me free.' There was a partly revealed tattoo on the inside of his right bicep.

'What's the tattoo?' Patrick asked.

He peeled back the sleeve of his T-shirt to reveal a circular design. 'It's double happiness. I got it for me and Annie after she left,' he said.

All this hippie shit. Patrick was delighted that it worked. 'Do you still do yoga?'

'The discipline. "You need a space to get to a place", she said. Every day of the week, man, I salute the sun. Not in a room any more. Now I do it in the park.'

'You've found your space.'

He nodded. 'It's sweet. The birds. The homeless guys in cardboard boxes. The sun.'

Patrick paid the bill. Back in his car, Patrick said "Mr Infinity" as a note into his phone. He found the two photos he'd taken of The Cleaner in Military Road and emailed them to Cooper. They weren't very good but the guy was recognisable. He texted *This is the guy I met inside Forest Street. Can u let me know if he sets off a siren?*

He tossed his phone into the console and turned the ignition. His car wouldn't start.

*S*he walked into his pharmacy and looked around, like any other customer.

She was back.

He saw her from behind the prescription counter and panicked. Why hadn't she texted to warn him like she used to ?

Seeing her in his front world like this, he felt he'd seen a banshee. She belonged to his back world, up those back stairs to the room and the danger they were in there.

She wandered up and down the small aisles, not looking at him, and circled around in front of the prescription counter, where he was serving a customer.

He didn't want to speak to her. He didn't want her here. If anything, he wanted her upstairs. His pulse raced. She was doing this on purpose.

Maybe she'd lost her phone? She hadn't responded to any of his playful sexts since she had left a couple of months ago.

Now here she was walking around in a floral dress, a canvas bag loose over one shoulder, as though she had a right to be here. As if he couldn't stop her.

BADLY. MADLY.

It turned out the weather was OK for tennis after all on Thursday. The predicted storms were now due overnight. Claire was busy at work but that would soon all be over, and she enjoyed the stress release that tennis gave her.

Denise was ten minutes late, which was unusual. It was made more unusual by the fact that Claire could see her sitting in her parked Range Rover in a street alongside the courts. She pretended to fuss with her kit, filled and refilled her water bottle, tied and retied her shoes. She walked onto court where Denise could see her and practised a couple of serves. Denise did not budge.

In the end Claire walked out and along the street, racquet in hand. When she stopped alongside the passenger door, Denise turned her face to her and burst into tears. Claire climbed in.

'I'm so sorry,' Denise said.

'It's OK.' She rubbed her shoulder. Waited. 'Do you want to talk about it?'

'I don't want it to be happening. Can you arrange that?'

'I'm guessing not.'

'Too right. Oh, I'm so stupid!' The car was vast and there was a box of tissues right there and Denise grabbed a fistful. 'Fuck! Sorry.'

'You can keep saying sorry if you want to, but don't feel you have to.'

Denise breathed deeply and dabbed at her eyes, checked herself in the rear-vision mirror. 'At least I don't wear mascara to tennis.'

Claire chanced it. 'What about when you're grocery shopping?'

Denise groaned. 'You picked it! Then I dress up like it's Christmas. Which I've ruined this year and probably for the rest of my kids' lives.' She shook her head.

'I've thought about you a lot during the week. Wondered how it was all going.'

'Badly. Madly. Deeply or whatever that film was. He booked a room. God, what was I thinking? I should have got my kids' faces lasered on my eyeballs when all this started.'

'So, what went wrong?'

'Just all of it. All of it! That's not true. For two hours it was...' She looked at Claire 'Awesome.' She smiled for the first time. 'But then we're outside saying goodbye and one of Andy's trucks is there with one of his drivers... what are the odds?'

'In this universe, or one far, far away?'

'That's what I think! It seems like we're not meant to have the lives we deserve. He's got twenty trucks, I think. Philip would know.'

She wasn't going to ask Philip. The relationships tangle they were getting into felt strange but she was warming to Denise. 'So was the driver waiting for you, or was it bad luck?'

'Bad luck. He saw us. He took a picture. Then he showed the boss.'

'Why would he do that?'

'He's a dumb man.'

'But how does he even know you?'

'We met at last year's company Christmas party, apparently. Andy's not much of a shopper but he knows our greengrocer when he sees me in his arms.' She sort of sighed and moaned all in one breath. 'He informed me that Luke will get the shit beaten out of him.'

'You've got to be kidding!'

'This is trucking, Claire, not the ABC. He wouldn't do it himself but there'd be plenty who'd do it for a Christmas bonus. I can't believe how quickly it's all gone wrong.'

They sat in silence. In every quiet house, lives were rejoicing or falling apart for Christmas. Generations heaved in and out, planted gardens, hoped for the best.

'I'm guessing Luke's your greengrocer. Does he know all this has happened?'

She nodded. 'I've warned him. If they all start fighting, someone will end up dead. I'm serious. I told Andy I'll take the kids and leave him if anyone touches Luke. He wouldn't care if I left but he'd miss the kids. Mind you, I've got nowhere to go.'

'Do you *want* to leave him?'

'Not like this! Not now.'

'Is there any chance he'd hurt *you*?'

'He better not try.' After that bravado hung in the air for a while Denise started crying again. Claire touched her shoulder. 'He never has. But then, I've never had an affair before.'

'Would it help if I asked Philip to talk with him? I think they get on well.'

'They do. But Andy would be furious if he knew I was confiding in you, or anyone else for that matter. He won't tell a soul. Just fucking fume like a kettle on the boil.'

'You can come to my place if you need to. There's room for the kids. He doesn't know where I live.'

Denise gazed at her. 'I can't do that, but you're amazing! Thank you. Sorry! Have you found Ben? God, I'm awful.'

She smiled. 'Not yet, but things are looking up. Patrick's actually been brave and useful. Some good can come out of bad. Trust me. And you're not awful.'

Denise shook her head. 'I'm not a *bad* person.'

'You're not. Think about my offer. Bully him back! And then start talking sense into him and planning your family Christmas.'

Denise slumped her head back against the headrest. 'I feel like hugging you right now but knowing my luck a truck will go past and then I'll be a lesbian.'

Patrick was furious about all the things he couldn't afford. He couldn't afford to run a shit car, he couldn't even afford a Christmas tree, he couldn't afford the rent, a Life. He needed that ghost with a wallet renting the front room.

It took him three hours to get home and $250 for a new car battery. Fuck that. He was going to sell the car. There was a Go Get share car on his street now. He didn't know the details but it was bound to be cheaper than keeping his own car, which he hardly used because he couldn't afford petrol.

He was in the back garden, trying to calm down, looking for something that might do as a Christmas tree.

Should he tell Cooper what he'd discovered? That Annie was some kind of serial drug angel? That she had a supplier named Mr Infinity? He didn't imagine Cooper would drop everything and get onto it. Onto what, actually, anyway? He hadn't even got back to Patrick about the photos of The Cleaner.

In his garden, there was a kaffir lime in a big blue pot. The shape wasn't bad but the leaves were yellowing and the caterpillars had ravaged many of them. He had neglected the garden and needed to get back out here and do things. The nasturtiums were no longer vivid. They belonged in the compost now and not in a salad.

But the lawn was long. Even the grave sites were turning green. Things grew or died apace at the end of a year. Rain and humidity.

Eve appeared, meowing and bumping into him. She rolled onto her back, legs akimbo and demanding attention. Who could resist? He rubbed her furry tummy. He thought about Evan and his yoga. Eve and Evan.

Evan was incredible. With all Patrick's family experience of schizophrenia and medication, it was beyond belief that Annie might have achieved what she had with Evan. But Patrick believed everything he'd heard. Evan was as credible as he was incredible. Annie warped the world.

Eve wanted food. He fed her. She thanked him with a meow.

There was a frangipani in a big plastic pot down the side of the house. It was a branch he'd cut off the tree because it was growing too low across the lawn. He went back outside and checked it out. It had thrived on neglect and was now chest high, six branches, green leaves. It was a Christmas tree.

He watered it well and used the hose to spray off the cobwebs and dust. When it had drained, he carried it inside and put it in front of the fireplace. He felt like a beer. He opened a stubby of pale ale. His phone beeped.

It was Cooper. *No sirens. Curious. Keep me informed.*

Patrick was disappointed. It had felt like things were moving and now they'd stopped again. The Cleaner. Mr Infinity. It sounded like the script for a bad superhero movie. He went back to his Christmas tree. The beer was nice. Sometimes he thought he drank too much red wine. Or at least not enough beer.

He retrieved the box of decorations from the front room. Opened, they smelled like a Chinese chemical factory. He wondered if Philip would help Claire decorate a tree this year. Would she have a tree? Were they broken apart in the same way?

Beer. Christmas cheer. He slugged at it, got another. Had an idea.

He got his phone and dialled the number Ben had given him, the burner phone. The number he dialled was not connected. Please check the number and try again.

Who was Ben calling with that phone, other than him? Annie? He had said it was an old phone that he didn't use much. It was probably Annie's phone. Somewhere in its untraceable chips, he was sure Mr Infinity was lurking. He must ask Cooper for whatever possessions Ben might have left behind, and suggest Alice did the same for Annie's things. Who knew what leads they might find?

Before long he realised his bargain box of decorations was too full of stuff for this spare, prehistoric tree. He decided to ignore the tinsel. He dangled the silver balls and the larger red ones clipped around the stems of the green leaves. They worked! He tried some stars, then removed them. There was nowhere to put the angel.

All the while his brain was processing things. Evan had mentioned a blue diary. Ben had talked about Annie's little red book. They must be her revolutionary versions of case files, her trials and mixes. One for each patient. Person. Body and soul. Where were those books now, how many did she have, and where was Ben's dictionary?

He wondered if Mick worked on Saturdays. He called him. 'Mick! Patrick Ireland!' He said it this time. 'Fish's dad. How's it going?'

'Too hot too often,' said the Irishman.

'Agreed. I don't know whether to blame climate change or you for knocking all the walls down. Look, I really need to have one last look in Forest Street. Are you still there?'

'I am, yeah. And I'm carrying the rent. I might scarper soon.'

'Could I come around? Just for ten minutes.' He recalled the atmosphere when he'd left last time. 'I'll bring beer. Reschs, wasn't it?'

'Aye. How about 3.30?'

'Great, see you then.'

It was awkward. When he got there, there wasn't really anywhere to sit except in that dismal lounge room.. Mick was dressed in dusty big work boots, tan shorts with a T-shirt. He wanted to be in the shower and Patrick wanted to be in the front room, so they agreed to that and then a beer.

Patrick walked back into that bedroom. It seemed smaller now, even though the mattress was still up against the wall and the bedframe too, like a lazy skeleton. He looked up at the serrated glass lampshade that was obviously original. It was strange how some fragile things had survived while the rest of the house was stripped and ruined time and again over decades.

The bookcase was still there in the corner, unharmed by the forensics team. He immediately saw the white lettering on the blue spine. THE CONCISE OXFORD DICTIONARY. He went across and tilted it off the shelf. It seemed to come alive, flexing like a muscle. Pieces of paper fell from it onto the floor. A small pressed yellow flower. He bent urgently to collect them.

He sat on the floor and crossed his legs. He smelled the worn dictionary. This was where Ben retreated when he felt the world no longer understood his meaning. It scared Patrick that he was now alone without it, surprised him too that Ben hadn't come back for it. He had a key, presumably.

The inside facing page had been altered with neat black censor lines to reduce the title to THE IS / OR DI ARY. Ben had even retained the backslash of the X as part of the equation. The Is/Or Diary. In the middle of the page below this, neatly written, was the number 83.

Patrick stroked the title with the pad of his middle finger. Ben, please be alive.

The tidiness of the front page was a mask. The next pages were covered with Ben's scribble in a variety of pens. There were names and childish drawings and bits of mathematics. Lots of question marks were drawn, like patterns. B1 + B2 written in neat lines like soldiers in rows.

The dictionary was swollen with the torn ends of prescription drug packets, bus tickets, scraps of newspaper articles, a small card with a blue smiley face on it, flattened silver foil. There was a sense of intimate and frantic madness. Paper clips bunched some pages together. There were stains. The meanings of words themselves were scribbled over throughout, or new meanings had been written in tiny print onto strips of paper, then glued over the original meanings. There were stars. Pages had wrinkled and warped under this treatment, reluctant in their transformation.

Mick reappeared at the door in a new pair of shorts. 'You find something, then?'

He looked up and realised that he'd hardly been breathing. He had to suck in air before he could speak. 'Yeah. I've found his dictionary. Ben's. Fish's. It's a long story.'

'Not much of a room to die in, hey?' He looked around now. 'I don't suppose any is anyhow. It gives me the creeps. I keep the door closed.'

'Where did they keep their stuff?'

'They never had much. Even Irish backpackers could learn a trick or two about travelling light from those two.' The room echoed to prove the point. Patrick knew Ben could travel light. He came and went like a shadow, survived on nothing. 'You ready for that beer?'

Patrick stood up. 'I'm sorry to ask but it actually could be important. Sorry. Did you ever hear Annie and Fish having sex?'

Mick looked him in the eyes for what felt like a long time and then shrugged his shoulders. 'Aye. Quite often, if I didn't put earphones in. Sometimes I got my own girl in and it was like a regular knockin' shop.' Patrick smiled. Annie and her cures. "The universe".

'I'm still very pissed off with Fish, by the way. That was a dog act.'

'I understand. He was scared.'

'Aye. And gutless.'

There was no point defending Ben, or arguing. 'There's one other thing,' he said. He went back to the bookcase and tilted his head to scan the spines. Some science fiction titles. A thick slab of DVDs. A book about wombats. It looked like the bookshelves in charity shops, jumbled and meaningless.

'Annie kept some small diaries. A red one and a blue one, at least. Did you ever see them or hear her talking about them? They're not here.'

Mick shook his head.

Patrick drank a beer with Mick in the awful orange lounge room and talked about something else for once. Apparently, small-town football teams in Ireland were losing all their young blokes to Australia. Some of them had to close the clubrooms.

'And now our girls, too,' Mick said, 'holding all those stop signs at roadworks around Sydney.'

Patrick had noticed them. 'Well, if you had better weather more of you might stay home.'

'Oh, our weather's better than this hot shite! There's just no jobs.'

He was a lovely bloke. Patrick stood to leave. 'Look, if you do move out and you're stuck for a few days, there's a camp bed at my place.'

They shook hands. 'You're a brave Sydneysider offering an Irishman a bed!'

'A few days.'

'What?' Mick asked and lifted his hand to his ear as if to hear better.

'A few days.'

'What?' Patrick got the joke at last.

He carried the precious dictionary home. He wanted to talk with Claire, explore it with her. There might be clues to Ben's life with Annie. His heart raced and he dreaded looking through it in equal measure. He felt closer to Ben, holding it, but Ben felt further away. Why hadn't he gone back to rescue it himself?

When he got inside, he laid the dictionary on the table like it was a live thing, or something that might spill.

He looked up *Ben*. It was the place to start the trail, the search. Ben would start with himself. There it was, with stars drawn alongside, on page 83 – the number handwritten in the front of the dictionary.

Ben1 n. Inner room.

Ben2 n. Mountain peak.

Even in the dictionary, he was a boy split in two.

FOUND AND LOST

This time it was Claire with the breathless news. They were a team. It was almost dark. He was still lost in the dictionary. The currawongs were calling the end of the day. No aeroplanes were landing or taking off. It was peaceful. His phone rang.

'Someone's seen Ben in Redfern,' she said.

'Wow! When?'

'Last night. He went to a food truck. One of his old social workers was there looking for someone else, and saw him.'

Patrick was grinning. 'Did they talk? How is he?'

'Dave didn't approach but he said Ben recognised him and then cleared off. He thinks Ben will go back underground now or move on.'

'Well, at least he's come up for air. He's alive, Claire!'

'I know!'

'How did he look?'

'Skinny. Nervous. He literally ran off, apparently.'

Patrick thought of the conjuring power of that dictionary. Ben was alive! 'God, I'm sick of not knowing if he's on drugs or off meds or where Annie left him. But he's alive! Did you let Dave and everyone know that Ben can come home? Get the message out that he's not in trouble?'

'Of course.'

Patrick breathed deeply and felt relieved and worried all at once. 'I found his dictionary in the house in Forest Street.'

'Oh, good!' she said. 'And strange.' Patrick was pleased they felt the same way. 'Why hasn't he been back for it? Anyway, he's alive.'

'Maybe he's scared. The room probably haunts him. It haunts me.'

'Any clues or contacts in it?'

'It's on the table in front of me now. It's a bit like taking an engine apart.'

'How would you know?' she asked, incredulous. Patrick never was mechanical.

'A jigsaw puzzle, then. With pieces missing. He's got you amended in the dictionary as ClairVoyant. You can see things that are out of sight. I bet he's wishing you could see him now. In a way you have. Well done.'

Silence.

'He's turned me from Patrick to Patriarch: the father and ruler of the family.' More silence. 'So, aren't we a couple of superheroes?'

'Aren't we just,' she said softly. Their failures hung in mid-air.

'On the bright side, he sees himself as a naked, winged child of love.'

'That's enough, Patrick. I get it.'

He wanted to share this with her. Needed to. He was stunned anew by the dictionary and its visceral definitions of Ben as a teenager and his moods and his meanings and interests.

'Sorry,' he said, brightly. 'But things are looking up. I want to tell you what else I've found. We're making progress and it's great that you've found Ben.'

'Found and lost. Yes, let's meet.'

All good. 'Somewhere nice this time.' Like a date, he wanted to say, but didn't. 'I want the glasses to have stems.'

'Ooh la la.'

They met at a restaurant that wasn't there when he had lived over in Balmain. Restaurants came and went faster than the seasons there. It was in another sandstone building with big lattice windows, linen tablecloths, fine glassware. It was so nice, Patrick asked who was paying.

'My shout,' she said. 'To say thanks for all you've done.'

'For what we've both done.'

He ordered two glasses of Tasmanian sparkling wine to start and a cheaper red off the list, to breathe. She suggested he pick another red. 'Something you want,' she said. Gesture versus gesture. It was like a first date. He stuck with the island theme and chose a Tasmanian pinot noir. Claire liked the lighter red style.

Ben was alive. They were together. The sparkling wine arrived. To Ben! They sipped and lapsed into silence, relieved at last.

'I'm sorry for what I did,' he said, eventually

'What did you do?'

'I made a mistake. The affair. The biggest mistake of my life.'

Claire tuned in, surprised. They'd never really talked about this. He'd never said sorry. The truth was she'd never given him the chance. It hurt too much. Or made her angry, actually.

'And all this, with Ben, seeing you both again, it reminds me every day what I'm missing. What we're missing.' Her green eyes had flecks that weren't there thirty years ago.

'Let's leave Ben out of this for now. And don't say you were drunk.'

'I *was* drunk. That has to be said. And I'm sorry. I always have been.'

'Sorry? Even that weekend you spent with her before you moved out of Balmain?'

'Was thrown out of Balmain – but fair enough. Yes. Even then I was sorry. I knew even then. Especially when she told me I was too old.'

'Something I've always wondered – was she older than Ben?'

'Yes! God.'

'Well, that's the kind of nonsense that's been inside my head, just so you know.'

The tall glasses sparkled, and they sipped in cautious silence.

'I can tell you about it if you want me to.'

'No thanks.'

'Right, in that case... I don't know how else to say this – let it go.'

'Let it go?' She wanted to, but found, bitterly, that she didn't know how.

He nodded. 'Yes. If we want a chance to be together again, for us, for Ben – and I do – then you have to put it in the past. I beg you to forgive me. Please. What can I do? Is there anything I can do?'

'Don't tell me to put it in a box.'

'You'd need to pay a therapist for that kind of wisdom.'

She'd enjoyed seeing him again, in spite of the circumstances. Or maybe because of them. He was helping. She felt it physically, too. 'Why haven't we talked about this before?'

'Well. We never saw each other. I didn't want to fuck things up again. You sensibly wouldn't let me. But I never stopped loving you.' They both smiled. 'I'm sorry.'

They were gazing into each other's eyes now. Connected. When their entrees arrived they both leaned back as the plates were placed, then they leaned forward and checked each other's serve. It was a kind of dance.

'Here's to us, this time,' she said. They touched glasses.

H e demanded more this time around.

He wanted to know what pills she was making, why, for who. He'd put his life on the line, his family and career, and she could no longer just wander in and out when it suited her, he said.

She told him not to get involved, knowing he was already balls deep in it and deeper.

He insisted.

One night in bed, pills and sex done, she explained that she was saving the world one person at a time. When she was ready, she would take what she knew to the world and fix millions of lives.

Lying back, spent, high in that bare little bedroom, he listened to her drone on and knew she was clever and crazy all at once. He wasn't sure where the border was. He didn't really care.

Now she was talking about her time in Mali. Then she was talking about her father. Then global drug companies ripping off the poor. Blah, blah, blah.

He got bored and started talking about himself as his way of joining back in.

He had taken over the pharmacy after his mother became ill and his father had left to look after her. He didn't really want the pharmacy. He was too young and still restless. He felt like his life was pushed onto him and he couldn't do anything about it.

He had a wife and family he loved, and a career opportunity that most of his friends would kill for. He didn't really want either of them.

THE SHORTER (HEAVIER) OXFORD
ENGLISH DICTIONARY

He woke early to the metronome tock of frogs in his neighbour Judy's backyard. Flight paths and frogs. Welcome to inner-city Sydney. Judy was a greenie who planted only native trees and shrubs and was doing her bit for the doomed planet by reintroducing a tiny frog that was once abundant in the creek down in the gully. It made a lovely, deep tocking sound. He hoped Eve wouldn't find her way next door and kill them all.

Stuart called and invited him to go sailing. There was a 'confuckingdition' they would not talk about 'the dead bed' – his tabloid headline for all that had gone wrong. Sailing would take the pressure off waiting.

Patrick had never sailed – he actively resented it, seeing it as evidence of Sydney's wealth and his lack of it – but he'd been on the ferries. Same-same, surely?

He drove across to Cabarita Marina, where the boat was moored among the clinking masts of hundreds of other white boats. Cabarita Point looked like a developer's blow job on whatever council ruled its waves. There were neat streets around low-rise, apartment blocks. Every courtyard garden had the same dwarf gardenias and mondo grass. Cars spewed up from underground car parks. It was another planet. There were no people. No shops. No harbour until he hit the point and then there were clinking masts as far as he could see.

Even here – which was nowhere, as far as he was concerned – there was metered parking. Maybe you were meant to have enough money that you didn't care.

Patrick had no idea what Stuart's boat was called. It was a beautiful afternoon, soft clouds in a blue Sydney sky, a bit of breeze, which even he knew would come in handy if you were mucking about in boats. As he wandered out along the narrow boardwalks, working his phone to call Stuart, he tried to guess what the boat would be called.

He heard Stuart's phone ringing and looked down and saw him right there, hairy legs in boating shoes, white shorts, an old T-shirt bent around his barrel stomach, wraparound sunglasses.

'Gidday, cock!' Stuart beamed, not bothering to answer the phone.

'Hello, Captain Ahab.'

'We might still see a late humpback on its way down south. There was one in the harbour last week. Can you climb down the ladder or do I have to carry you?'

'*Can* you carry me? I'd enjoy that.'

'No.'

He climbed down onto the deck without injury but then the water glugged underneath and immediately tilted him and he had to steady himself against the cabin.

'Jesus Christ,' Stuart moaned.

Soon the engine coughed water and then purred as Stuart backed them out of their berth and steered out between rows of money.

'What's your boat called?' he asked, holding onto a rail, the breeze already a wind out on the water.

'For sail,' he called back. 'S.A.I.L.'

Patrick grinned. 'I get it. That's piss-weak.'

'Yeah, I know. I was filling in a form. I made it up on the spot. They say there are two good days when you own a boat – the day you buy it and the day you sell it. It's bullshit. I love this thing.'

It took Patrick time to get the hang of where he should be without being in the way. Stuart did all the work. The breeze was not enough, Stuart reckoned, but it meant that he needed little help. It was only when they got towards Balmain that Patrick had any idea where they were. He recognised the ferry stop at the end of Birchgrove, the jetty just around the point where he and Ben and Claire used to go fishing.

Suddenly there was the city and the Harbour Bridge.

It was an amazing location for a city, lazing by all that blue water. He felt they were ripping along; the sail was taut and the water sprayed up on him in energising bursts. He breathed full lungs of air and closed his eyes and hoped they didn't hit a whale. The sunlight was warm on his eyelids.

Christmas party cruises pumped out music so blokes in board shorts could charm girls in pink bikini tops. The promenades around the Opera House were teeming with tourists. Some of them waved and he waved back at a camera flash, a photo for Japan or China. An aeroplane wrote an advertisement in the sky. Patrick looked at the curves of the Opera House and wondered if Suzy was still playing her violin.

They sailed for hours and it was brilliant. Everyone was rich and happy. Sons weren't missing and daughters weren't dead. Or mentioned. All hands were on deck. His lips dried out and he could feel his skin burning. They got back to the marina at five o'clock and agreed to go back to The Nag's Head for a couple of drinks.

The earth moved, but not properly, as he walked back to the car.

He got to the Nag's first and ordered beers. He looked around and the pub felt enclosed. No-one else here had spent the afternoon on the harbour. All these suburbs with people spinning around the harbour like a solar system, never intersecting. When he went for a piss, he saw himself in the mirror. His hair was swept back and he looked vividly alive and healthy.

Back at the bar, Stuart had arrived. They drank for hours, the waves still affecting his sense of balance. Even when he was sitting down, he swayed. Sailing was a drug. He could see why people with money and canvas shoes and big houses got hooked on it. He tried to explain all this to Stuart, who was unsympathetic.

'You are, without a doubt, the worst sailor I've ever encountered. In fact, you're not even a sailor, you're just a person who was on my boat.'

'For Sail.'

'Fuck off. I explained that.'

Nancy showed up at some point later on and startled Patrick. She kissed him on the cheek. What was she doing here? Her hair was too red, like it was coloured in by a pre-schooler. He almost said something. Stuart seemed less surprised that she was here and put his arm around her waist.

'We must have won the meat tray,' he said, dangerously. 'Have we got time for another or are we off?' he asked, producing his wallet in an attempt to influence the answer.

'I think we're off,' Nancy said, looking deliberately at each of them. Patrick refused a lift. 'Are you sure?' Nancy asked.

'It's not far,' he said, standing unsteadily and patting various pockets as if there was something somewhere on him that he should get into one of his hands. Was he driving? He couldn't remember.

He was pissing up against a tree when he heard Stuart call out of the car window behind him, like a cop with a megaphone, 'Drop the toy and put your hands on your head.'

Patrick leaned back and laughed and heard Stuart roar laughing as well. What a great day.

· · · ·

When he woke in the morning his hangover was almost defeated by enough sleep. His body was a machine. He should treat it with more respect. He would treat it with more respect. Would that be his new year resolution? He was never very good at them because they generally included a resolution to drink less.

Another year was almost over. This time last year he had been moving out of Balmain. The first time he had spent any time – real time, not bed time – with his new young lover, she had told him he was too old. He hadn't disagreed. He had felt old. He had known he was making a big mistake, and was more than capable of feeling sorry for himself.

He was glad he had apologised to Claire. He should have done it sooner.

Eve jumped up on the bed and walked all over him. His bladder, mainly. It was way past the time when she should have been fed. He obliged her. After a pot of coffee, he decided to go Christmas shopping. The frangipani Christmas tree looked more like a decorated indoor pot plant. It needed presents. He used this as an excuse to phone Claire and ask about the Christmas rules.

'Any more news on Ben?' he asked.

'No. People are being great. They're looking and they're calling me often.'

'We'll see each other for Christmas this year, won't we?' he asked. She agreed they would, and hopefully with Ben as well.

'Like a family Christmas, but with Phil,' Patrick said. He was his own worst enemy.

'Leave Philip out of this,' she said.

'Great idea.' There was silence on the line. 'He won't be there, will he?'

'No. He has a family in Hobart.'

Patrick felt for him before he could stop himself. Christmas. Kids. Separation. But it was good news he would be somewhere else. On another island.

'I've bought you a Christmas present,' he lied. Why would he do that, he wondered.

'Is it a T-shirt?'

'It's better than a T-shirt.'

'Just in case you're unsure, everything is better than a T-shirt.'

'I want you to remember you said that when you see what it is. Have you got a Christmas tree?'

'I do. I'm afraid it's very David Jones this year. You pull a lever and it stands up and there it is, already decorated.'

'I bet the decorations are purple.'

'They are! How did you know that?!'

'You won't throw away our old decorations, will you?'

'Of course not. Why would I? Will you have a tree? I saw a box of decorations in your sunroom.'

'I've got a tree, it's decorated and everything.'

'Well done!'

'If – when – Ben appears, let's get those old decorations out.'

'Absolutely. We'll get a real tree and hang them if that happens.'

'Together.'

'Hopefully.'

'I love you,' he said.

'I unsensibly love you too,' she said.

'Shouldn't that be insensibly?'

'No. They're different things but don't argue.'

He wanted to say that was what they did well, but didn't. 'Thanks for dinner the other night.'

. . . .

Parking in King Street would be a nightmare, so he drove down Australia Street and parked not far from the Courthouse Hotel. He could hear the buzz as he walked past and wasn't even tempted. Or maybe a little bit. All those good-looking young people with their lives ahead of them.

King Street was teeming. It was the best street in Sydney these days. Everyone was welcome. He joined the throng.

He checked out some of the music shops. Vinyl was back. He still had their record player and a hundred albums. If he could get Claire over, he was sure he could spin her back down the years and start again. It was a testament to his love that he wanted that, and not something new.

On the street there were addicts and athletes, girls holding hands, bald men with dogs, thin young men in checked shorts with long bodies like Ben's. There were plenty of great clothes shops. He found somewhere that sold antique kimonos. Better than a T-shirt. He bought one for Claire.

When he walked past a bookshop and saw the display, he knew it was perfect. He went in and bought the two-volume *Shorter Oxford English Dictionary* for Ben. Something to keep him busy for what he hoped would be a long life.

There was a volume in each of two plastic bags that sagged towards earth as he wandered back to the car. The word carrier. Three and a half thousand pages of words and meanings for Ben to play with. Patrick was ecstatic with his gifts. Normally he was shithouse at presents. He couldn't wait to wrap them up and put them under the frangipani tree.

It was starting to feel like Christmas. That summer article deadline loomed, or had it passed? If he didn't make it, he knew they wouldn't pester him. Those days were gone. They'd syndicate something or ask a staff writer to invent a list of the best movies of the year, or write about whether the length of shorts was going up or down.

He wrapped the presents. He was feeling buoyant and sober, which didn't often happen. He had a feeling Ben would find his way back to them.

He went to his desk and had a spur-of-the-moment crack at writing something.

THE CHRISTMAS THAT WASN'T THERE

This is the first Christmas where I haven't got a single merry card in the mail. All I got were texts and emails.

It's the Internet of Things.

One card did arrive in the mail but it wasn't for me. And it wasn't merry. It was for some long-gone previous occupant called Doreen Robinson. I can't imagine someone called Doreen living in my house. Which room did she sleep in? Does her ghost still wander the corridor in curlers?

There was no return address on the envelope, so I opened it. It was from Joan.

'Dear Doreen. I hope this finds you well. Clarence died in June after being kicked in the head by his horse. It was a terrible shock for us all. He loved that horse. I'm sorry we lost touch but it's hard to keep up now that you are up there in Sydney. Merry Christmas. Love Joan.'

I didn't know whether to laugh or cry. I wished I hadn't glimpsed those lives. It was handwritten, with dry paddocks in the wide spaces between the lines.

It was a card from a landscape where it was still possible to lose touch. Clarence could get kicked in the head by a horse, and die, and it wasn't on Facebook. The card wasn't mine but it belonged to the house and so it went up on the mantelpiece.

Whenever I open the window to a breeze now the card blows onto the floor. Like it should. That used to be one of the rituals of Christmas.

This year a client gave me a device with a Christmas tree in it. It's about the size of a cigarette lighter. You sit it on a side table, point it at a blank wall and press a button. Wow! A zig-zag, blinding, decorated tree appears, like a child's drawing.

It looks great and saves space. With not many sleeps to Christmas, the projection is sadly mesmerising. I go to the wall and try to touch it. It ripples across the back of my hand like a tattoo or a virus.

There's no Christmas tree smell. Or actual tree. The cat can't prance on its back legs and wreck the decorations and cause a house fire. Sooner or later – probably sooner, possibly before Christmas – the battery will run out.

Joy to the world.

Regardless of battery life, when the tree isn't turned on, it isn't there. This is the Christmas that wasn't there. Isn't here.

Meanwhile, in my inbox there are e-cards and best wishes and year-in-review chain letters. None of my friends got kicked in the head by a horse.

This is not an unbeautiful world. It's more connected than ever. It's just weird and different and kind of disappointing. It feels like Santa spam and not jingle bells.

If you get any Christmas cards this year, lucky you. Open the window and let them fall where they will. Maybe the breeze connects our lives better than the ether.

· · · ·

When he finished, he checked the word count: 500 exactly. He still had it!

It wasn't very Christmassy after all. That sometimes happened when he sat down to write. The words took the story from him and wrote themselves. It reminded him vaguely of what he had written in the first piece, all those years ago. His brilliant career. Anyway. It was publishable, he thought. The older demographic would relate.

He hadn't confessed that it wasn't the Christmas cards that were missing, it was Claire and Ben and their lives together.

PROFESSOR BIGUS DICKUS

The cafe at the Seymour Centre on the Sydney University campus was in a big air-conditioned space behind soaring glass walls.

Claire had come up with a contact who'd talk to Patrick about Professor Benson. It wasn't just the fact that the prof had punched him in the face that made him want to find out more about him. It was that he and Annie had argued. That he was so aggressive and aggrieved.

Patrick sat on a faux leather couch and read a uni newspaper. It was astonishing how much stuff was going on. Bands, poetry, plays in small theatres, debates, exhibitions, even politics. He'd formed a notion that his old uni was more or less a business school these days. He was wrong. It was deserted at this time of year except for aimless boys and girls with fresh skin, mostly Asian. He felt old, was old.

Jacob had described himself as "black haired and unkempt" when they had set up the meeting. He wandered into the cafe with a serious limp and Patrick admonished himself for wondering why he hadn't mentioned that too. They shook hands. Jacob was unkempt in a university staff way, unshaven – was that a beard or not? – a worn leather jacket, a whiff of body odour, slightly overweight.

Patrick was paying. He could afford coffee. 'Thanks for meeting with me. What'll you have?'

'Long black and fudge. Adam knows.' Patrick ordered a fudge too and when he brought everything to the low table, they both leaned forward. Jacob emptied three paper cylinders of sugar into his cup and stirred.

'Thanks for this,' he said.

'I haven't done anything yet,' Jacob said.

'You know Stephen Benson?' Patrick asked, and bit into the fudge. It was poisonously sweet.

'*Professor* Benson. No human names, please.' He wasn't a fan, obviously. Good.

Patrick had rehearsed a background speech to provide context for their chat but he decided to drop it. 'Would you say he's a complete prick or a work in progress?'

Jacob grinned. 'Oh, so you know him then?'

'Not really. I met him once. He punched me in the mouth.' He pointed to his lip, which still wore a tiny split.

'That's how he'd like to greet most people, given the chance.'

'I was at his daughter's funeral. I wasn't invited. My son was his daughter's boyfriend.'

Jacob theatrically computed this configuration. 'Annie studied here. I guess you knew that.'

'Yep. You knew her?'

He sipped his coffee, looked out at the light with lovely grey eyes. 'No. *He* was here. Been here forever. Then *she* was here. Reluctant daughter, it seemed to me, but who wouldn't be reluctant? She was kind of intense.'

'I gather he's quite a personality.'

'That's one way of putting it.'

'I've heard they argued a lot. He and Annie.'

'I wouldn't know, but he's a bully and a prick.'

'Why do you say that?'

'I'm a shit kicker. I arrange things for him and others. Meetings, conferences, flights, rooms, cars, cancellations. He's in it for whatever he can get, even though he's rich. He thinks the sun shines out of his arse.'

'He's a professor at Sydney uni. He's got tenure.'

'That's half the problem. Do fuck all. Expect everything. It's like they've retired but stay on for the perks. This prick would have us carry him around in a sedan-chair if they found one in the drama department.'

Patrick laughed. Jacob felt appreciated. 'So why are we chatting?' he asked. 'I probably should have asked that sooner.'

'I'm not sure. I just want to get a sense of who he is. My son Ben was Annie's boyfriend, like I said, and since she died, he's done a runner. He's done that before but I'm worried, obviously. I guess I'm wondering if there are any networks, or...'

'Did you know Annie?'

He thought of the intimacy of seeing her dead and naked. 'No.'

Jacob put the last of his fudge in his mouth and licked his fingers, chewed quickly. 'This is confidential, but what the fuck – you didn't hear it from me.' Patrick nodded. 'This all happened before I started working for him, but she had a boyfriend with mental health issues, apparently. He was an arts student and there was a scandal when she was accused of messing with his medication.'

'That all sounds a bit familiar.'

'Professor sorted it.'

'What's that mean?' he asked.

'He kept it in-house. I don't know the details but I know things happened. He charmed or paid or intimidated them. He has a lot of clout.'

'Who's "them"?'

'The boy's parents? The university? Who knows?'

'But if he and Annie never saw eye to eye, I can't imagine she would have agreed to all that?'

He hunched his shoulders and his leather jacket creaked. 'I dunno.'

Patrick thought about it. 'So, it worked? Nothing happened? Annie graduated.'

He nodded. 'It didn't work for everyone. The boyfriend's dead. Suicide in a caravan park on the Central Coast.'

Patrick felt like the world was spinning to a stop. Not even Annie could save it. Maybe she wreaked havoc as well as helped. 'Did Annie know about that?'

'It was after she left here. But if I know, she'd surely know. I think they stopped seeing each other as part of the prof's deals.'

Maybe she hadn't had her six months to fix him. Or maybe he was "fucked", and she left anyway. Maybe Annie's Mix had led to his suicide?

'Did Professor Benson ever teach Annie? They were in the same faculty.'

'No. They were still using chalk last time he did any work in a classroom.'

'So, they were both here on campus, fighting like cats and dogs, but they never saw each other?' It didn't make sense.

'They saw each other.'

'Why do you say that?'

'There was a minor shit fight a couple of weeks back because the professor was late when he was supposed to be at a sponsor's soiree. They're providing big bucks and Bigus Dickus missed the canapes. Apparently, he'd found out his daughter was living nearby and went to see her.'

'Really? When was that?'

'It was the first function of what we like to call "the festive season". Exams are almost finished, most students have already pissed off, but we're still here. It was November twenty-fourth.'

Patrick leaned back and looked out at the courtyard and the trees.

The day before Annie had died, she had a surprise visit from her angry father.

UPRIGHT IN INDIA

It took Patrick a bottle of red before he could get to sleep, then a koel woke him at 4am. Koels arrive in Sydney from Asia and drive everyone crazy over summer with their manic calls. This one kept calling, loud as a fire alarm, until the kookaburras joined in. They were even louder but at least they were native. And at least they were laughing.

He lay awake and waited for dawn, Eve asleep on the bed beside him, both of them too hot for a cuddle. The forecast was for a week of hot weather.

Alice had said the professor visited Forest Street with the police. That was *after* Annie was found. Not before. Why would he lie to her about that? Had he lied to the police? He grabbed his phone from the bedside table and texted Cooper.

Maybe her father had her diaries? If he knew about them, he'd want them, at the very least to protect her again from the risks they had exposed her to. He'd done something similar before, according to Jacob. No wonder he was angry. It seemed like the only person who ever defied him was his own daughter.

Then he remembered, after the funeral, after the punch, the professor had said Annie was dead because of 'your bloody hopeless son'. Had he met Ben in Forest Street too?

He was startled when his phone beeped. It was Cooper, at this hour of the morning! *Benson said he didn't know Forest Street. When was he there?*

Patrick dropped the phone onto the bed. Holy shit. What was he getting himself into? It was no use talking to Alice about her husband because Patrick already knew more than she did. The last thing he wanted was the first thing he had to do. Talk to the professor himself.

He wanted to update Claire – hear her voice, have her on his side – and grabbed his phone to set up a meeting, although his brain called it a date. Another one. He suggested a bar. When she got back to him, she suggested his place. Again!

He tidied up a little and picked some coleus for a vase on the table. Claire arrived. Her perfume. If he knew what it was, he'd buy her more for Christmas. A cheek-to-cheek kiss. She headed through to the sunroom out the back as if she lived here. If only.

'What a great room this is!' she said, kindly.

'Yeah, we live out here.'

'We?'

'Me and Eve.'

'Eve and I,' she corrected and bent to rub Eve under the chin. She was curled up on a striped cushion on the red couch. 'Hello again, Eve. Is she easier to live with than me?'

'Easier. Less fun.'

'Well, here I am! Let's have a drink and that update. Any chance of something white?'

'Milk?'

'Gin?'

'No tonic. We can drink it straight.'

'I could have got some. Or you could have got some.'

Eve was purring like a percolator. Claire looked out the window. The garden was a wonderful bright tangle. She liked it. It was much smaller than Balmain. She no longer had the time or the impetus to garden. Now she paid a teenager to mow the lawn.

Patrick reappeared with a bottle of red wine and two glasses. 'I love having you over here but how come I never get to Balmain?' It was nagging him.

She sighed and seemed on the verge of saying one thing, then said another. 'Philip's not at Balmain and he's not moving in,' she said. 'So, cheer up!'

He did. Instantly. He never considered himself a complicated man but he surprised even himself at how quickly that made him feel better.

He opened the wine. 'Remember when we were young and wine bottles had corks?'

'We still had bottles with corks. You took them all when you left.'

They sat on the red couch. 'I drank them all when I left too. This one's a cheeky little 2020 from the bottle shop down the hill. It hardly needs a screwcap, let alone a cork. It's like eating grapes.'

They touched glasses. The sun shone through the mulberry tree next door and tangled shadows onto the floor. The room was bright and quiet and theirs.

'Are you drinking less?' she asked.

'Less wine. More slop.' They sipped. 'Like this. Sorry. I did suggest a bar.'

'Here and this is fine. I wonder where Ben is right now?'

He wondered too. 'What generation are we up to now? I can't remember.'

'What are you on about?'

'Is Ben Gen Y?'

'I didn't know you spoke Mandarin. No. He's Gen Zee.'

'The end of the alphabet.'

'He'd find a way out of that.'

'Yes, he would! Professor Benson visited Annie the day before she died,' he said, getting to things. Claire turned her body and her knee touched his. He noticed. Did she, he wondered? 'But he never told the police.'

'That's odd.'

'Odd! That's an understatement.'

'I wonder why not.'

'I'm going to ask him.'

'Are you sure that's a good idea? Can't Cooper do that?'

'I told Cooper. He didn't offer,' Patrick said. Yet again, it was only sort of true. 'I think they've closed the case.'

'He might assault you again.'

'He might. I'll be ready this time.' He made a fist. She smiled.

'But why? What are you going to ask him?'

'What happened? What does he know? Why didn't he mention it to the police? That sort of thing.'

They sat in silence for a while, knees still touching. There was a double bed in the house, and he thought of it now. He wondered if Ben was half-mad because of him, because of a crowded brain, because he also warped the meaning of words and things until nothing was real.

'The universe will cough him up,' he said, and she wasn't baffled by his change of tack to Ben. He pressed his knee back into hers and she smiled upside-down. He leaned towards her and they kissed on the lips, a front-door kiss, parents-under-stress kiss. Her hand slid onto his thigh but stopped there. His brain kind of exploded. She removed her hand and faced back into the room.

'Come to bed,' he said. 'The room's messy as a cheap motel. It'll be exciting.'

'That was exciting enough,' she said primly.

'Well, let's make it boring then. Less exciting than India that time when we fucked standing up and then went back out into the streets with all those people.'

She shook her head.

He could tell it was over, in spite of the available bedroom and the perfect dappled sunlight. Life is a series of moments lost to routine but Patrick knew this moment would shine and last for him. Like India. He sat upright too. 'Thanks for the kiss.'

'I remember that fuck,' she said, and held up her hand before he had a chance to bend back into her.

He poured more wine although she had hardly touched hers.

'I've got some news too,' she said. 'I've got a family of four living with me in Balmain.'

Patrick was flummoxed. No wonder Phil wasn't moving in.

FIND A FLATMATE

It happened quickly after that. If Claire could move Denise and her family into Balmain, and not him, he could rent out his spare room. Except that it wasn't spare yet. He still worked in it. If he could line up a tenant, he felt sure he could sort the room soon enough.

He thought about the awful Christmas that was coming the Bensons' way and wondered how much worse he might make it by visiting the professor. His own Christmas was starting to look – feel – better. He trusted his instincts and they were beginning to buzz.

He Googled *Find a Flatmate* and got 32,400,000 results in 0.48 seconds. Not a bad start. Bed start. Within a minute he was astonished. It was like the dating sites he had tried when he found himself single again but instead of wanting to watch Netflix and chill, these were people who wanted to move in and live with him.

There was Emily, nineteen, studying arts and law and looking to live with some chilled people. She liked cooking and gardening. Great! His postcode was one of her preferred locations. A student at the university. Life just starting. They could talk about books.

Celine, thirty, was a management consultant who often travelled for work. A ghost! She was tidy and respectful and liked wine. Patrick wondered if he was dreaming all these people up. From her photo he guessed she might be Japanese. Very good looking. She could pay up to $300 per week. *Depending.* Depending on what? Whether he was in the room as well? Or maybe she had a room of her own in mind, with a built-in wardrobe and ensuite?

Having Celine move in would be like winning Lotto. She could move in tomorrow as far as he was concerned – except for the room thing. He didn't really expect to get anyone in until the new year anyway. Who moves house so close to Christmas?

An hour passed. Voyeurism. There were women from England who loved the beach and had their tongues out in every picture. Blokes

142

with beards moving down from Byron Bay. Transgenders seeking happy households. Tattoos and piercings and recent divorcees. He was amazed that most of them seemed like plausible housemates. Except maybe those two English girls.

He forced himself to stop surfing, to stop wanting to meet them all and write about their lives. Instead, he checked out what sort of places were up for rent and how they were presented. He would need some pics. He decided to post a pic of his bedroom – as if it was available – and not his front room, another pic of the cute terrace frontage and an arty angled pic of a section of the back garden and view.

He was a 'young, early fifties' freelance writer with a black cat, a wild garden, easy-going, wine lover, keen to share in 'funky Forest Lodge'. Etcetera. He ticked the various boxes and then posted. He was live.

He went and made a pot of coffee. Eve was stretched out on the warm boards of the back deck and he asked her who she would choose. What was she looking for in a human? He didn't tell her he had already made his choice. He took his coffee back to the spare bedroom and looked at Celine again. Feeling ridiculous, he waited as if she was somewhere else waiting too.

A contact from Helln – that's how she spelled it – appeared. She was a musician, troubadour, twenty-eight, nose pierced, a pile of hair. Could she look at the room this afternoon at 3pm? Holy shit! He went and poured a second coffee. His heart was racing and he had to force himself not to imagine a shared household with Helln. It was all too soon.

Maybe it was her stage name, or maybe she actually *was* an idiot, but he didn't like the 'Helln' thing in spite of his own way of mangling words. He decided she wasn't the right match but he also decided she could come around at 3pm anyway, and messaged back with his address. It was a chance for him to get an idea of how things worked and how to behave when Celine walked through his door.

He would tell Helln straight that his work room was the available room and hoped that would curb her evident enthusiasm. He thought about tidying up but didn't. He muddled about, nervously waiting for 3pm, wishing he hadn't been so hasty.

There was a knock on the door ten minutes early! She was more than punctual, she was frantic. When he opened the door, it wasn't Helln standing there. It was a man with a beard and blue eyes. It was The Cleaner from Forest Street.

'Remember me?' he asked.

Patrick nodded and stood there, adjusting. 'Yes. But I don't remember telling you where I live.'

'Not everyone's hard to find,' he said. Was that a reference to Ben? His visitor seemed in no hurry and they stood looking at each other. 'Can we talk?' he asked.

'Who are you?'

'Andre.'

'Andre who?'

'Take your pick. Smith. How about that?'

Patrick looked him up and down. Blue jeans bulging around thighs. A black shirt tucked in, old-school, black belt, black leather shoes. He looked and sounded at ease, which was more than Patrick felt.

'I'm not going to hurt you,' Andre said.

'Why on earth would you say that?'

'You look like you're sizing me up for a fight.'

He couldn't believe who knocked on his door these days. Police. Claire. Thugs. 'But you do hurt people?'

He shrugged his thick shoulders. 'I'd rather not.'

'Why have you been following me?'

'It's more that we're both on the same trail.'

'You don't work for the police.'

'No.'

'Who do you work for?'

'I'm not enjoying this, out here. Can I come inside?'

'I'm expecting someone.'

'I think that's bullshit.'

On cue, a woman in a loose cotton dress appeared on the footpath behind Andre, like a conjuror's trick. Patchouli perfume. 'Don't tell me someone's beaten me to it!' she said. Andre spun around. 'Which one of you is Patrick?'

Andre pointed to Patrick, who stepped down and shook Helln's outstretched hand.

'Hi,' he said. 'This is my friend Andre.' Andre reluctantly shook her hand too.

'So, you're not taking the room?' she asked him.

'No.'

'Good!' She smiled a big, open smile. What looked like chopsticks held her sun-bleached brown hair in a messy pile. She had big brown eyes and dark eyebrows and a small silver nose ring.

It was a complicated doorstop. Everyone stood there until Helln broke the spell. 'So, this is a little bit weird. Can I see the room, or should I come back later? We did say three o'clock.'

'No! Now's fine.'

Andre lifted his phone from nowhere. 'I'll go. Can you give me your number and I'll text you?' Patrick was reluctant. 'Look, I can find it online if I want a room.'

He relented and gave his number. 'Text it now,' Patrick insisted.

Andre turned and headed back out onto the street. 'Yes, boss.'

'Come in,' Patrick said to Helln, wondering which room to show her and feeling flummoxed yet again.

TOGETHER APART

Claire sat with a gin and tonic on the patio overlooking the sweep of lawn and found it difficult. And wonderful. She had an hour to herself.

Difficult because the big house was full again, and noisy, but it wasn't filled with the people she most wanted there. Her own family.

She had inherited the house after her mother died. Her father had died five years before that, after all that pipe smoking. Mother left the house to her and a substantial portfolio of superannuation and investments to her older brother Peter. He took the money and ran and had been living in America for a decade now. He had a New York wife and two children and was apparently happy ever after. They Facetimed now and then. His face was fatter. Fat time, Patrick and Ben called it.

Peter was a Republican. What a journey from that swing at the bottom of the garden.

Claire had finished work that day and was starting a four-week Christmas break. Hers was one of the last shows to wrap because it was one of the cheapest. There was a party on at a small bar in Chippendale, but after a few drinks she had left them to it. She was too weary. Too anxious. Not that she told them that. She told them she had a family to muster.

They weren't here now and Claire enjoyed the respite. They were down at the Dawn Fraser Baths, built into the harbour. It was just one of many magical water places in Sydney. The kids couldn't get enough of it and, right now, anything that kept the kids happy got a tick.

There were three of them. Brian was fifteen. Jodie was twelve. Lucy was nine. Denise confided that Andy was missing them all. The plan was working. They were talking again. 'We'll be back home for Christmas, don't worry,' Denise promised Claire. 'You won't need to buy a bigger turkey!'

That was good news. She didn't want another family smashed apart. But how far could she rewind hers? Could it work again? The three of them? Hearing kids' loud footsteps running in the hallway almost broke her heart.

Meanwhile, Philip was down in Hobart for Christmas, celebrating his failing family with string and wrapping paper. He would understand if things changed here, she knew that. She sipped her drink and felt weary. She was glad the year was almost over. May it end well, for everyone.

· · · ·

Patrick was weary too. He'd spent the night tossing and turning. He hadn't heard back from Andre. All he could think was that he'd been hired by the Bensons. That put them on "the same trail" he'd talked about. He texted Alice and suggested chardonnay.

Helln's imminent arrival irritated him like a radio not quite tuned in. He'd agreed she could have the front room. He didn't need to move his stuff, she said, they could work around each other, see how it worked. She would be out a lot.

But the timing was wrong. He decided to renege on all that. He felt bad, but he would tell her straight.

Then she was there. It seemed all her possessions fitted into a giant tote bag like the kind tennis players carry onto court, filled with racquets. Everything except her acoustic guitar, which she had slung over her other shoulder, for balance.

He didn't tell her straight. He lied to her and said instead that his son Ben was suddenly coming home, unannounced.

'Well, that's great!' she said, crestfallen. 'Home for Christmas! Bummer for me.'

'Sorry about that.'

'I'm joking!'

'Obviously I didn't know he was coming so soon. He's unreliable. Unpredictable is a better word. And I'm sure it *is* a bummer for you. Is it hard to find accommodation at this time of year?'

Her hair was wildly up again and moved when she nodded. 'It is, but hey, I'm an expert. Not a very good expert, obviously.' She smiled and looked forlorn.

'Can I make you a coffee?' Her hair moved. They were sitting out on the red couch – Eve on Helln's lap already, tart! – he offered her a camp bed just for the night if she needed it. 'So you've got some time to plan your next move.'

'That would help me big time. Otherwise I'll have to plan my life from a park bench. I know my bed in the hostel's gone already.' She was nice. He really did feel bad. 'Only don't bother making up a bed. I've got a sleeping sheet in my stuff. I want to sleep on the couch in there and look at that frangipani Christmas tree. I think it's beautiful.'

She was better than nice, she was lovely. He went to brew some coffee.

He was tempted to change his story again so that flaky Ben was no longer arriving. Then he felt like that was tampering with the universe and might make Ben disappear altogether.

His phone rang. It was Alice. He wandered out the back to answer it. They agreed that he would visit her at home. The professor was away, which suited Patrick, though he knew at some stage he'd have to talk with him.

When he came back inside, Helln was already on her phone, trying to sort her accommodation. Or renting a truck to empty him of all his possessions. He poured them both coffee and they sat outside together.

Helln told him a potted history of her life. Men are bastards.

SOMETIMES YOU CAN'T LIVE FOREVER

Not far away, Ben was dying.

He knew that now. Sometimes you can't live forever.

He floated up in flames and saw himself lying down there on the floor with all the rubbish he had made. That would burn too. The towers of words.

He was Fire. Leaving Earth. The Elements, like Annie said. That's all we are.

She was on fire once too. He had put her out.

His mouth was tingling. Water.

His bones ached. *His bones.*

FINDING INFINITY

It was immediately strange having a stranger in his house, leading another life, kind of in his way. Patrick told Helln he needed to go out.

'Cool,' she said. 'Hey, what if something comes up while you're out? If I find somewhere? Can I just leave? Sorry, but...'

'Of course. Look, I'm sorry too. Just pull the door shut behind you. It locks.' Maybe Mick was right. Ghosts come and go in a house. 'See ya!' he said. He was trying to sound like Mr Funky of Forest Lodge, as he had advertised. Fraudulently.

He walked the long way to the shops, around Blackwattle Bay. There were people out and about, a Christmas party complete with silly hats, cricket games with no umpires, or too many, kids everywhere. He felt happy and lonely all at once.

The harbour air cleared his head before his trip across it to visit Alice. Annie had *known* Mr Infinity, he decided. It hadn't bothered Evan or Ben that she had disappeared now and then, sometimes overnight, but Patrick reckoned she had been fucking Mr Infinity. Not in a 'universe' kind of way. She was dealing.

He bought baklava from a cafe on Glebe Point Road. On the way home, wet dogs greeted him, the sky was blue and a boy in board shorts dived off the back of a yacht moored in the bay and came up slick and shiny as a seal.

When he got home, Helln was sunbathing or asleep on the sun lounge on the back lawn. She'd hitched her dress up around her already-brown thighs. It seemed she'd found somewhere to live, or given up. He left her there. Part of him was unsure if he really wanted her gone when he got back.

He drove across the dinosaur bones of the Bridge to the lower North Shore.

The Benson residence was so nice you couldn't see it from the street. Big old trees cast shade onto a sandstone wall and behind that, a green lawn merged into a border of rhododendrons and fading hydrangeas. It was ragged and perfect and he got the sense that Alice and the professor didn't spend much time down on their knees, pulling weeds.

Maybe he was wrong. On the flagstone front porch, elastic-sided boots sat under a wooden-slat seat with a pair of dirty gardening gloves.

He rang the doorbell. Alice answered in a patterned summer dress. She was barefoot and her hair was down. She was tanned and looked at home in this rambling, beautiful universe, and just a little worn with the effort. They air-kissed on both cheeks.

She thanked him for the baclava and offered coffee. 'Or something stronger?'

'It's a bit early for that,' he said politely, not meaning it. He asked for a long black and she clattered the enormous bench-top machine with confidence.

'Let's go out on the patio,' she said. It was covered under a shady pergola beyond open French doors. He looked across the lawn.

'It's beautiful. I love gardening but mine's about as big as your patio. Did you grow up rich?'

'Born and raised in Maitland. My father worked in the coal mines. He was a foreman, though – I'm not rubbish.'

Birds sang. Alice was wonderful. He wasn't at all surprised that Annie had been smart and renegade.

'Class is a strange thing,' he said.

'What about you?' Alice asked as she brought the coffees out on a wooden tray. The baclava was on a plate with a green border.

'Oh, I'm rubbish,' Patrick declared. 'Dad died when I was young, in an industrial accident. Mum never remarried. Single mum, more or less. She worked as a stenographer. I don't suppose they do that anymore.' He thought about it. 'Stenographer: it even sounds like a dinosaur.'

'No brothers or sisters?'

'Nope.'

'And Ben is an only child?'

'Yes.'

'And Annie was an only child.'

'Yes,' he confirmed on her behalf.

'I'm one of six kids,' she said, matter of fact. 'You didn't risk losing everything back then. Not if Dad worked down the mine. You had a lot of kids in case some of them died.' She picked up a sweet pastry and bit into it with her eyes closed.

He sipped from a big white cup. 'It's good coffee. If you were thirty years younger you could get a job on Glebe Point Road.'

'If I was thirty years younger, I might take it.'

'And not do nursing?'

'Not the second time around. It's a bloody hard job, and getting harder if anything. But I've enjoyed it in this life. Is your mother still alive?'

'No. I'm an orphan now.'

She half-smiled. There was a strange, liberated intimacy between him and Alice. Even their small talk was confessional and bare. Annie's death had changed the rules again for Alice and she was coming to uncomfortable terms with the rest of her life.

'What did you want to see me about?' she asked.

He wasn't going to ask her about Stephen's visit to Annie the day before she died. He felt sure she didn't know about that, and in her own garden it didn't seem right to start there.

'I wondered if you've hired a private eye.'

She tucked her chin in and looked astonished, as if he'd turned into a trout.

'You know – an investigator.'

'I know what you're talking about,' she said. 'I just don't know what you're talking about.'

'That's a no, then?'

'Yes! It's a no! What would we hire one for?'

'None of us seem convinced the police have solved what happened to Annie; they've just stopped looking. I had a visit yesterday from someone I've seen around since she died. He was somewhere nearby when you and I met in Military Road. He told me yesterday we were "on the same trail".'

'Well, what does that mean? Who is he?'

'Andre. I don't know who he is. I was busy with someone and he left before I could get any more details. He promised to text me but I've heard nothing.'

Alice looked at the garden again. Her oracle, it seemed. Green grass and flowers and calm. 'I should have known Anne wouldn't go quietly.'

'Maybe Stephen hired him?'

'Maybe he did,' she said flatly. 'I'll find out.' That seemed to be the end of the discussion.

Patrick waited a while, finished his coffee. 'Maybe someone from uni days was supplying Annie with the drugs she used to help Ben and Evan?'

'Where are you getting this from?'

'Nowhere, really. Just things Ben and Evan said.'

'Oh, you saw Evan! What's he like?'

'You never met him?'

'No! I never met any of her experiments.' Their eyes met. 'Sorry. What should I call them?'

'Boyfriends, maybe? Clients? Anyway, Evan is amazing. He's healthy and happy and claims that Annie cured him of all his ails. Body and soul.'

Alice beamed. 'That's good to hear. That must be why she gave me his details. "In case something happens", she said.' She looked at the garden, still smiling. 'Thanks for following up on that, and for letting me know.'

Maybe Annie's paranoia had been justified. 'Be proud of her. Evan also said she used to meet someone else now and then. Maybe an old boyfriend, or someone she travelled with? I wondered whether he might be the one who supplied medications for her... boyfriends? Actually, "cases" sounds better, doesn't it? Let's go with cases.'

Alice stood up and left the room. He heard her footsteps soft on the stairs and then there was a kind of silence. She reappeared with a cardboard box and put it on the table.

'This is all sentimental. Annie's real achievements are framed on the wall in the library, along with her graduation photo and the other set pieces. This is just stuff that I kept as a mother.'

There was an old scrapbook, a bunch of cards stuffed one inside the other, a menu that he saw had the Sydney University logo across the top. She produced a booklet and passed it to him. 'That's from her graduation day.'

He opened it and saw endless lists of students from various faculties. He imagined the scene in the Great Hall, hundreds of kids in hired gowns and mortar boards, proud parents crammed up the back. It probably would have been hot.

Alice found a small photo album and sat, turning the pages in slow motion.

He kept looking through the booklet and found her. Anne Benson. B. Sc. (Pharm.) He looked down the list of her graduating classmates. No clues there, not that he knew what he was looking for. He closed the booklet.

Something clicked in his head then. A word thing. He went back to the page listing Annie's graduation class. There was a name there. He leaned across to Alice and pointed: *Jeremy Finnearty*. 'How would you pronounce that surname?'

Alice looked at it. 'Finity,' she said. 'It's Irish, I think.'

Another Irish connection. Patrick put the booklet onto the table and leaned back. He breathed in like he had just discovered air. Or infinity. Mr InFinnearty.

Alice looked at him. 'What?'

'It's nothing,' he said. It was something. It was *the* thing, he was already sure of it. 'What are you looking for in that box?' he asked to get the focus off him and his belting heart.

'Well, you asked about someone she knew so I'm looking for him, I suppose. And you said travel. There's some photos in that album there of her trip to Bali.'

He picked up the small album that Alice had put aside. He flicked through it. Blurred shots of a coastline in a blue sea, taken from the window of an aeroplane. Coconut groves taken through the window of a mini-bus. She was no photographer. She looked good in a red bikini, though, with a blue patterned sarong wrapped around her hips and the sea tumbling small waves behind her. He was mesmerised. That was Annie alive.

'Who did she go to Bali with?'

'On her own,' Alice said, exasperated.

'Who took the photos?'

'Oh, she met people. She never had troubles there.'

'I'm not surprised,' he said. 'She was a good-looking girl.' Alice nodded sadly, still fossicking in the box. He watched her. 'What are you doing for Christmas?'

Alice sat up and rubbed her lower back. 'Something quiet.'

Of course, it was difficult. Every helpline professional knows Christmas is the hardest time of year. The ads are full of happy families. The houses are full of despair.

'Let's think about catching up on Christmas Day,' he suggested. Alice looked at him. 'Near to my place, so I don't have to drive.'

She laughed. 'You sound just like Stephen. You might get on.'

'I doubt it.'

'He likes smart people.'

'I'm more smart-arse.'

'Well, he'd probably find you out then.' She leaned back down to her box and picked up a prize ribbon.

'Are you two OK?' he asked. Should he tell her about the professor's visit to Annie?

'We'll see. Yes, is the obvious answer. People like us don't fall apart. We have a big house. We can live our lives separately if we need to. What about you?'

'I don't have a big house. Or anyone to avoid.' Then he remembered Helln.

'What's your wife's name?'

'Claire.'

'You're not living together?'

'No.'

'Does that suit you?'

'No.'

She shook her head. 'We're not very happy, are we?'

'No.' A staccato sprinkler spat into life on the back lawn, on a timer. Or maybe it was magic. 'I meant what I said about Christmas,' he said.

'I know. Thank you. I'll consider it.'

BEER WITH THE DALAI LAMA

Patrick sat in his car for a moment and breathed deliberately to calm his nerves. His phone was tempting but he wanted to be home at his desk when he Googled Mr Jeremy Finnearty. He was annoyed again that he'd Found A Flatmate so soon. Bad timing. Maybe she'd be gone.

When he parked, a raucous flock of corellas swirled into view. The flock had been building for weeks and now there were hundreds of them, wheeling and screeching over the valley. One day early in the new year the suburb would wake up and they would be suddenly gone. Inland. Outback. Somewhere else.

He knocked on his own front door in case Helln was in the shower or turned out to be a nudist. These scenarios occurred to him not because he was chivalrous. He was mad in the head. Helln was back on the red couch.

'How'd it go?' he asked.

'Yeah, pretty good. I think I should be OK to leave tomorrow.'

'That's great! Good for you. I've got some urgent work to do in the front room but I'm going to have a glass of red. Do you want one?'

'Thank you.' He poured two glasses and walked back out to the sunroom.

'This is a beautiful place. So calm,' she said.

'Thanks.' He didn't feel calm. 'Here's to the shortest rental in history. Sorry.' They raised glasses.

'No more sorries! One-night stands aren't unusual for me.'

He heard that in a way that wasn't intended. 'I better get to work,' he said.

He closed the door to the front room – which he never did, it was like there was a beast that might escape, or get in – and typed.

JEREMY FINNEARTY: 1,720 results in .31 seconds – and one astonishing thing. There was only one Jeremy Finnearty on the internet. One! He operated a pharmacy on New South Head Road, Double Bay, Sydney. The World.

A cornucopia of prescription drugs.

Click. There he was. Dark hair back from his forehead, thick eyebrows, lots of white teeth in a puffy face. Unattractive in a pale chemist sort of way.

Click. A photograph of the nondescript pharmacy shopfront with part of a passing car blurred in a Google global moment. He soon confirmed, through LinkedIn and other accounts, that this was Jeremy Finnearty who had graduated from Sydney University with Anne Benson. Now he had to confirm that he was also Mr Infinity and what that meant, if anything.

He was nervous with excitement, and gulped down some wine. Maybe this would lead to Ben somehow? He wanted to tell Claire. He should tell Cooper. He called Stuart instead. Stuart was good in a crisis.

'I've got some drink vouchers I won in a raffle,' Stuart said. 'I'll pick you up in half an hour.'

Patrick took the bottle of red out to the sunroom and told Helln he had to go out again but she was welcome to the rest of the wine.

'Wow! Busy,' she said, twirling a strand of hair around her finger.

• • • •

They sat at a table outside a sailing club. Patrick didn't know which one. The Iron Cove Bridge clattered with traffic. Across the water, the turrets of the old Callan Park Hospital thrust into the blue sky. He had conducted a writing workshop in a room over there one weekend, years ago.

Stuart was wearing his sunglasses with loops of black cord that disappeared behind his ears. It annoyed Patrick. His glasses weren't going to fall overboard here. Stuart put two beers on the table.

'The barmaid's nice,' he said.

'They usually are.'

'It's the happy coincidence of breasts and beer.'

'I'm not sure that's a coincidence. It might be capitalism.'

'Do you have to spoil everything with your yoke?'

Patrick laughed. It was a fair complaint here in the sunshine. 'Speaking of which, I feel bad about the other night with Nancy. I forgot to wish her a merry Christmas, I think.'

'Well, you forgot to do up your fly, so it's possible you forgot the Christmas thing.'

'How is she? I can't remember.'

'She's well. Her mother's dying.'

'Oh shit. I'm sorry to hear that.'

'Nancy spends a lot of time at the hospice with her now. She keeps offering her Christmas at home, hoping it will rally her. They wouldn't let her out anyway. I reckon that's one cracker that won't be pulled this year.'

'That's no good.'

'No. Actually, I'll miss her. She's had an incredible life.'

'Well, here's to her, then.' They lifted their glasses and drank. Then they got talking.

'If it's Finnearty, it ties so many loose ends together,' Patrick said. 'Maybe they were working together? Maybe she left the diaries with him?'

'Or maybe he killed her *for* the diaries?'

Patrick slumped back. 'I don't see how. But maybe. I want Ben's. It could help him. And Evan's diary. She fucking cured him! It's huge.'

'If it's true. It's all illegal.'

'Listen to you in your old age.'

'I'm just warning you that this isn't Biggles, and neither are you.'

He laughed. 'You think I should tell Cooper, don't you?'

'Of course you should. Or at least tell your imaginary friend Andre.'

'He'd know what to do. And he'd do it this afternoon. He thought I wanted to fight him.'

Stuart leaned back and laughed like a tugboat. 'You! Even the professor knocked you out!'

'But that was before I knew I was in a fight! I was at a funeral.'

Stuart produced two more tickets. 'Go and get us some beer while I sit here and laugh at you.'

Patrick felt light-headed at the bar. Adrenaline. Free beer. Helln, if he let himself think about her. What he really wanted was Claire, and he felt pleased with himself for that.

'You've done well.' Stuart welcomed him back. Patrick wasn't sure if he was referring to the beer or the breakthrough. 'If Finnearty's got the diaries and Cooper gets hold of them in an investigation, they'll be tied up as evidence for years.'

'I don't want that.'

'No. You should tell Cooper, but before that, go and see Mr Infinity yourself. You found him. He's yours.' It was old newspaper advice. A source. Work him and work it out. 'Make sure you're handing over the right guy.'

'I'll do that. Now that I know it's not crazy.'

'And besides, how will Annie ever get justice unless someone tells the cops? Mind you, they dropped the case.'

'That's why I'm here drinking beer with the Dalai Lama. To find out.' They sat a while. 'But to answer your question, it would be justice if Annie's research didn't go to waste, if I get the diaries and save Ben.'

'Mmmm,' Stuart muttered with a mouthful of beer, unconvinced.

'I'm not saying we *don't* tell Cooper.'

'No. Tell him after you've stolen the diaries that might help to convict this prick.'

'Stolen might be a bit strong.'

'Thieved?'

Patrick laughed and relaxed a little. Beer did that. Henry Lawson said beer makes you feel the way you should feel without beer. The harbour sparkled, right there. He missed Balmain. Stuart leaned forward and grabbed his forearm.

'You're not going to kiss me, are you?' Patrick joked.

'No. But be careful, mate. There are already dead people in this story.'

He got the message. Part of him was scared.

'By the way, I've got a young female musician sleeping over at my place tonight,' he said, to change the topic. That cheered Stuart up no end.

· · · ·

'Come into my room.' He didn't say it out loud, he hoped. He said it in his head.

It was late and he was lying awake in bed, so wired and so tired. Come into my room and just hold me. You don't have to sleep on the couch out there beside the frangipani tree. You don't have to leave. You can stay.

I've lost my family. All of them.

Helln said farewell the next morning with a prim hug. 'When's Ben arriving?'

For a moment he was baffled by his own lies. 'Who knows? Maybe today. Maybe tomorrow.' They chatted about him for a while, his illness, his unpredictable self.

'This house has a good tune.'

'Really?'

She nodded. 'You should take it off the website, though. It's still up there.'

'Oh shit! So I should.'

She hitched her guitar over one shoulder and hoisted her bag off the floor. 'Thanks again.'

'Thank you. Of course, you'd be mad to rely on me, but if you find yourself stuck again, you're welcome back.' She smiled and walked out of his life. Funny old world, he thought, as he walked back through the house to make sure Eve had food and water.

He noticed a small present wrapped in newspaper under the frangipani tree. *TO PATRICK!!!* It was obviously a CD – one of hers, he hoped. He sort of missed her already and had to force himself to get on with things. It would be so nice to just sit down and listen to some music and try to bliss out.

He still hadn't heard back from Andre. He could only think the professor had hired him and hadn't told Alice. The old prick. Anyway, he felt like he knew more than Andre now. He didn't need him. He went to his computer to delete his Find A Flatmate account. Celine had responded to his contact!

'In another life, maybe,' he said to the screen, and shut it down. He grabbed his car keys.

Out in the bright day, the traffic was shocking. As he wound down the hill into the shopping strip in Double Bay, pedestrians walked among the cars as if they were invincible, talking on their mobile phones behind enormous, expensive sunglasses.

He parked up a side street and walked back down to New South Head Road. There it was, Finnearty Pharmacy, wide open and air-conditioned. It seemed strange somehow that he could just walk in.

He wandered the short aisles, looking at jelly beans and anal creams, and around. There were two counters. At the cash register near the front door, a young woman with too much make-up was selling someone corn pads. At the prescription counter down the back, a middle–aged Asian woman in a white coat was tapping away at a keyboard. Mr Finnearty was nowhere in sight.

The young cashier appeared at his side. 'Can I help you with anything?'

He was startled. He was so focused he'd forgotten where he was. What did he need at the chemist? 'Um... eyedrops.'

'Are they for you? What's the problem?'

'Stingy eyes.'

She led him to a selection and chose a couple and talked about lubrication and bacterial infection. He chose the cheapest one and she took it back to the counter.

'Is Jeremy in today?' he asked.

'No, he's got a school Christmas thing on today.'

'He's got kids?'

'Yeah, two. A boy and a girl.' She accepted his twenty-dollar bill.

'Is he normally in?'

'Yep. Try and keep him away!' She smiled and handed back his change. 'Do you need a bag?'

'No thanks. I think I went to uni with him.'

'Oh, right,' she said. They looked at each other. She seemed bored or baffled.

'Will he be in tomorrow?' She nodded. He turned and walked out and stood on the busy footpath. Surely Annie didn't walk in the front door like that and up to the prescription counter when she came to collect.

Finnearty's a family man. Maybe he has a fuck flat?

Patrick crossed the street. Now he could see there was an upstairs above the pharmacy. There would be a back lane behind the shops. He counted the buildings down to the next corner and crossed back at the traffic lights.

An enormous poster with vanilla ice cream oozing between a woman's lips filled the side wall of the corner shop. He turned left into an untidy lane of wheelie bins. There was already a dead Christmas tree lying on its side. The runt of the litter that wouldn't sell. He counted his way up the lane to a green roller door fitted into a high brick wall with razor wire on top. He backed off and could see a metal stairway up to a door with a security screen on the upstairs level. There was a room up there above the pharmacy.

A security camera aimed back down the stairs. Patrick couldn't read the small plate next to it, so he took a photo with his camera and blew it up. *Brick Security.* If he *was* Mr Infinity, Patrick was confident Annie would have met him there. She would be on CCTV. Dates and times. Maybe she had a key. Was it in her bag in that dismal room? Did she have a bag? Evan said she had lost the one she had carried into his life.

Cooper could help. A key that meant nothing might now mean something.

But Patrick wanted to discover Infinity before he asked for help.

H e woke early. Eve was curled up heavily on his bladder. He tipped her aside and called Claire. He should have done it yesterday but he was starting to feel very tired.

'What's happened?' she asked, sleepy and jangled.

'Sorry. I didn't realise it was so early. How's life in the hostel?'

'Oh. They leave tomorrow. It's been good.'

'I've had a tenant too. Helln.' He didn't spell her name because he knew it would irritate Claire. 'She's gone now. She slept on the couch.'

'And where did she come from?' She sounded irritated anyway.

'The internet. It's a long story about a short stay. One night.'

'Hardly a tenant then?'

'No. I'm ringing to tell you that I think I've found out who was supplying those off-prescription drugs to Annie, for Ben. He's a chemist in Double Bay. I'm heading there this morning.'

'Hang on.' He heard the phone drop. He could hear what Claire called 'atmos'. Script shorthand for atmosphere. Birds. An early-morning aeroplane. Then a long sigh and her voice again. 'Sorry. I had to tell my brain that I'm awake. Tell me about this chemist. That's good news.'

'Well, I have to make sure it's him. He graduated with Annie. Beyond that it's just a hunch.'

'How are you going to decide if it's him?'

'I'm going to tell him I knew Annie and see how he reacts.'

'That's your plan?'

'Yep. And then rely on my everyman skills.'

'Why don't you tell Cooper and let him rely on his policeman skills?'

'He's on Christmas leave. He has a young daughter. So, this chemist is Jeremy Finnearty and his pharmacy is on New South Head Road in Double Bay. Oh, and Helln's given me a lead on how I might find Ben.'

'How could she possibly do that?'

'She's a hippie.'

'You're being very cryptic. Actually, you sound a bit odd. Are you OK?'

'I'm tired. This is all exhausting, right?'

'Right. Tell me about the lead on Ben.'

'Downward dog. That's your clue.'

'Maybe I should come with you to Double Bay?'

Yes. 'No. But I want you to know that's where I'm going. In case something goes wrong.'

'Like what?'

'I don't know. It's a public place. I'm not going to try to arrest him or anything.'

'No. Text me when you get there and text me when you leave. Straight away, OK?'

'OK. I miss you. Talk later.' He pressed end. He wanted to talk like this forever but had to head east and heave himself into possible danger. He tossed back the blankets.

The traffic. The pre-Christmas static in the air and in the people. He parked up a side street again with a two-hour limit. Down on New South Head Road there was a community choir singing carols outside a bank. They all wore red Santa hats. He tried to feel purposeful as he waited to cross at the lights.

Inside the chemist, he immediately saw Finnearty behind the prescription counter, wearing a white coat over a pale blue shirt. No Santa hat. Patrick strode up to the counter and Mr Infinity turned his eyebrows and teeth towards him.

'Can I help you there, sir?'

'I hope so. I'm a friend of Annie Benson.' Surprise is the best form of attack. He hoped. He watched for a reaction. The eyebrows furrowed.

'Right.'

'I think you know her as well?' Putting Annie in the current tense just came to him when he opened his mouth and he hoped it might rattle Finnearty.

'Knew her.'

'What do you mean?'

Finnearty looked hard at him. Was he sensing danger, planning a defence? 'We were at uni together. Long time ago.'

'Have you seen her lately?'

Another customer appeared alongside Patrick at the counter. Finnearty smiled at her. Those teeth! 'Is there a prescription I can fill for you, sir?' he asked Patrick.

'No, it's OK. You can serve this customer,' Patrick said, and smiled too.

Finnearty accepted the script and turned back to the shelves of pills behind him. Patrick grabbed a small packet of jelly beans and tore them open and tossed a few into his mouth. A sugar hit. When Finnearty returned to him he glanced at the opened jelly beans.

'Tell you what. It's Christmas. You can have those for free but I need to get on with things here. It's a busy time.'

'Is there somewhere we can talk?'

'I just said. I haven't got time to talk right now. What's your name, by the way?'

'Patrick Hyland.'

Finnearty leaned forward over the counter and extended his hand. They shook. 'Jeremy Finnearty. Have you got a card or something? Maybe we can talk in the new year.'

'That's too late. My son's missing and I want to find him before Christmas.'

He looked baffled. 'I'm sorry, but what's that got to do with me?'

'You were supplying Annie with prescription drugs. For him. Without a prescription.'

He stood upright and stared down at Patrick. 'I've got no idea what you're talking about but I'm now asking you to take my jelly beans and leave my pharmacy.' The jelly beans were becoming ludicrous and Patrick shoved the torn packet into his pocket.

'If I leave now I'm going straight to the police.'

'And if you think all you've just said is true then why haven't you been to the police already?'

'Because I want to save my son before I do that.' Patrick was flying.

Finnearty's shoulders sagged a little. He looked up and around, lost. He had a wife and young children. He sponsored a school nativity play. Hay bales and tinsel halos. Surely he hadn't killed Annie.

'Let's talk,' Patrick said, dialling things back a bit.

Finnearty looked at him for what felt like an eternity and then nodded. He turned and picked up a telephone. 'Wendy, can you come to service? Sorry. I need fifteen minutes.'

They walked down a short corridor past a staff tea room and into the rear courtyard with a four-wheel-drive BMW and a metal staircase up to the security door Patrick had seen yesterday. Their footsteps clanked on the stairs. Finnearty produced a thick jangle of keys and unlocked the security door and then the door behind that.

It was a spacious room, sparsely furnished with two deep chairs in brown leather, a low wooden table, a standard lamp. It was like walking back into the 1950s and he thought of Claire's father. Over by the window to the street, a chest-high bench screen hinted at a kitchenette beyond.

'Can I get you a drink?' he asked, tossing the keys onto the bench. He was still in his white coat and made a weird bartender.

'Scotch,' Patrick suggested. 'Ice, if you've got it.'

'$C_{10}H_{15}N$. You shouldn't ask a chemist for ice.' They looked at each other. 'It's a joke,' he said. Patrick smiled. Finnearty was cool. He wasn't rattled.

A large metal safe stood against one wall like a giant wood heater. There were two rooms off, doors open. One was a bedroom with a glimpse of a well-made double bed, the other was a small windowless bathroom.

Finnearty put a crystal glass of gold whisky and ice on the table in front of Patrick and sat down.

'So,' he said. 'You know her father came back into her life?'

Patrick took a slug of whisky. He'd been in control, journalist, interviewer, half-filled with the facts, but now Finnearty was taking back control. He hadn't denied supplying drugs to Annie so he *was* Mr Infinity. Tick. He hadn't admitted it either.

'Yes,' Patrick said lamely. They both sat there. He could hear the choir singing *The Little Drummer Boy* down on New South Head Road. 'He visited her the day before she died.'

Finnearty moved those eyebrows. 'Did he now? That's interesting.'

'You didn't know that?'

'No. He abused her, you know.'

'Her father?'

'Yes. The great Professor Benson.'

This had spiralled out of Patrick's control already, but at least they were talking. 'She told you that? What kind of abuse?'

'Don't be prurient. Does it matter?'

'When she was a girl?' Patrick asked, dumbfounded. 'I know they argued.'

He snorted. 'Yeah. Well. She wasn't happy when he waltzed back into her life. Neither was I.'

'Why would you care?'

'It upset her.'

'When did he reappear?'

'A few weeks ago. Don't ask me how. She wouldn't tell me. She just complained that "Dad was back". Or "sniffing around", I think she said.'

'So, you and Annie have been friends since uni?'

'No. We weren't really friends back then. We bumped into each other by accident a while back.'

'And that's when you started supplying her with drugs?' Finnearty gave no response.

'What about your son? The reason I agreed to talk with you,' he said.

'He's gone missing. Do you know where I might find him? Someone Annie mentioned? Networks?'

'Of course not. Why would I?'

Patrick put his glass back on the table and stayed leaning forward. 'She was medicating him with your drugs.'

'I know nothing about that.'

'Really?'

'Really. What does "missing" mean? Do you think he's OK?' He seemed genuinely concerned.

'He's alive. Did you ever go to Forest Street?'

He shook his head. 'No. Where's that?'

'That's where they lived. Annie and my son. Where Annie died of a heroin overdose. Did you know Annie was a smack addict?'

'No! A heroin overdose?' Patrick nodded. Finnearty looked down at the worn carpet.

'I'm surprised you don't know all this. You were close.'

'Not that close, as I said.'

'She confided to you about her father's abuse.'

He sighed. 'Maybe she did heroin. I know she tried different things.'

'Did she try different things with you?' He looked annoyed. Something occurred to Patrick. 'Do you know Andre? Or did Annie mention him?'

Finnearty shook his head uncertainly. 'The name sounds familiar. Not someone I know. Maybe she knew him.'

'I know about her diaries,' Patrick said, to startle him. It seemed to work. 'I want them. I think they can help my son. Did Annie leave the diaries with you?' Finnearty considered this, as if a gear had shifted.

'Let me get you another whisky,' he said.

Patrick stood too and wandered to the bedroom door. There was that neatly made bed and a wooden set of bedside drawers. All very spartan. No pictures of his family by the bed. Or Annie.

'The bathroom's the other door,' Finnearty said, blocking Patrick's exit. He handed a whisky to Patrick. Ice clinked. 'Maybe I can help you. How much of all this do the police know?'

Patrick wanted out but Finnearty was still there in the door. 'Not much, but other people do.' He was glad Claire knew where he was, then realised he hadn't texted her when he had arrived, and that Stuart knew the back story.

'Let's sit in here,' he said. Patrick looked back into the bedroom. There were no chairs. 'On the bed is fine.' It was getting weird. 'Please.' Patrick did as asked and sat on the edge of the bed. Finnearty sat next to him and sipped his whisky.

'When her father reappeared in her life, she was rattled. It wasn't easy to rattle Annie, but he did. He'd rattled and shaken her since she was a girl. She saw her mum but never told her about the abuse.'

This all rang true. 'Why not, I wonder?'

'She thought it was her fault when she was little and later on it seemed too late or too pointless to tell her. She thought her mum would lose everything.'

'Why did Annie study at the same university where he was teaching?'

'That's not unusual. Victims can detach from their own pain and remain in thrall to someone they know isn't good for them. Being on campus was an act of defiance for Annie. She went there and tested his boundaries on so many fronts. Both of them knew she could ruin his career and his life at any moment. It was a kind of vengeance.'

Patrick thought about the havoc Annie had threatened and caused. The cover-ups and defiance and the boyfriend in a caravan up the coast. All that pain for everyone. He was sitting on a bed with Mr Infinity.

'I'm guessing Annie came up here,' he said.

'She did,' Finnearty said. 'Do you know what a compounding pharmacy is?'

Patrick shook his head.

'Basically it's an authority to prepare medication from scratch. You can make tablets from powders. You can turn tablets into liquids for those who can't swallow a pill. You can avoid allergies by removing flavours and binders from what are otherwise across-the-counter prescription medicines. You can manufacture prescriptions that work for a patient but the drug companies no longer make because they don't sell enough. It's endless.'

There was no noise from the street now, no Christmas carols. It felt to Patrick like there was pressure in the room that blocked out all the noise.

'Annie used the room out there for compounding medications,' Finnearty said. 'It's no lab but it's well enough equipped. It's where she made whatever she gave to your son and her other starfish. She knew what she was doing but it was illegal.'

Patrick was astonished that despite Ben's illness he had never been informed about compounding options. Through all those years and doctors and tampering with medications, no-one had explained this to them. Starfish?

'And you helped her?'

'No. But I didn't stop her.' He gulped at his whisky.

'You enabled her. Facilitated her. Do you think she came up here because she loved you?'

'No! I was probably abusing her as well in my own way, but it was her choice.'

'She was here for the drugs. You know that?'

'She was. But there was more to it than that. We'd take some pills –
the joys of being a chemist, two chemists, she was always smarter than
me – and we told each other all sorts of things. She might be trying
to save others but I was helping to save her. This room was a kind of
confessional. She could walk out of here cleansed and get back to the
fucked-up world she thought she was saving.'

'You're kidding yourself! This world was fucked up too.'

He shrugged. 'Depends how good the drug mix was.' Annie's mix.
He finished his whisky. Patrick did too. They sat side by side on the bed,
holding empty glasses. Finnearty said 'I *know* Annie. Not some sanc-
tified version I'm sure you've dreamed up for yourself. Her world was
fucked up. *She* was fucked up.'

'But she *was* doing some good. I've seen it.'

'Bloody risky,' he said matter-of-factly.

'Where are her diaries?'

'She gave them to me, when the professor showed up again. They're
in the other room. You can have them if you want.'

Patrick tried to hide his astonishment. 'Yes. I do want.'

'To "save" your boy, I assume. Be careful.'

Finnearty stood up and left the room. Patrick followed. Out in the
kitchenette, Finnearty put his glass down and picked up a pair of latex
gloves. The confession seemed too easy. Patrick panicked.

'I want you to promise me something in return for these diaries,'
Finnearty said, snapping a glove onto each hand. A professional. He
fixed Patrick in a stare. 'I want you to leave me alone. I have a wife and
two children. You can judge me about all that, of course. I'm not proud
of it. I feel like I've been given a second chance and I mean to take it.
Will you leave me alone now?'

Patrick was in turmoil. He couldn't believe he was about to get the
diaries. Finnearty was so compelling Patrick was sure he hadn't killed
Annie. How could he have? He hadn't been in that room. Ben had

been, with Annie and misadventure. And who doesn't want a second chance? Like he wanted to be back in Balmain.

'Promise,' Patrick said.

Finnearty stooped in front of the safe and fiddled with a circular dial. The thick door swung open and he reached inside and produced three small diaries. Red and blue and green. Green? He closed the safe again and spun the dial, stood and held the diaries out to Patrick.

'Why the gloves?' Patrick asked.

'Because I've never touched them. She asked me to keep them safe when her father reappeared. He was on a rampage to stop all her "nonsense" and she was frightened he might get hold of them somehow. I've looked through them since she died. There's something to it all. They're worth saving. If I "enabled" her, as you put it, I'd be better off burning these, but I'm giving them to you.'

'And denying all knowledge.'

'Yes.' Patrick looked at the diaries in his hand and wondered if he'd made some sort of big mistake. He wished Cooper was here. 'A second chance. Remember?'

'No second chance for Annie.'

'No. But for the rest of us. You too. I hope you find him.'

Everything was off kilter. 'Thanks.'

'Merry Christmas.'

CCTV, Patrick thought. Annie's ghost, clanking up those stairs. We don't need your fingerprints.

H e phoned Claire when he got back in the car. He was dizzy with adrenaline and a couple of whiskies on an empty stomach.

'How'd it go? Is it him?'

'It is.'

'Wow! Well done. Did he admit it?'

'Admit what?'

'Supplying Annie with drugs.'

'Actually, she was making her own. She was manufacturing the meds she supplied to Ben.'

Claire went silent as she absorbed this. On some level this made the whole arrangement even more dangerous than they had previously thought.

'Are you home? Can I come over?' He wanted to leave the diaries somewhere safe. Safe from Andre, whoever he was. Safe from Finnearty, in case he had a change of heart. Safe from the professor on a rampage.

'Maybe I should come over to yours again,' she said. 'There's a houseful of people here looking for lost shoes and packing up.' Even though they had talked that morning, he'd forgotten about them. All these people crowding their lives.

'I managed to get Annie's diaries and they're making me nervous. I feel like there's people who want them, who know where I live. I was hoping to leave them at yours for a bit.'

'Jesus, Patrick! Do you think that's a good idea? Call Cooper.'

'I will but I just want to get away from here. I don't want the diaries at my place.'

'OK, come over. When's this nightmare going to end?'

'Soon, I think.'

'I want to find Ben and just want things to... start again. Is that too much to ask?'

'Probably. I can't wait to see you. Let's sit down the bottom of the garden, far from the madding crowd. What have you got to drink?'

'Gin.'

'Perfect. Easy on the tonic. See you soon.' At this rate he'd be pissed by mid-afternoon, but he'd been that way before.

And so, it happened. He drove back to Balmain a year after he had left.

There was a white Range Rover parked behind Claire's car in the driveway. Off-street parking. The old luxuries of family life denied to him by another displaced family. He had to drive more than a block to find a park in the street. Balmain was a bastard that way. A two-hour park. He must try to remember that.

He grabbed the diaries and checked his rear-vision mirror. It was ridiculous but he felt quite rattled.

He walked home. The small front garden was still overgrown with oleander and a struggling cotoneaster he had planted three years ago. There was a cricket bat lying on the ground and a plastic ball. The front door was set back in a portico with several pairs of kids' Crocs shoes piled in front of it. The door was unlocked, like it often was. Family life was a shield they all believed in. Claire had grown up in the house when no-one locked their doors and she carried on the tradition. Their house rule had been to lock up when no-one was home but otherwise live like the world was fair, even in Sydney.

Having gained entry, he decided he had better knock. He could hear kids' voices.

'Hello! Hello, Claire!' Maybe she was out the back. Maybe he should phone her. A small blonde girl appeared and stood motionless, looking at him from the end of the corridor. 'Hello. My name's Patrick.'

'My name is Lucy.'

'Do you know Claire?' She nodded. 'Can you please go and tell her that Patrick is here?' She disappeared. The house smelled different. Takeaway chicken? It made him hungry. Sweet perfume – not Claire's.

She appeared and walked right up and hugged him and he hugged her back for a lovely long time.

'Lucy the maid let me in.'

'Did she now? Come through.'

He followed. There used to be a table there with a bowl for tossing keys in.

The corridor opened out into the big kitchen and living room they had created with major renovations a decade ago. There was a white synthetic Christmas tree with purple decorations against the far wall and many brightly wrapped boxes underneath. The double French doors were open to the flagstone terrace and there was the lawn that sloped away to the big tree with the tyre swing at the bottom of the garden. It was beautiful and spacious and it had a blue sky.

A buxom woman with hair in a ponytail appeared with Lucy trailing behind her. 'Hello, I'm Denise. You must be Patrick?' She offered a handshake and he took it and shook it. She was bustle and confidence, on the surface at least. 'We'll try to stay out of your way. Kids! Kids, come and say hello to Patrick. I believe you've met Lucy.'

'Yes, Lucy has been very helpful.' He bowed to her.

A chubby teenaged boy and a slim younger girl, older than Lucy, appeared and walked up and both offered a handshake too. It must be a trucking thing.

'I'm Brian,' said the boy.

'I'm Jodie,' said the girl.

'It's nice to meet you all,' he said.

'We're going back home,' Lucy said, partially hidden behind her mum.

'Well, that's good! Are you looking forward to that?' She nodded. 'Have you told Santa, so he knows where to go?' She smiled and nodded again.

Denise clapped her hands. Maybe they were Pentecostals? It all seemed to be hand shaking and hand clapping and he could imagine them praising money and the Lord.

'Righto, kids. Keep moving and keep packing,' Denise said. They all turned and disappeared into the rest of the house like mice in a maze.

Patrick and Claire looked at each other and smiled. Understood. 'Drink?'

'Yes please!'

They went out onto the terrace. The chairs needed oiling. The sweet taste of gin seemed to absorb and offer all of Balmain as a botanical.

They stayed out on the terrace, not down in the garden. Denise was true to her word and kept herself and the kids away. Patrick and Claire talked and pored over the hieroglyphics of Annie's diaries. They were graphed pages with columns of figures, weights and volumes, chemical symbols, unpronounceable compounds and dates, written in tiny, tight writing. Arrows pointed up and down or side to side in a private language. Smiley-face emoticons here with an exclamation mark. Sad face there. Random words in the margins. *Placebo! Syrup.* Unlike Ben's dictionary diary, they were highly ordered, in spite of the scrawl.

Patrick would need a chemist to make any sense of them, and Finnearty hadn't offered. Maybe he could bribe him? Not surprisingly, he was getting drunk, but trying not to show it. Claire prepared sandwiches and he ate greedily.

She insisted they deliver the diaries to Cooper, along with a full account of his strange morning with Finnearty. Let the police handle it. He agreed but felt bad about his promise to Finnearty, maudlin even. And first they needed the diaries to help medicate Ben, if he needed it, when they found him. Neither of them – but Patrick especially – wanted to go back to square one and the prescription medicines that had so often failed them all.

'She cured Evan!' Patrick kept saying.

Claire promised to take photographs of the diaries cover to cover and send them in a folder to Patrick for back-up. Then they would go to Cooper.

The red diary recording Ben's treatment never mentioned him by name. He was FISH, as they both knew. It was a glimpse into the kind of mad other world where he'd been living. Evan's blue diary was MOON. The mystery green diary was TIDE. There was a theme.

On his second gin, Patrick started calling Claire GRASSHOP-PER, the name of a Buddhist character from a 1970s TV show.

They were getting closer to Ben, and Patrick felt closer to Claire. In the morning she was coming over to his place. They were going to follow up on a question Helln had put into his head: where did Ben do his yoga?

'You need a space to get to a place,' Evan had quoted Annie saying this about yoga practice. Evan did his yoga in a park these days but he had mentioned a room. He and Claire were going to find that room, and maybe Ben.

It was a long shot.

AS IN FLUTE

ive days to Christmas and Patrick was happy to let Claire drive back over to Camperdown. It was nice to get back into the silver Peugeot 308 and it reminded him to sell the shitbox he now drove. She wasn't an aggressive driver but was easily annoyed and spent much of the journey swearing at others who cut in, and at lights that turned green and back to red with only a few cars moving through. Car horns heralded the season of joy.

He directed her to a car park in the shadow of the tower block. 'It's got a certain Soviet charm,' she said, looking up.

'No wonder you work for the ABC. I think it's less charming if you have to live here.'

'I'm sure it is.'

The lifts were working. They waited with a short woman holding onto a floral shopping trolley as if it might escape if she let it go, and all her small world with it. In the lift, she pressed four and Patrick pressed eight. The machinery clunked and whined. When the doors opened at four, she said, 'Merry Christmas' without looking at them and dragged her trolley away behind her.

'Merry Christmas!' they chorused as the doors slid closed.

There was graffiti sprayed on one wall. FUCK THE PO-LICE! and various tags. Other graffiti had been semi-removed into a grey smudge. The doors opened onto level eight and late morning shone into the lift like a spotlight. Out on the walkway, Claire gasped at the city view, just as he had done.

'Affordable housing with an unaffordable view,' he said.

'It's beautiful.' He took her hand like a schoolboy and walked along to 815. Knocked loudly. The dog barked. They waited. He listened. Claire looked out at the Christmas city that was teasing the residents. There were no sounds from inside the flat. He knocked again, long and loud like a proper policeman.

The curtain next door along opened and a whiskered old man in a white singlet looked at him. 'Is Evan in?' Patrick asked. The curtain closed. He tried to peer in through the window of Evan's flat but a holland blind was drawn down. He knocked again.

It was unbelievable no-one had phones. Ben. Evan. Annie. Or none that he knew of. He should have asked Finnearty about that. Did he have Annie's phone in his safe too? With a lock of her hair.

'What do we do?' Claire asked.

He didn't want to leave. He was with her. They were together trying to find Ben. He leaned on the railing and looked down. A young girl in pigtails ran ahead of her mother. A police car swerved into the car park like a shark. Patrick heard the beep as the constable locked the door remotely. He looked out at the city and heard its soft hum.

'Let's wait,' he said.

'Not here. Stunning as it is. Let's find a cafe and come back.'

They went to the same cafe where Evan had revealed his miracle. He told her about it again. 'There's a big story in it,' he said.

'There is. It'd struggle to get past our lawyers but I'm impressed with what you've done, Patrick. And what you've found.'

'Any jobs going at the ABC?'

'That's the problem. They're *all* going. Years of "efficiency dividends" and bastard governments.'

'No job for a retired cadet, then?'

'I didn't know you'd retired!' It was nice to be at a table with someone who knew where to jab. 'It's mostly twenty-somethings now. They record interviews on their phones. It's broadcast quality. No sound guy with a furry mic anymore.'

'When we find Ben, where are we all going to go?'

'Balmain. It's home.'

'Home is where the cat is. That's my place.'

Claire smiled. She'd been replaced by a cat cliché. 'You don't have a spare room.'

'Ben and I could sleep together and you could have the camp bed.'

'Mmm. That works on every level.' She sipped her coffee and looked good.

'Excellent. Now that's settled, I think you should know that Helen spells her name H.E.L.L.N. In case you ever meet her, please don't call her Helen, call her Helln.'

She laughed out loud. He was flirting with her and she liked it. He was ageing well, without the gym fees and hard work and tennis that she pursued. He had the metabolism of a thoroughbred. She was enjoying him and his sudden doggedness.

'I thought she was gone,' Claire said. 'If she reappears, it will be Hell 'n back. Ben will be thrilled.' He laughed. They were a family of nerds. 'She'll have to sleep with you two instead of joining me on the camp bed, I'm afraid.'

Before he could respond to that, he saw Evan walk into the cafe. He had a rolled blue yoga mat slung over his shoulder on a strap, and his wild hair and black glasses and pale pink shorts. Hairy legs. All of them here now in the synchronicity of the universe.

'Evan's just walked into the cafe,' he said to Claire. They had finished breakfast. She had some coffee left. 'I'll collar him when he comes out.'

A minute later, Evan reappeared, sucking on a large cardboard cup of something.

'Evan!' Patrick called out and Evan spun around, grinned.

'How you doin', man?'

'Good. Can I introduce you to my wife, Claire?' Not ex-wife. She stood up, her metal chair scraped on the footpath, and Evan juggled his drink to shake her hand.

'Nice to meet you.'

'You too,' she said. 'Patrick's told me a lot about you. Have you been to yoga or on your way?'

'Been.'

Patrick complimented him on how well he was looking. Evan struck a pose like an archer pulling back a bow.

'Is that yoga, or have you slaughtered a goat as well?' Patrick asked.

'Calm, not harm.'

It was a bit like turning over the pages on an old-fashioned desk calendar, all pith and discipline. Claire sat down again. Evan did look healthy.

'Actually, we were hoping to run into you. Have you got a minute?' Now Evan scraped a metal chair and sat down. He put his drink on the table and leaned forward, wedged between the table and the yoga mat slung on his back. 'Before you started doing your yoga in the park, saluting the sun, back when you started with Annie, where did you practise then?'

'There's a place in Redfern.' Patrick and Claire locked eyes. Redfern was where Ben was last seen. 'Not a proper place. It was a space Annie found in this old building.'

'Do you remember the address?'

'Shit Street, that's what I called it. She wore me out there in the early days and I used to complain. But the real name is Shute Street.'

Claire reached into her bag and grabbed her phone, called up Google Maps.

'As in Shoot? Bang?' Patrick asked.

'No, Rambo. As in flute. Music.' He held his hands up beside his face and fingered the air.

'Got it!' Claire said. 'Do you remember the address?'

'No. It's a brown brick building, sort of like a triangle. You have to go around the back. It's all locked up.' Claire was using her phone.

'Could we take you there?' Patrick asked. 'Could you show us?'

'What's all this about?'

'We're still looking for Ben. Annie got him into yoga too and we thought maybe he's gone there. Maybe he's living rough there, or someone's seen him.'

'Maybe,' Evan said, and that casual plausibility seemed like a gift from an oracle.

'Is this it?' Claire asked and held her phone up in front of Evan. He looked at the Google photo and nodded.

'That's it.'

Planet Earth. Air. Water. Fire.

THE SPACE PLACE

C laire drove patiently this time, though the traffic was just as bad. It was as if she didn't want to crash on the last lap. At first, they talked excitedly about the chances of Ben being there, but soon descended into silence, with only the phone calmly advising them to turn left and turn right.

Shute was a nondescript street a couple of grids back behind the railway station in Redfern. There were narrow houses squeezed between single-storey warehouses and dilapidated factories. Wooden pellets were piled in overgrown delivery bays. The area was in transition, lost between its light industrial history and the inevitable apartment blocks that would soon nail it back down. Already, new apartment blocks loomed like tiered seats around a boxing ring, waiting for the fight to start.

The 'space' place was a brown-brick, single-storey building with a bungalow pitched roof. Evan's triangle. Identical windows either side of the security front door were covered by link-chain security screens. There was an old business sign bolted to the wall beside the door. *Flagrant Inc.* A listed phone number didn't seem to have enough digits. All this stood behind a six-foot-high chain-mesh fence. There was an ancient, dying cypress on the right hand side.

Claire stood out the front and took a picture with her phone. He squeezed her hand and kissed her quickly on the lips. There was an obvious breach in the chain-mesh fence and they both crouched and slid through, diving in. A worn path in the dust and weeds steered them under the cypress and down the right-hand side of the building.

Out the back, there was a small concrete courtyard with weeds rampant in the cracks. There was a brick outhouse in the back corner. The green door was open and Patrick could see an enormous plastic pack of toilet rolls sitting on the floor. His heart pounded.

Ben was here. Patrick thought he could smell him. Not his shit. Him. His presence. His ephemera. He could hear Claire's phone camera clicking behind him, recording, being the journalist, the proof of whatever happened next.

There was an ugly, low extension across the width of the building out the back. The glass panel in the back door was smashed. Patrick opened the door into a narrow room. The ceiling lining bulged down in one corner and spilled leaves onto the floor. A metal sink sat above a cupboard with no doors and the draining board was a grid of rinsed plastic milk bottles arranged neat as an art installation. Mania.

Claire's camera clicked. 'He's here, or he's been here,' she said. Patrick turned to look and her and nodded. She slipped her phone into her back pocket. 'Ben!' she called out suddenly and startled him. 'It's Mum.'

'Ben!' he joined in.

They walked into the next room, which was much larger. It was strewn with cardboard boxes, newspapers, a yoga mat on the floor, empty wine bottles, milk bottles, water bottles, juice bottles, clothes, books in small piles. Ben wasn't there.

There was an open door on the left that led into a dark corridor. Claire went first. Slowly now. The adrenaline had given way to caution, fear. Of what they might find. Or not find.

A room on the right. Very dim. So dim they stood there together and adjusted to the gloom. There was a smell. There was a dark bulk on the floor in the corner, a mattress. Someone breathing. Them breathing? Was anyone breathing?

She grabbed her phone from her back pocket and turned on its torch. The pool of light revealed a man in tartan trousers, a mane of matted black hair, asleep, breathing noisily, face down on a bare mattress. She turned her phone to Patrick and his eyes glowed like an animal in the headlights.

'Turn it off,' he said quietly.

He walked out of the room and she followed. Further down the corridor was another room, brighter this time, with light coming in through the meshed window that faced out into the street. Another mattress. Less rubbish on the floor. Another body.

This time it was Ben. No noisy breathing.

The image of him seared Patrick's brain. Effigies on alabaster tombs he had seen in cathedrals; clerics in robes; knights in armour, pale and still. All dead. He stepped slowly towards Ben. Movement might shatter him. He knelt down beside the mattress, as if to pray.

Ben was on his back, bearded, dirty, blistered lips, pale as a ghost. He looked arranged. Annie had looked similar. Maybe the Grim Reaper had a sensitive side. His hands were clasped across his chest in repose. The weak light into the room was dusty, still as a crypt.

After a long moment. 'He's breathing,' Patrick said softly.

She knelt beside him and they both silently watched Ben breathe. It was regular breathing and theirs joined his until the room seemed to balance again. There was a half-full plastic bottle of water on the floor by the mattress. Patrick picked it up and unscrewed the lid.

'I'm going to wake him,' he whispered, but she shook her head.

'Let me do it.' He nodded. She settled herself on the floor and gently laid her right hand on Ben's knee, let it sit there a long time. 'Ben,' she said softly. 'Ben, it's Mum.' She squeezed his knee. 'Mum and Dad. We're both here.'

'Hi, Ben,' Patrick said. 'Just wake up slowly, son.'

They'd been through this before, back in the days when his medication knocked him sideways and he slept and slept. They woke him more briskly then.

He was wearing pale green canvas trousers and a brown cable-knit jumper. Strangers' clothes. In this heat. The room was stifling and stuffy.

Claire reached up and put her hand on his clasped hands and squeezed again. Ben breathed in and stirred. He opened his big green eyes and looked up at the ceiling, not sideways at them, not down at her touch.

'Ben, you're OK. Mum and Dad are here with you. We've found you. We're with you.'

He turned his head and looked at them, from one to the other, and then back up to the ceiling.

'This is real, Ben,' Patrick said, as calmly as he could. 'We're in the room where you've been sleeping. We found you. Would you like a sip of water?'

Ben nodded his head and slowly propped himself up on one elbow. He took the bottle from Patrick and suckled while he looked at them again, one and then the other and back again, and back again.

Claire smiled and squeezed his free hand. 'We're here, Ben. Everything's going to be alright now. You're not in trouble.'

He stopped drinking. 'You're hurting my hand,' he said to her.

She let go and laughed, and then started crying. Patrick felt hot tears on his cheeks too and Ben looked at them both as if they were strange creatures in a zoo.

THE MAGIC CARPET RIDE

H e recognised them. They called an ambulance.
Standing back while the paramedics checked and stabilised
Ben, they looked around the room. Behind the graffiti tags there were
spider-scrawl rows of text in black felt pen. Up close, the walls of the
room were handwritten.

*Gender: classification of objects corresponding to the sexes and sexless-
ness.*

Inquiline: animal living in the home of another.

Row after row. In the messy chaos of the room, the rows of writing
were thin columns almost to the ceiling. Ben must have found another
dictionary. Of course he had. Patrick searched the room, lit by LED
torches now, but couldn't find it.

The ambulance took him to the RPA hospital in Camperdown. He
was back in the system – that brutal, beautiful, bastard of a thing that
had helped and hindered him over the years of his illness. There was no
belligerence from Ben. Before they left Shit Street, he asked the female
paramedic if she could give his squat mate, Jock, some 'juice' because he
was pretty worn out.

They supervised Ben's admission to RPA, filled in what they knew
of his recent history without mentioning Annie's Mix. The doctor nodded, asked questions. The paramedics updated their treatment so far.
Patrick pleaded with them not to resume the last treatment on Ben's
Health Record. He'd been off that for a while, Patrick explained, living
rough, but doing yoga, reducing his medication. 'Scan his brain. Start
again.' The doctor smiled politely.

Was he 'fixed or fucked', according to Evan's assessment of things,
Patrick wondered. Had he been with Annie long enough to be on the
right side of being alright? After hours of exhausting bureaucracy, waiting and then joining Ben, who was in a crowded ante room, on a gurney

with a drip in his arm, commercial TV blazing, they finally got a hospital bed for Ben.

'Keep a close eye on him,' Patrick told a nurse who was standing at a lectern in the corridor and apparently supervising the chaos. 'He's prone to wandering.'

They went back to Patrick's place, five minutes from the hospital and Forest Street, where this all started a short lifetime ago. Gin and tonic out the back. He felt sure Claire was drinking more now that she'd been seeing him again. The black cat curved around their ankles under a sky of puffy white clouds. A sweet life, but for the mangled and dead.

'We found him!' he declared and they clinked glasses.

'We did. You did. He seems OK.'

'I agree. He's got good genes. To go with those bad ones that put him in hospital.'

She grabbed her phone from her bag and started swiping through the photographs she'd taken, zooming in on some to read the scrawled definitions. 'He's been there for a while, based on how much he's written on those walls. He wasn't sleeping entirely rough. Or even alone.'

'No. And all those vegie boxes and milk bottles suggest his diet may have been OK.'

'Did you see the yoga mat rolled out on the floor in that front room? Back room.'

'I didn't notice it.'

'The magic carpet ride.' They sat in silence for a while. Worn out. The gin was helping, though. 'Do you want to stay here tonight?' he asked. 'It's closer to the hospital. I'm only being practical.'

She grinned. 'Of course you are. Much as I'm enjoying this, I'll stop at one and head home, I think. I need space to absorb everything and I haven't lived or slept in a quiet house with just me for what feels like forever.'

'Fair enough.' Even he could do with some downtime in his own empty house. The family was still atomised but coalescing. 'So, where's Ben going when he gets out of hospital?'

'Balmain! Home. His own room. We've talked about this.'

'And can his father come too then?'

She looked at him and trailed her hand out for him to touch. He touched it. 'Yes. I'm sure that'll help him recover. And I'm sure the single bed in the spare bedroom will be long enough for you.'

Message happily received. He'd be back in Balmain! 'You'll want to tell Phil the good news.'

'I will,' she said without missing a beat. She sipped her gin.

'You know who I want to tell?'

'Hell 'n back?'

He laughed. 'That's a good idea! She helped us find him. No – I want to tell Alice. Annie's mum.'

'That's a good idea too. I thought you were going to say Cooper.'

He let his head slump back and surveyed the sky. 'Yes. There's quite a line-up.'

They met up and visited Ben in the morning. He was clean and looked better already, in spite of that ragged beard.

'I think I might keep it,' he said. 'One of the nurses likes it.'

'Well, make sure you keep the nurse as well,' Patrick said. 'She'll come in handy when you get home.'

It was so close to Christmas now and they spoke to the doctor about Ben's chances of being home for it.

'Unusually for someone living rough, there was no alcohol in his system. He was dehydrated. There was acetaminophen and codeine in his system – he was taking Panadol for headaches, apparently,' the doctor said. 'Very sensible self-medication.'

A psychiatrist was seeing him later in the morning. Ben had displayed no signs of psychosis since his admission, though he was confused by his surroundings at times. He had responded well to treatment. All things considered, the doctor said, Ben was 'remarkable'.

Claire and Patrick looked at each other and beamed as if they had a newborn. Claire stayed with Ben.

Patrick headed across to Kirribilli, as suggested by Alice. 'Neutral territory between Mosman and Forest Lodge,' she said.

It wasn't neutral for him. He and Claire had spent light years there, in careless energetic sex, Guinness at the pub on rainy Sundays, bottles of wine and seafood down in the secret pocket parks that dotted the harbour.

Alice was already at a table on the footpath in the late morning sun, with a bottle of water and two glasses. She had her funeral sunglasses on. The bones of the Sydney Harbour Bridge loomed at the end of the street and made it feel like they were in the pit of an archaeological dig. Alice looked older too. Maybe it was the bright morning sun. She was wearing an orange shirt that didn't suit her.

He sat down. It was unsettling looking into those big sunglasses that covered half her face. Nothing felt quite right.

'Coffee or chardonnay?' he asked.

'Let's start with a coffee,' she said without missing a beat.

A waitress appeared. She wore a trim apron and had North Shore skin and a ponytail and perfect teeth. There is absolutely nothing wrong with being gorgeous, Patrick decided, putting aside his class warfare for a moment. They ordered, and Patrick told her they'd found Ben.

'Wonderful news!' Alice laid her hand over his. 'Tell me all about it. How is he?'

'Unusually well, according to his doctor. He was in a squat in Redfern where Annie took him to practise yoga. She's still protecting and guiding him.'

Alice smiled. 'Was it squalid?'

'Yes. But don't focus on that. It was dry and safe and we think he might have been there the whole time he's been missing. He was still doing yoga there.'

Alice watched a car pass. Who knew what was going on behind those sunglasses? Their order arrived. Latte and baclava for Alice. Strong flat white and blueberry cheesecake for him. They chatted about Ben and the chances of him being home for Christmas. He talked up Annie, gladly.

'I've found some other things too,' Patrick said after they had finished the coffee and sweets. 'I've found out who was supplying her with the drugs she used to treat Ben and Evan, and others before them.'

Alice sat upright and looked at him through dark lenses. 'Who?'

'I'd rather not say. I haven't told the police yet. I want them to follow it up.'

'Of course. But do you think I'm going to go and confront them?'

'No.' A pause. 'But maybe Professor Benson would. This guy went to Sydney uni.'

She exhaled. 'You're right. Stephen may go off. Do you think he knows him?'

'Possibly.'

Alice absorbed all this and carefully licked the sticky flakes of pastry from her fingers. 'You've been telling me everything Annie was up to was going to save the world and now you're telling me you're going to report it all to the police. Why?'

'Well.' Patrick pondered. 'Where's that chardonnay when you need it?'

'Order a bottle,' Alice said flatly. He did. The conversation stopped and he took the time to think things through and what to say now they were here at a wooden table in the increasingly hot sun. Alice seemed resolved not to break the silence. She was waiting for his answer. White wine was served and the bottle clattered into a metal ice bucket between them.

'Well,' he resumed. 'The police knew nothing about this guy. His motives. His whereabouts. His relationship to Annie. They never looked into him.'

Alice pondered. 'You think he might have killed Annie?'

'Who knows.' He didn't think so, really. Maybe Annie *had* died in a misadventure.

Another silence. 'I can't say that Annie being murdered cheers me up but the possibility – I don't know – *relieves* me of something,' Alice said.

'I think I understand. Anyway, I'll take it all to the police. It was all illegal, at the very least. What he did, what Annie did.'

'Thank you for the drink,' she said. He was paying, apparently. He hoped his card would still work. They both drank in silence for a bit. This was a slow-motion lunch, or whatever it was. He'd already had had time to absorb all the news and now Alice was taking her time.

But not too much time. 'You're saying the man who may have killed my daughter is in that class photo I showed you back at the house?'

Was he saying that? 'I don't know. There's more.'

'More what?'

'More things I've found out.' He wasn't sure if he was doing the right thing.

'And more chardonnay in that case.' She lifted the dripping bottle from the cooler and refilled their glasses.

'You may already know this.' Behind her huge dark glasses he could feel her eyes on him. 'Professor Benson re-entered Annie's life in the days before she died.'

'What's that supposed to mean?'

'He visited her at her house.'

'We didn't know where the house was!'

'He did.'

Alice took a sip of her wine and put the glass carefully back onto the table. She lifted her sunglasses up and set them on her head. She had a black eye. 'Did he now?' she asked.

He was startled. 'Alice, what's happened? Did he do that?'

'More or less. It was an accident, of course.'

'Are you OK at home?'

She nodded and slid her sunglasses back down and sipped her wine. 'I wasn't going to tell you. He didn't hit me. He never has. I just got in his way and then I stumbled. He's been so angry since Anne died. Now *I'm* angry. I can't believe he's lied to me. Tell me.'

He told some of what he'd learned from Jacob at the uni but left Finnearty's testimony out of it. He wondered how much Ben might know about all this. Would he corroborate what Finnearty had said about Annie living in fear? It didn't take Alice long to wonder whether Stephen might have been involved in what happened to Annie, inadvertently, by accident rather than design.

'He's a bull in a china shop,' she said. 'We both know that.'

'It might just be a coincidence that Annie died soon after he found her again.'

'It will be. But why is he lying about it?'
The question hung in the air between them.

P atrick drove home with a promise from Alice that she'd call him if she needed to. He knew she wouldn't. He wasn't sure how much use he would be if she did.

He walked over to the hospital. The nearer he got, the more sick people he saw. He didn't blame them for wanting to be outside, but seeing them in hospital gowns, smoking cigarettes while attached to a drip, made him feel like he was in a zombie movie. It must drive the medical profession mad.

Ben had been moved into a four-bed ward. There was an old woman in the next bed with a bruised face, asleep or drugged or dead. Opposite Ben's bed, a man with his baby spoke in Arabic to his grey father, and in English now and then. Something about a party.

Ben looked well. 'Is Nurse Beard still looking after you?'

'No.'

'Did you get her number?'

'Yes.'

'Seriously!'

'No. I don't have a phone anyway.'

'That's a good point. You used one to ring me that morning after Annie died. Do you remember?'

'Yeah.'

'Well, whose phone was that?'

'That was mine. I don't have it anymore.'

'Where'd you get that phone?'

'Annie gave it to me.' Patrick thought about that. 'What's the big deal?' Ben asked.

It wasn't worth pursuing now. 'Nothing. How are you feeling?'

'Yeah, OK.'

'Better or worse than you felt on Annie's mix?'

'Better than when I ran out of her mix. I felt bad in the squat. I had really bad headaches and fevers. I thought I was dead once or twice.'

'The doctor praised you for not turning to drink and drugs. We're proud of you too.'

'I couldn't afford them.'

Patrick laughed. 'No.' His hair had grown since they had faced each other in the doorway to hell of Forest Street. 'Did you want them?'

'Not really. Yes and no. I've been really sad.'

Patrick was sitting in a clunky vinyl chair with solid arms so that patients could push themselves upright. That's what he did. 'I understand. I've been really sad too. I'm going to give you a hug.'

Ben nodded, instead of disagreeing. It was awkward and sublime. Patrick stooped and Ben sat up and leaned into him. They felt muscle in each other's shoulders. He could feel Ben's bones too and his beard against his cheek.

'I love you so much, Ben. So much.'

'Where's Mum?'

He was speaking into his ear while they hugged. 'She's in Balmain, making your bed. But she'll be over to visit you soon.'

'Is that where we're going?'

'You have to get out of here first, but yes. It looks like you'll be home for Christmas.'

'I don't like how it smells in here.'

'Me either.'

'And there's always people coming and going. Different people. All the time.'

He patted Ben's shoulder and stood back up. 'Well, you've been in hospital before. You know how it works. It'll be great to get home.'

'Will you be there too?'

'Yes, I will.' Ben grinned at him. 'I think I've got the spare room.'

'Wow! The spa room. That sounds good.'

Ben was back! In a hospital gown, but you couldn't have everything. Not all at once.

• • • •

Patrick fed Eve. He hadn't bought her a Christmas present. He wasn't one of those stupid cat owners. He knew the only day Eve knew was today over and over again. It was the same for people. You don't notice that your life ticks away like that, one day at a time.

He walked into the lounge room and looked at the sparse offerings under the frangipani. Ben's giant dictionaries dominated, wrapped in red. Claire's kimono wrapped in yellow. Helln's CD wrapped in newspaper.

They needed that Christmas tree in Balmain! A real one. They'd agreed to get one if Ben was back home and now that looked likely. Replace that shit tree that Claire had. Get out the old decorations. He texted Claire to remind her of their plan, and told her to leave it up to him. He was becoming quite the man. Even Stuart might be proud of him. His phone pinged. He expected Claire.

It was Andre. The fun never stopped, now that it had started.

Christmas drinks? The Nag's Head. 3pm?

At least Patrick had his number now. Everything was connected but he had no idea how. Part of him wanted to ignore the invitation but it was already after two. Meeting in a public place was a good idea. The diaries were safely over in Balmain.

See you there.

• • • •

He took off his sunglasses when he walked into the gloom of the bar. He'd set his phone to camera and, when he saw Andre sitting by the window, he snapped a couple of secret pictures. Or not so secret. In the last photo, Andre was staring directly at him and giving him the finger.

'You don't need to do that,' he said when Patrick approached. They didn't shake hands.

'Good,' Patrick said and headed to the bar. Facial recognition might turn something up but he doubted it. Andre seemed to know what he was doing and he didn't seem worried.

'Did your friend with all the hair take the room?' he asked when Patrick returned.

He smiled. 'Yes.' Sort of true.

'Lucky you,' he said.

'Thanks for meeting somewhere where you won't hurt me.'

Andre looked around theatrically. 'I've been in quite a few bar-room brawls.'

Patrick looked around too. 'Not in this bar.' An old guy with a sad moustache. Two fifty-something women drinking white wine. Silent TVs showing silent sport. He felt like the world was on a loop. He'd been here before, plenty of times.

'Let's go up to the balcony outside,' Andre said. They took their cold beers upstairs. There was an office Christmas party in the bistro but outdoors they were alone. The Italianate flourishes of Glebe Town Hall posed across the street and beyond that, the city glittered. Packer's monstrous casino tower was visible. It was visible from everywhere.

Andre had had a buzz haircut but kept his beard and very blue eyes. He was handsome and scary all at once. They settled on their stools. Drank.

'A is for Andre,' Patrick said. 'Tell me the rest.' His nervous brain veered into overdrive. B is for Ben. C is for Claire. Stop! Concentrate. This is what you do well. Sitting in a bar and getting a story out of someone. You've been doing it for years.

Andre removed his mobile phone from his pocket and turned it off and displayed it to Patrick. He put it on the thin wooden ledge next to his beer.

'You're kidding, right? Or are you going to strip search me?'

Andre gazed ahead. 'You've already photographed me. I don't want you recording me as well.' He sipped his beer and waited. Patrick produced his phone and turned it off. He placed it carefully on the ledge, like he was lowering a needle onto a record.

'Will you talk now?'

'I will.'

'Who are you working for?'

'I work for a pharmaceutical company,' Andre said.

Patrick hadn't expected that. 'What were you doing at Forest Street?' he asked.

'I was looking for something.'

'Who let you in?'

'I did.'

Break, and enter. 'What were you looking for?'

'Her diaries.' Patrick wasn't sure if he had wobbled on his stool but it felt like it. He was in the middle of something bigger. Too big. He drank his beer to slow things down. 'I told you we were on the same trail,' Andre kept going.

'Did you find them?' Patrick asked, breathing again.

'No. That's why I let you in. I was hoping you'd lead me to them. Have you found them?'

'No.' Yes. They're in a drawer in a spare bedroom in Balmain.

'You obviously know about them. You're not as dumb as you think.'

'You might be surprised,' Patrick said.

Andre grinned. 'Would you like another beer?'

'I would. A pale ale. Any variety.'

Andre grabbed his phone and headed inside. Patrick gathered his wits. What else did he need to know? Almost everything. Andre wasn't supplying drugs to Annie, Finnearty was, or at least letting her make her own. What was the connection?

A boy clattered down the footpath on his skateboard, dragged by a muscular dog on a lead. Careless youth.

Andre returned with the beers. 'A micro-brewery. I've already forgotten which one.'

He tried it and it was good. 'Why did you take so long to get back in touch with me?'

'I was being mysterious.'

'I think I can decipher that. You kept looking for the diaries but got nowhere.'

'Pretty much.'

'So now you talk to me again. Why do you want her diaries?'

'Why do you?'

'I don't,' he lied.

'For what it's worth, I'm asking you to keep all this to yourself.'

'For what it's worth – that's not worth anything.'

'No. We'd recently started supporting Annie's work. The sort of work she was doing with your son.'

'What sort of work's that?'

'Medicating him. Mentoring him. I know you know about that, so no need to be mysterious. In our assessment, it showed promise. Would you agree with that?'

'I would.' He decided not to mention they'd found Ben.

Andre nodded. 'Good. That's good. Like I said, we'd recently started supporting her work. It was very preliminary.'

'Off the books?'

'Her diaries might suggest our company was involved and as I say – we weren't.'

This bullshit confounded even Patrick. 'All care, no responsibility.'

'Her earlier diaries also could be useful to us. To follow what she'd done.'

'So, the "support" you weren't giving her was supplying medication – helpful medication, I admit – to my son Ben?'

'No comment.'

He sighed. 'Annie was in a dangerous place. Home and away. She hated big pharma.'

'She did.'

'And there you were "supporting her." Unless anyone asked.' Andre shrugged, took the jibe, drank. The Christmas party inside started on a boisterous version of *Ghostbusters*. Patrick felt like the jigsaw puzzle now had the edges joined together. Now there were only a thousand pieces left. 'What's the name of your company? I'm guessing you're not in sales.'

'That doesn't matter.'

'What if it matters to me?'

'Find out.'

'Andre Smith. I'll Google you. Do you think Annie died of an overdose?'

'I doubt the autopsy was wrong.'

'Death by misadventure, then?'

Andre turned to face him, instead of gazing out at Sydney. More than one siren blared in the distance. There were always sirens in the distance here – most of them heading to or from RPA hospital, where Ben was lying in bed with a weird beard.

'I think a lot would be explained if we found out who was supplying drugs to Annie before we didn't get involved. Any idea who that might be?'

Those blue eyes almost made him confess. They could see through him. 'No.'

'They'd want the diaries too. Maybe more than us.'

They had *had* the diaries, though. Annie had handed them over for safe keeping from her father, but maybe from Andre too? Maybe she was scared of everyone in the end. What a place to be. Fucked up, as Finnearty claimed. He wondered how much support Ben was to her in all this quiet terror, how much he knew.

'Why are you finally telling me all this?' Patrick asked

'We want to help boys like your son. Girls. Parents. We want to carry on Annie's work. You said you thought it was working for Ben. We want the same thing.'

'And you've found fuck all.'

'As I said, pretty much.'

'Maybe because you're not involved?'

'That hasn't helped.'

Patrick was beginning to relax. There was a calm certainty about Andre that he realised he'd been craving. He *wanted* Andre on his side. He wasn't working for the professor. He wasn't Annie's heroin dealer. All he was was a thug from big pharma with blue eyes.

'You weren't the one who was "supporting" Annie,' Patrick said after a long break in their conversation. 'I'm guessing that person is a chemist in a white lab coat. If it's a woman, she'll be beautiful when she takes off her glasses and shakes out her hair.'

Andre leaned back and laughed. 'I've seen that movie!'

'I thought it was a TV show. How am I doing?'

'Pretty good, Sherlock! Better than you think, actually.'

'I want to meet that person.'

Andre gazed at him. 'Why?'

'Ben's their lab rat. He's my son. It's something about duty of care. I want to know why they think it's worth finding those diaries.'

'They do.'

'That's why we're here?'

'It is.'

'I've just realised you're trying to recruit me.'

'Speaking of beer,' Andre said, and stood up and left. The glasses were piling up. As usual, Patrick felt vaguely drunk. He stood up and stretched his arms above his head, swivelled on his hips. He would *definitely* ask Ben to teach him yoga out on the lawn in Balmain! Life resumed.

If all this was true, Patrick now had a chemist who could decipher Annie's diaries and help Ben. A compromised chemist. Someone who didn't exist, according to Andre. Perfect. He allowed himself to think that he was getting good at this.

Andre eventually reappeared with the beers. Neither of them spoke. They sat and sipped beer and looked into the distance like old blokes.

'She'll meet you,' Andre said eventually, speaking towards the Town Hall in front of him.

'Who will?'

'The lab coat.' He seemed pissed off for some reason. 'Our chemist. I just called her.'

'She's a she!' Patrick couldn't believe how quickly things were moving. At last. 'Nice touch.'

'She doesn't wear glasses, though. You got that wrong.'

When he got home, Claire called. She had news. The doctors had told her that afternoon Ben would be home for Christmas Day, at least, even if he had to go back in after that. 'But it's unlikely,' she said. 'They told me again that he's remarkable.'

'Finally someone else sees it!' he said happily, intoxicated in more ways than one.

'So, you can go and get that Christmas tree,' she said.

'And you can put that shit tree you've got back in a box.'

'You've put that so nicely I might let you do it,' she said. 'I'll find the old decorations.'

He told her about his meeting with Andre. 'Tell Cooper,' she said. 'You have to tell Cooper and let them take over. I just want our family back, not all this.'

That's what he wanted too. He felt high and reckless. Things were moving towards their end. He called Cooper.

'Patrick Hyland! Merry Christmas,' Cooper said.

'You too, copper Cooper. Sorry! I'm sure you've got a first name.'

'Wayne. But I'm not the famous fashion designer.' He hardly needed to explain that. Patrick remembered his tight brown suit.

'I've got some good news. We've found Ben. He's recovering in hospital but he's OK.'

'That's great! Wow!'

'He's been in a squat but hopefully he'll be back home for Christmas.'

'That's wonderful. Thanks for letting me know. I'd been wondering.'

'Will you still need to interview him?'

Cooper paused. 'For the record. There's no hurry. Early in the new year? Just enjoy Christmas together for now. That's great news.'

'What are you doing for Christmas?'

'The Central Coast. My wife's parents. Bigger house. Beach. My daughter Polly loves it. So do I.'

He thought about Annie's ex-boyfriend and a caravan park up there somewhere. All these connections and disconnections. He felt like a voyeur into lives that didn't belong to him.

'Sounds great!' He left a polite pause before letting life and death crash back in. 'The thing is…I've also found out some other things about Annie. I know who was supplying her with drugs. And I know she was afraid of her father. We need to talk.'

Cooper sighed into the line. 'Her father? OK. I agree.'

'Can this wait until after Christmas?' Patrick asked.

'Do you think anyone's in danger? Ben? Yourself?'

He thought about Alice. Finnearty and the nativity. The diaries. 'Not really.'

'Good. Call me straight away if that changes. I'm back at work on the third. Can it wait until then?'

'I was hoping you might say something like that.'

'How did you find all this stuff out?'

'Looking for Ben.'

THE DEAD BED

'Well done, Dad.'

BETH AND BENSON

Patrick was ushered into a bland meeting room above a large furniture shop in Auburn. They hadn't entered through the shop but through a locked glass door at street level between other shops. It felt cloak and dagger and fish and chips all at once.

He was nervous. Andre had driven him there and taken him up to the room. He took Patrick's mobile phone this time.

'Beth will be up in five,' Andre said and headed back down the carpeted stairs. It felt like Andre didn't like him anymore.

There were no windows but he could hear the muffled sound of traffic from outside. An electronic whiteboard was unplugged from the wall. A long black table divided the room. He walked all the way around it and counted eight office chairs, for something to do. He heard the glass door lock click down on the street. A woman appeared silently at the top of the stairs. Eurasian, mid-thirties, her black shoulder-length hair parted in the middle. She smiled and extended her hand. 'I'm Beth.'

He stepped forward and shook her soft hand. 'I'm Patrick. Thanks for agreeing to meet with me.'

She looked around the room. 'This is nice.'

'Not your regular meeting room, then?' She shook her head. 'Did Andre take your phone as well?' he asked.

'I'm used to it. Shall we sit down?' They did, the black table between them. 'I'm glad you found Fish,' she said.

He wasn't expecting that. He was back on the other side of the Ben divide, on Annie's side. He took a moment to regain his composure. 'How do you know we found him?'

'Andre said.'

'Did he now?' It wasn't worth wondering right now how that had happened. 'I'm glad we found him too. Describe Annie to me.'

'What she looked like?' He nodded. It occurred to him that Andre could have delivered any old flack to tell him what they knew he wanted to hear. 'Late twenties, blue eyes, slim, angry, smart.'

'How often did you meet her?'

She estimated with a shrug. 'Half a dozen times?'

'How did all this start? Who set up the meetings?'

'Her father.'

'Her father!' Patrick reeled. Beth nodded. 'Professor Benson?' Beth nodded again. He slumped back in his chair and then stood up and walked around the table again. For something to do. Sat down. 'Her father.'

'That's what Annie told me. I don't think she was supposed to, but she did.' She was calm, in spite of his agitation.

'Why would he do that?'

'I don't know the back story.'

'Join the club.' Beth had dark brown eyes. He trusted what she said. She was no Andre flack. He sighed. 'Are you a chemist?'

'I am.'

'How did you get involved?'

'I was offered a confidential project. Everything's confidential at Semper and Hodge, so that wasn't unusual. It turned out to be Annie. That *was* unusual.'

'Why?'

'Well, *she's* unusual, but it was a strange brief. I wasn't sure if I was recruiting a spy or conducting a job interview.' He expected Beth to continue but she didn't.

'It was a job interview, wasn't it?'

'In hindsight. They wanted me to assess and then hopefully recruit Annie if I thought there was potential in whatever it was she was doing.'

'And did you think there was potential?'

'Yes.'

'And what did you decide she was doing?'

'Illegal trials of homemade drugs. I say homemade but she's intellectually and professionally qualified for complex compounding of medicines, and that's what she was doing. Without meeting the procedural and reporting requirements, etcetera.' Beth implied a sort of freedom she wouldn't have minded having herself. 'But it was more holistic than just drugs. Lifestyle too. Exercise. Diet. Meditation. She believed you could rewire the brain over time, change its chemical balance.'

'Cure people?'

'So she claimed. Some people, she said. Not everyone.'

'Did you believe her?'

'Put it this way. I haven't seen any evidence of it.'

He wanted to yell to Beth, 'I've seen it!' But had he? 'So your company started supplying her with the drugs and paraphernalia she needed to continue her research.'

A conspiratorial smile. 'A well-equipped, sterile lab was helpful to her.'

'Do you know about her diaries?' he asked.

'Her little workbooks?'

'I guess. That's a better description, actually.'

Beth leaned forward. 'So you've seen them, too? Do you know where they are?'

'Well. Fish told me about them. His was red.'

Beth nodded. 'She had them at our meetings, so I've seen them, but she referred to them herself when we were talking, never offered them. Refused, actually. *We* got on well but she made her disdain for our company very obvious.'

'Do you think she was in danger? From Semper and Hodge?'

'No. She was keen for our help, but not our influence. *We* two thought we could manage that, but this is a powerful company.'

'So, there was no way Semper and Hodge wanted her dead?'

'Not that I'm aware of. It wouldn't make sense. Certainly not without her workbooks.'

'According to Andre, Semper and Hodge remained interested in her workbooks after she died.'

She nodded. 'Based on what I told them. They'd officially deny it. I'm sure Andre would swear on a Bible he's never met me.' The room fell silent and he noticed Beth's perfume for the first time, faint and fine. 'What's your son's name?' she asked.

'Ben.'

'Ben. Do you think Annie helped him?'

'Absolutely. The doctors at RPA think so too. He's there now, but he'll be coming home for Christmas.'

'So, he's OK?'

'Seems to be. "Remarkable", according to the doctors.'

Beth smiled and shook her head, as if acknowledging what Annie had achieved. She had full lips.

'If Ben became ill again, back home, if you had those workbooks – his red workbook – do you think you could use her notes and help him?' Patrick asked.

'Manufacture drugs for him?'

'That sort of thing.'

She shook her head. 'I'm a scientist,' she said.

'That should help.'

She smiled. 'Theoretically, I could. But as I said, the work Annie was doing was illegal and dangerous, though she evidently knew what she was doing.'

'I'll take that as a "yes".'

'Take it as a "no". Anyway, we'd need the workbooks first.'

'I reckon I'm a chance to find them.'

'That would be fantastic.'

He liked her. She was more pharma fun than Andre. 'I'm guessing you're pretty good with numbers?'

'Not bad.'

He recited his mobile number to her, twice. 'Got it,' she said. 'Do you want to try the same trick with mine?'

'Old dog here. No. Text me. No need to tell Andre.'

ack home, confounded again by the prof, and Claire phoned. Ben was being released into her care! They'd be back in Balmain within the hour.

After everything. All of them.

'Do you need me there at the hospital?' he asked.

'No, I need you back in Balmain to welcome us home.'

'Will my key still work?' He'd left it on his ring. The key to his old life.

'Do you think I'd change the locks on you?'

'Um. Possibly.'

'Well, I didn't. It's a lovely day. Open the terrace doors and make it all feel calm and welcoming. Now get going. I don't want to beat you there.'

Patrick picked Eve up and explained what was going on. He gave her a big bowl of dried food and told her not to eat it all at once. Would any of his clothes still be at Balmain? He threw some things into a gym bag and put it by the door. He put together a toiletries kit. He went to the frangipani Christmas tree and grabbed Ben's big red presents, Claire's kimono, and put them by the door too. Helln's gift lay flat and alone on the wooden floor. Maybe he should call and offer her the house? And Eve.

The family back together. Happily ever after? He loaded the car hopefully and left. He needed a Christmas tree! There was a runt in a bucket outside a greengrocer on Glebe Point Road and he put it on the back seat of his car and drove to Balmain.

Homes have a smell. Now that Denise and her kids had been gone for a couple of days, Balmain was beginning to smell of itself again. He couldn't identify what it was but he recognised it.

The white Christmas tree seemed to have lost most of the presents that were there a few days ago. Transported over to the trucker's house.

Poor kids. Christmas isn't meant to be moved around in the boot of a car.

He folded the fake tree and took it to the garden shed and found a plastic bucket. Within five minutes he had his Christmas tree upright with a couple of bricks to hold it in place. He filled the bucket with water. All it needed now was those old cardboard and clag decorations, and the family. He put his trio of presents under the tree and looked to find one with his name on it. Already he wished he'd bought more for Claire. Christmas and its old despair.

Now he opened the doors to the terrace and the sloping lawn as Claire had requested. It was glorious. More than 30 degrees outside. He wandered back inside. Waiting. Just looking. Not snooping.

There was an accounting magazine on a coffee table. There was Phil's aftershave in the ensuite bathroom cupboard. Maybe he was snooping. Crappy sandals sat in the bottom of the wardrobe in the 'marital' bedroom. He wanted to put it all in a box and take it to the Salvos, or throw it off the ferry wharf at the bottom of Darling Street.

This was spoiling his mood, so he went back out to the bright kitchen.

He finally discovered where the coffee grinder was now kept and put it on the bench. Claire still kept the coffee beans in a sealed jar in the fridge. He rattled some into the grinder and pressed the button. The sound, the smell, the routine was bliss. He looked out over the back garden. He had missed all this but now he physically felt how much had gone from his life, and reduced it.

Where were they?

He filled the stained coffee maker with filtered water and completed the routine, flicked a switch and saw the orange light go on. When would Phil come back to Sydney, he wondered.

The coffee machine coughed its perfume just as a car pulled into the driveway. Perfect. Car doors closing. The front door down the corridor rattled open. He stayed leaning on the bench in the kitchen, watching and waiting with a kind of lightness in his head. Footsteps in a long stride and then there was Ben. Green canvas trousers and a white cotton shirt, big beard and clean, wild hair. He was carrying a bag with the RPA hospital logo on it.

'Hiya, Dad.'

'Hiya, son.'

Claire appeared with the strap of a stuffed backpack across her shoulder. Black T-shirt, jeans, red runners. Gorgeous. She looked around the warm, open house and smiled. 'Hi, Patrick. Coffee smells good!'

Patrick stuck his hand out and Ben shook it, then swung his hospital bag up onto the bench.

'I'm gonna put some shorts on,' Ben said, and disappeared back into the house. Patrick and Claire smiled at one another.

'Remind me how you like your coffee.'

She dumped the backpack on the couch and rubbed her shoulder. 'Very funny. And I'm sure you remember how I like my hugs too.' They walked to one another and embraced. 'Thanks for finding him. I'm going to say that every day, so get used to it.' Every day, he thought, holding her. That implied day after day.

Ben reappeared in a pair of long checked shorts with no shirt. 'Get a room you two!' He was terribly thin and pale. There were canula bruises on his arm and Patrick thought of Annie with her dart bullseye bruise. Later. Not now. Never.

'Who wants coffee?' he asked.

'Me,' Claire replied, putting her hand in the air like a schoolkid in case no-one had noticed.

'Me too,' Ben said, walking out onto the terrace in the bright sunshine. Doctor Singh had given advice on diet but Claire was going to leave it up to Ben for now, within reason.

'OK! And I baked some muffins too,' Patrick said. Claire looked at him, astonished by this new trick. He'd been gone a year. He shook his head guiltily. She wandered outside and joined Ben on the terrace, rubbed his shoulder.

'How are you feeling?'

'It's all a bit trippy.'

'I'm sure it is. It's great to have you home. Just take your time to get used to it.'

'Where's Annie now?'

She was glad he had waited until getting here to ask. He must have been tormented by this in hospital but never raised it. 'There was a funeral. Your dad went.'

'Did he? Why?'

'For you, I think. For us. She was your girlfriend.'

Ben nodded. 'Do you reckon that swing would break?'

She looked down the garden. Denise's kids had been using it and some of them weighed more than Ben. 'No.'

He stooped and did a somersault to start his trip down the lawn. He used to do that as a boy! Her heart broke. Patrick appeared with a tray of coffees. They stood and watched Ben lean his pale frame back on the swing seat for momentum, then he was away.

They sat and drank coffee and watched Ben play. He stayed on the swing until they began to worry but then he jumped off suddenly and walked back up the lawn, chest puffing. He drank his coffee cold. He said he liked it like that now. He was talkative, chatty even, and seemed keen to fill them in on his survival methods at the squat.

'You could live forever there!' he told them seriously. 'Get up early. Salute the sun. Go out foraging. Five-thirty, even 6am there's hardly anyone about. Boxes of veggies outside cafes. Crates of milk. Bread. Bottles of water. Boxes of wine on people's doorsteps. Everything! I got my mattress. Some lounge chairs. Clothes and blankets from outside Vinnies. There were TVs and everything but we didn't have any power.'

The city was a cornucopia, it seemed. They needn't have worried.

'Someone thought they saw you at a soup kitchen one night,' Patrick said.

Ben nodded. 'That was me. It was nice to have something hot now and then.'

'I'll bet. Especially when you weren't feeling well?'

'Yeah.'

'The doctor said you were on painkillers.'

'Yeah, for the pain. I'd beg a bit to get money. I got headaches. Had a sore mouth.'

'Yes, I've got you in to see a dental hygienist in the morning,' Claire said. 'The doctors recommended it. At 11am. It's on Glebe Point Road, Patrick. I thought you could take Ben and call in and feed Eve.'

He nodded. 'What about The Magical Mystery Tour, Ben? Voices?'

'Some. Not too bad.' The animation was draining out of the conversation and Claire was going to change tack when Ben brightened again. 'Sometimes Jock would scare them away for me. He'd stand right in front of me, looking at my brain, and shout at the top of his voice, "Get out of his fuckin' head right now or I'm coming in there!"'

They all laughed.

'And that worked?' Claire asked.

Ben nodded. 'Sometimes. He's quite scary.'

The strange and wonderful afternoon passed that way. Salads for lunch. Sunhats and talk. Ben seemed well. "Remarkable". There were odd moments. Strange segues and non-responses. Ben went inside to the toilet and came back holding a pair of scissors. They both panicked.

Patrick stood up and walked towards him.

'Will you cut my beard off, Mum? It's too hot.'

They took before and after pictures on their phones. Ben sat on a chair while Claire cut off clumps of hair. She put them down by her feet but blond tufts of Ben soon rolled and bounced in slow motion across the lawn, or drifted into the air like splinters.

Then they went inside and decorated the Christmas tree. Ben sat on the floor with his legs crossed like a kid, remaking angels.

WITH GODS ON OUR SIDE

B en went to bed early and got up later to watch some TV. He couldn't sleep. He was wearing long, stripy pyjama trousers that Patrick remembered from years ago. They were too short for him now. Claire and Patrick stayed out talking on the terrace. Tomorrow was Christmas Eve.

He would take Ben to the dentist. There was a link between schizophrenia and dental health. Bad hygiene and medications often led to gum disease. Poor Ben. Claire would shop for Christmas lunch. Seafood and salads. Nothing too rich until Ben's system adjusted after weeks on his subsistence diet.

Beth hadn't texted Patrick yet. Maybe she couldn't memorise his number after all. He told Claire more about the meeting, the cloak and dagger, the new role Annie's father had played in getting big pharma onboard. Professor Punch never ceased to amaze. That reminded him of his offer to Alice about Christmas Day.

'Well, I don't think she can come here!' Claire said, annoyed and amazed that he would even suggest it.

'I offered before I knew that I'd be back here. I thought I'd be on a park bench at the end of Glebe Point Road. Christmas lunch in a brown paper bag from Tim's bottle shop. But I will contact Alice, make sure she's OK, let her know where things are at. She'll understand.'

'I'm sure she will. Can you take Ben to the supermarket tomorrow on the way home? See if there's anything he wants. Shaving stuff at least. That beard trim I gave him looks awful.'

'He looks like he escaped from a hairdressers, not a hospital. I like his longer hair, though. I hope he keeps that.'

'Me too.'

'There's no bloody doubt he's remarkable.' They lapsed into silence that the warm sounds of the harbour and the city soon filled. 'Do you reckon my board shorts are still here? Maybe we can get a swim in to-morrow.'

But Claire had fallen asleep.

When he eventually got into his own single bed in the 'spa' room, his mind raced in every direction. He said goodnight to Eve out loud in the darkness. He tried to focus on his breathing to clear his mind and eventually dozed off to the distant clinks and clanks of yacht masts. He was in the family home with his family. In the wrong room.

· · · ·

Next thing he knew it was light and morning and someone else was making the coffee. He could smell it. He tried to recall the last time someone brought him coffee in bed. It had been a long and mostly lonely time. There was a knock on the door.

'Time to get up,' Claire said, appearing with a big black mug. He sat up and took it. She sat on the edge of the bed. 'Well, this is weird, isn't it?'

'Sure is. Nice and weird, though. What time is it?'

'A little after nine.'

'Is Ben up?'

'No. I'll let you wake him.'

'Which shower am I using?'

'The shared shower.'

'But I left all my stuff in the ensuite bathroom.'

'When?'

'A year ago. Toothbrush?' She shook her head. 'Shaving stuff?' Shook her head. 'Hair gel? Wet towel?' She smiled but it was kind of upside down. 'I'm gone, am I?'

She stood up. 'No, Patrick. The opposite. You're back. Let's not do this. Enjoy your coffee and then get up.'

He did. He knocked and opened Ben's bedroom door and was star-tled to see him sitting up in bed, wide awake. 'Are you OK?' he asked.

Ben nodded. 'Good morning, then.' He handed him a glass of orange juice.

'Hi.'

'We're off to the dentist in an hour. Time to get up and have a shower.'

'Yeah, right.' He gulped his juice down, looking at the wall past the foot of his bed. Patrick looked too. There was an action poster of Harry Kewell that had been there for years.

'Harry Cool,' he said, reviving one of their old word plays.

'No, not him.'

Patrick knelt down on the floor beside the bed while Ben sat up bare chested, still bruised. He looked down the room. 'What are you looking at then?'

'Ganesh.'

Panic. 'The Hindu god, right?'

'That's him. He's there,' Ben said calmly.

'What's he look like again?'

'He's got an elephant's head and four hands.'

'How does it make you feel to see Ganesh at the end of your bed?'

'It's good. It's great.'

Patrick breathed.

'It's cool. He protects you,' said Ben.

'That's good then!'

Ben nodded, transfixed, not scared or tormented. His eyes moved as he gazed at Ganesh, followed his swirling arms, his trunk that rose and fell. Patrick's panic began to subside. Even still.

'Dad?'

'Yes, son.'

'I'm visualising. I know he's not there.'

Wow! This was new. The vocabulary. The apparent technique. Ben was learning how to bend his mind. Part of the service, part of the cure.

Annie's cure. Patrick wasn't sure how long they stayed like that – the room seemed to pulse, even to him – and his legs began to ache.

'I've got to stand up now.' He leaned on the bed and groaned and stood up carefully. 'I need to do some yoga, I think. Maybe you can teach me some moves?'

'They're called poses, Dad. It's not hip-hop.'

'I think my hip just hopped.'

'That's lame.'

'Did you mean to say that?'

'Yep.' Ben was still staring at Ganesh, but with a small grin on his face.

'I thought we might go for a swim this arvo.'

Ben nodded.

'But we've got the dentist first, so get up and have a shower.'

Ben threw back the bedcovers and breezed past Patrick as if he wasn't there. The bathroom door slammed shut. Out in the kitchen, Claire was at the sink, rinsing dishes.

'You were gone for ages. Was he hard to wake up?'

'No, he was already awake.'

She half turned. 'You're kidding?'

'No. There's good news and bad news.'

Now she looked alarmed. 'What?'

'The bad news is that he was seeing things. The good news is they were fucking fantastic.'

'What's that mean?'

'It means he's now got a Hindu god on his side.'

. . . .

Patrick didn't think Ben was planning to disappear again but he sat with him in the waiting room until the hygienist called him through. Now he had half an hour to feed Eve and still be back reading year-old magazines in the waiting room when Ben came out again.

Eve was pleased to see him. She wrapped around his ankles and deliberately got in his way. Her food dish was empty. Her litter tray was full. He opened the back door and Eve headed out onto the lawn and started chewing on her catnip plant. She would be right for a while. He phoned Alice, absently watching Eve.

'Hello you,' Alice said.

'Hello you, too. How are you? Have you finished the Christmas shopping?'

'He gets a bottle of scotch. I get a bottle of gin. Job done these days.'

Patrick thought the professor would be dangerous with a bottle of scotch in him, but said nothing.

'How's Ben going?'

'He's back home! We collected him yesterday.'

'Fantastic. That's good. Give him my love. I feel like I know him.'

'I feel like that too. I'd like you to meet. That's partly why I'm calling. I know I suggested you and I might meet up on Christmas Day but now that Ben's home I'll be spending it at home.'

'Of course. And where's "home"?'

'It's a good question. We're all at Balmain for now and we'll see what happens next.'

'Good luck.'

'Thanks. Will you be OK?'

'I'm fine, but I must tell you something, Patrick.'

'Yes?'

'I challenged Stephen for lying about Annie.'

He sucked some air in. 'I thought we were going to leave that to the police?'

'We were. Blame the chardonnay and a miserable bloody house.'

Patrick was in no position to judge. He didn't *have* to be drunk to make bad decisions but it seemed to help. Why would Alice be any different? 'And what was his explanation?'

'Plausible, I thought. He wants to speak to you.'

'Me? What for? Round two?'

'No. He feels bad about that. He says he wants to apologise.'

'Tell him to text it. I'd feel safer.'

'No doubt he also wants to pick your brains.'

'About what?'

'Whatever else you know.'

'Did you tell him I'd found Annie's supplier?'

'Not really.'

'What's that mean?' He couldn't keep an angry tone out of his voice.

'This is my *life*, Patrick. Back off.'

He felt rightly rebuked. 'I'm sorry.'

There was silence. 'He said he could meet you in his university office this afternoon,' Alice said. 'If that suited.'

'It doesn't suit! Absolutely not. I'm going for a swim with Ben this afternoon.'

'Fair enough. I'll let him know.' Alice sounded worn by the whole fiasco. Men and their egos.

'It's Christmas Eve!'

'So it is,' Alice said.

There was another period of silence.

'This has all gone wrong. I'm sorry, Alice. Are you going to be OK?'

'Of course I am. You enjoy your swim.'

Patrick had all the different versions of Stephen's involvement in his head. No-one else did. Maybe it *was* time to talk to him and see if he could unravel them, find where the truth lay. He had a sense too that it would be a favour to Alice.

'Tell Stephen I'll meet with him after Christmas. In his office, if that suits.'

'Thank you, Patrick,' Alice said, relief in her voice now. 'I'd like to hear what you think of it all.'

'Sure. Have a good Christmas, Alice. I know this has been a terrible year. Call me any time.'

'You enjoy Christmas with the family. And thanks for all you've done.'

He went and joined Eve on the lawn. She rolled on her back, full of catnip, and let him stroke her stomach. 'Christmas Eve,' he said, cat and calendar synchronised.

TILT

The Boxing Day cricket test had been down in Melbourne and Australia had been dominating. Patrick had spent time on the couch yesterday, watching it with Ben. Neither of them had really been interested. Ben had spent most of the time with his new pencils and a colouring-in book Claire had bought him for Christmas.

Now Patrick was wandering around the old sandstone quarter of Sydney University, looking for professor Benson's office. Campus was deserted. A white security vehicle circled slowly and aimlessly. Workmen in high-vis vests were replacing paving stones. You needed a high-vis vest to change a light bulb these days, it seemed.

The office was on the second floor and Patrick was surprised to find the door into the stairwell unlocked. He took the magnificent wooden staircase up to a heavy door. He had never gone anywhere near here when he was a student. He knocked.

'Come,' professor Benson called from inside.

He opened the door to a room filled with books and light. It was a corner office, with stained glass in some of the windows. The professor was on his feet, circumnavigating an enormous wooden desk, hand extended, his checked shirt tucked into belted brown corduroy trousers.

'Patrick! Thank you for coming.' They shared a bone-crushing handshake and the professor covered it with his other hand and leaned in. 'And I apologise for knocking you at Anne's funeral. That was unforgiveable.'

'That'll explain why I haven't forgiven you.'

He rasped a loud laugh, still hanging on. 'Well done! Well done.' He let go. 'Take a seat.' He gestured to a green leather chair facing the enormous desk. 'Drink?'

'Scotch on a block of ice, please.' The key to the adult world.

'No ice, I'm afraid. They're thawing the fridge.'

Patrick guessed he was talking about the servants. He sat while the professor went to a sideboard. Floor-to-ceiling wooden bookcases displayed the spines of books. There was a photo of a younger Alice in a frame and sundry academic group shots.

The Professor handed him a heavy glass and placed a coaster on the desk in front of him. He went and sat back in his creaky chair on the other side of the desk and held his glass aloft. 'Here's to a better next year.'

'Indeed.' He sipped. Single malt. Glenmorangie, Patrick guessed. Sweet, citrus, easy.

They looked at one another.

'You got me into some trouble with Alice,' the professor said.

'I think you got yourself into that trouble.'

He nodded and drank. 'She likes you, by the way,' he said, as though his assessment was necessary. 'How did you know I'd been in touch with Anne?'

'Various sources.'

'Yes, but who?'

'I'd rather not say'

'Why not?'

'You might assault them.'

'Oh, nonsense! I've apologised for that. Please remember it was my daughter's funeral. I was overwrought.'

'I don't doubt it.'

He leaned forward. 'You know things about *my* daughter's death – and won't tell me. Have I got that right?'

He was intimidating and easy to dislike. Patrick was glad there was a desk between them. 'You've been keeping stuff to yourself too. Even from Alice.'

The professor frowned and leaned back. The chair creaked as it tilted. There was pressure in the long silence. 'A colleague who was drinking at the pub on the corner saw Anne go into that dreadful little house and told me. It was dumb luck that I found her.'

'Are you sorry you did?'

'Why would I be sorry?'

'You visited her one day and the next day she was dead.'

He leaned forward again and glared. 'How do you know when I visited her?'

'You were late back for a uni function.'

The professor looked momentarily baffled. 'Who the hell told you that?'

Patrick didn't answer. 'Is Alice OK?' he asked. It was a deliberate prod.

The professor drank and put his glass down carefully. 'I've told her the truth. I found Anne by chance. I went there to try to convince her – *yet again* – to do something with her life.'

It was plausible, Patrick thought, depending on other truths and secrets.

'You've got me pegged as some dangerous liar but Alice kept her own secrets from me. These are scenes from a marriage, Patrick. She'd been seeing Anne off and on. Trying to do just what I was trying to do, as it turns out.' All of that was true, Patrick knew. 'How's your marriage going, by the way?' the professor asked.

'Much better, thanks.' What a pissing contest. He'd asked Ben what he knew about Annie's father. He'd said, not much. He had never met him. Annie didn't like him, though.

'Do you think Annie was frightened of you?' This was Finnearty's version of her last days.

'Possibly. A lot of people are. But generally, I can see what's best.' He challenged Patrick with a stare.

He wasn't doing a very good job of picking Patrick's brain, if that's what they were here for, as Alice had said. He was too aggressive. 'How was your meeting with Annie?'

'Bloody terrible. You've seen the house, no doubt. Your boy was there, zonked out in bed in the middle of the afternoon.' His mentioning Ben and the room and Annie alive threw him off kilter and the professor saw it, and pressed it. 'Not so much fun, is it?' he asked.

So far, he'd been plausible. Nothing contradicted other versions Patrick had had of him.

'Had you seen Annie recently, before your day of dumb luck?'

Professor Benson shook his head slowly, wondering where this was going. 'No.'

'See, I think you're still lying. You got her a job with Semper and Hodge Pharmaceuticals a month before then. How did you manage that?'

'Well, well,' the professor said, leaning back, the chair creaking again. 'That's impressive. I don't know how you could possibly know about that. I don't even think Anne knew that.'

'She did.'

He was startled. 'Really?' He stared at the desk and seemed to be processing this.

'According to my sources,' Patrick said, softening. He tried not to move. Waited. Another scotch would be good. He wished Cooper was here. Why hadn't he left all this to Cooper? It was Alice's fault.

'I think I killed her,' the professor said, remorseful, eventually. 'With my interfering. Just by interfering. Why can't I leave her alone?'

Patrick breathed out. 'Why do you think that killed her?'

'Oh, I don't have to explain anything to you. Christ.'

'Why *did* you get her that job?'

'To get her out of the gutter she'd gotten herself into! Anne was a bright girl. She could have done so much more.' He stood up. He was very tall but no longer entirely upright. Gravity had got hold of him. He sat back down again. 'Tell me this. Who was supplying drugs to Anne?'

The room had tilted without a creak, so Patrick only felt it after it had happened. 'I don't know,' he lied.

'Really!' he shouted, suddenly furious. 'You know so much but you don't know that. What kind of fuckwit are you?' He stood up again, reinvigorated, and angry. He went to the bookcase and took down one of the framed group photographs and set it up on its stand on the desk, facing Patrick.

Patrick recognised the same photograph Alice had shown him in Mosman. Annie's graduation photo. When he shifted his gaze from the photograph, the professor was ready and waiting for him.

'Well, I've figured it out, you dumb cunt. It's Finnearty. The little shit! I knew his father.'

Patrick said nothing but panic coursed through him.

'I think we're about done here,' the professor said.

'Let's just leave all this to the police,' Patrick said.

'I'll take that as a confirmation on Finnearty. "Leave it to the police!" We tried that, didn't we? Both of us. They did two-thirds of fuck all.'

'Detective Cooper's still investigating,' he said. He wasn't. Not until the bold new year.

'Sorry,' the professor said. 'I need to lock up here. Would you mind?' He gestured to the door.

Patrick walked back to Forest Lodge. Thinking. He fed Eve. He phoned Alice. He avoided a drink. 'Is Stephen home yet?'

'No. How did it go?'

'Not well. He knows who was supplying drugs to Annie. I've got a terrible feeling he might go there. Can you call him? Stop him if you have to.'

'How does he know? Who is it?'

'Jeremy Finnearty. He owns a pharmacy on New South Head Road.'

There was a pause. 'We knew his father. That was his pharmacy.'

'Maybe Stephen's still on his way home. Will you call him?'

'I will. You sound odd. What kind of mood was Stephen in?'

'He threw me out of his office.'

'Sorry,' Alice said and ended the call. Patrick was sick of being a lone ranger. They had Ben back and all he wanted was for this to end. That's what Claire wanted, too. He wanted to swim with Ben again in a blue-green harbour, the world muffled by water.

His phone beeped a message. It was from Beth. *Hello old dog!* She had remembered! Bad timing. He had too many balls in the air.

He phoned Cooper and got his voice message. The world would resume on January 3. He left a voicemail. *Things are going wrong. Chemist Jeremy Finnearty on New South Head Road was supplying prescription drugs to Annie. Her father, professor Benson, is angry + might be on his way there now.*

He thought about phoning Andre, and decided against it. On the other hand, Andre might be the only one capable of stopping Stephen on a rampage. Semper and Hodge wouldn't want all this back in the news. Was he catastrophising? Would Benson really drive across town to confront Finnearty? Was the pharmacy even open between Christmas and the New Year? He Googled.

It was open. But was Finnearty there?

He texted Alice and asked her to let him know immediately when Stephen showed up. He watered the fading frangipani Christmas tree, then decided to put it back outside in the garden. He unclipped the sparse decorations.

He drove back to Balmain. It was a warm afternoon and the house was empty. The terrace doors were wide open. Ben's Christmas yoga mat was rolled out on the lawn. This is how life was meant to be, he thought.

Unless something was wrong. No. Claire would have called. This was just a summer's day. He walked back inside and turned on the cricket. The Australian tailenders were in. He went to the fridge and grabbed a beer. The air felt heavy.

He texted Alice again. *Is he back yet?*

Almost immediately, she texted back. *No. Not answering his phone.* Not good. Patrick felt adrenaline leaking into his bloodstream. His heart was suddenly belting. Where were Claire and Ben? He wanted them home and safe, though he knew they couldn't possibly be tangled in all this. Could they?

He Googled Finnearty Pharmacy again and pressed the number. After a long ring, a female answered.

'Is Jeremy at work there today?' he asked.

'Yes, he is.'

'Can I speak with him, please? It's important.'

'Well, he's got someone with him at the moment.'

'A customer?'

'Yes. He's down at the prescription counter.'

'Well, can I wait or can you transfer me through?'

'I can put... Sorry. There's someone...' There was a scream and the clatter of things falling over.

'Are you there?' he asked. 'Hello!'

More screaming. Men's angry voices. A woman's voice shouted at them to stop it. A gunshot exploded, impossibly loud through the phone, followed by sudden silence and then someone saying no, no, no.

'Are you there?' he asked. No answer. End. He dialled 000.

• • • •

'Where are you?' he asked Claire in a hurried call, straight after. 'We're nearly home. Ben wanted to see Jock in the squat. Is everything OK?'

'Just come home safely. I'm fine. I'll tell you when you get here.'

He texted Cooper. *I just called 000. Gunshot at pharmacy.*

His phone rang immediately. It was Cooper. 'Are you at the pharmacy?'

'No, I'm in Balmain. I was on the phone to warn Finnearty and I heard it all through the phone.'

'Stay put,' Cooper said. He ended the call.

Patrick wanted to stay put forever. What a clusterfuck. He was about to call Alice when she texted.

Stephen's on his way home now.

What? That didn't make sense. *How do you know?*

He texted.

Patrick wondered if he'd got the whole thing wrong. Maybe it was a just robbery gone wrong at the pharmacy. A coincidence.

But the timing and his sense of dread said it wasn't.

He texted Alice. *I think you should get out of the house.*

Texting Alice was unfair, he decided. He called her.

'What's going on?' Alice answered.

'How did he sound on the phone?'

'He didn't phone. He texted.'

'Sorry. Yes.'

'Patrick, what's going on? Just tell me.'

He took a breath. 'Stephen was angry when he threw me out of his office. I think he was planning to go and confront Finnearty and I phoned the pharmacy to warn him.' Another big breath. 'While I was on the phone, I could hear something going wrong. There was shouting and things breaking and there was a gunshot. And people screaming.'

Alice heard all this in silence. 'Are you saying Stephen may have been shot?'

No. 'Not if he's texted you. I called the police. Maybe Stephen had the gun.'

'But he hasn't got a gun!'

'I know all this sounds...'

She interrupted. 'Are you saying he made all that mayhem and then texted me to say he's on the way home?'

'All I'm doing is warning you. Letting you know as much as I know. If Stephen *was* there, whether he had a gun or not, he'll be dangerous when he gets home. We know what he's like.'

Patrick heard a car pull into the driveway outside. Claire and Ben were home. Things were normal. Staying put.

'Where would I go?' Alice asked.

'Sorry?'

'If I left the house, where would I go? We've got a garden shed.'

'No. Don't go there.' Patrick thought about it. Claire walked in and saw him and looked worried. 'Come here,' he said. 'Get in a taxi and come here. Fifty-three Nelson Street, Balmain.' Claire was shaking her

234

head and saying a silent no. To what, or to who? She didn't know, but she wanted the house to themselves.

'He'll need me,' Alice said.

'It's up to you. I think you should get out of there. You can be there for him once we know what's happened.'

She hung up.

'What was that all about?' Claire asked. Ben stood in the background with his hands on his hips. Patrick smiled at him. He hoped it was a smile. Maybe it was a grimace. What must he be thinking of this 'real' world?

'You saved Denise. Now I'm trying to save Alice. That's Annie's mum,' he said to Ben over Claire's shoulder.

Ben nodded. 'I know.'

'Things have gone wrong,' Patrick said and went and hugged Claire. She hugged back and he held her and let her soothe his bones.

Then let go. 'I've got to text Cooper.'

Prof texted Alice. He's heading home. She's coming here for safety.

THE FUCKING WORLD

The Rose Bay police attended four minutes after several 000 calls. Armed police cordoned off New South Head Road. Ambulances arrived from St Vincent's Hospital in Darlinghurst. Sirens approached from every direction. Fifteen minutes after the first contact, a crime scene had been established and the shopping strip had been evacuated and locked down. Witnesses were being interviewed.

There was chaos and control in equal measure. Luckily half of Sydney had already headed for the coast, otherwise chaos would have won.

Soon media helicopters swooped in loud circles overhead and journalists did pieces live to camera from the hastily arranged cordons. They prodded locals who couldn't believe this was happening in their neighbourhood.

Stuart phoned him. 'Are you OK, mate?'

'Yes. Though feeling worse by the minute.'

'Is this all what I think it is?'

'Very likely. I've let Cooper know. We're all in Balmain. We're OK.'

'Well, stay put.'

'That's just what Cooper said.'

'Do as you're told.'

'Thanks, Stuart. Will do.'

· · · ·

Stephen arrived home and parked the Audi in the driveway. It felt like there was a glaze on things. He couldn't feel his fingers on the door handle as he got out of the car. He couldn't feel the keys in his hand as he unlocked the house. He was surprised the door opened.

'Alice!' he called. 'I'm home.' Silence thrummed in his ears. 'Alice?'

He looked out at the garden. It was quiet and green. Eden beyond a double glaze. They both loved gardening, and then a drink on the patio at the end of the afternoon. Sometimes they left their gardening gloves on for the strangeness of drinking such clear gin with such dirty gloves. And no sense of touch.

No-one knows what goes on in a family.

Why couldn't he feel his fingers? It was strange. Standing there, he couldn't feel his outline either, or his shape. He didn't feel like a person any more.

It was only days ago he and Alice had shared a bath after a sad and silent afternoon pruning the burnt edges of the summer garden. Alice was beautiful in the bath, her breasts worn and low, her limbs finely lined with age like a pencil drawing. She had pressed the arch of her foot gently against the loose swell of his balls. It had been a perfect moment in a house somewhere.

'Alice!' he called again. She wasn't there. No-one was there. Not Anne. Not Alice.

Where was the gun? He'd left it in the car. On the passenger seat. What a passenger. He supposed the police would be here soon. You can't just go around killing people, even if they deserve it.

Annie, get your gun. He smiled. He went out to the car and got it. It felt lethal in his hand, now that he'd used it. He could hear sirens in the background. They were coming for him, he knew. It wasn't a fire or a crash at an intersection. Where was Alice?

When he went back into the house, he saw her on the back lawn in her yellow dress. She was standing barefoot. He was suddenly unsure of he was seeing. She didn't move, just stood there, looking at him. She seemed to be floating. He opened the door.

'Where have you been?' he asked. 'I've been calling.'

'Why have you got a gun?'

He looked down at his hand. What was she talking about?

Wrong hand. He looked at his other hand and saw the gun. It was so heavy. The grip had beautiful fine serrations in the metal. Who designed these things? The fucking world.

He looked back at her. 'Well, that's the thing, my love. Our family's dead,' he said. 'Are you with me?'

'I'm with you, but I want you to put the gun down. Where did you get it from?'

'There's still things to be done.'

'What things?'

'Us. There's us to be done.'

'That's nonsense. Put the gun down.'

'You'll be pleased to know I've killed the man who killed our Anne. Jeremy Finnearty. He admitted it! He confessed to the monster. That's what he called me. A monster. Him! The little shit!'

Sirens arrived on the street. The dog next door started barking. Molly. Stephen walked out onto the patio and looked up as if the sirens might be there in mid-air. 'That's all for me, isn't it?'

'I think so. But we can explain it.'

He shook his head. 'All that fucking...' he gagged and vomited on the flagstones.

'I'll get you a glass of water,' she said. She walked across the lawn and rubbed her hand on his stooped back as she passed. Felt his spine.

'Don't let them in!' he hissed.

'I won't. We can take our time. Why don't you sit down out here?'

He stood upright instead. The gun was the weight of the world.

Alice went and opened the front door. There were police cars in the street and red and blue lights that lit the underside of leaves on the trees. Their trees. There were police in the driveway in black bulletproof vests, with rifles. She put her hands in the air. Surrender. Surrender that life you had with its familiar faults and occasional bliss.

'He's out the back,' she said to the nearest person – a man in a suit. 'He has a gun.' The man motioned with his hand for her to come towards him. 'He's having a stress attack,' she said.

'Madam, please come to me now. Now!' He stepped towards her and she stepped towards him. She was whisked away into other arms. The dance was over already.

Out the back of the house, Stephen went to the wooden garden shed. He could smell potting mix and see cobwebs in the window in the afternoon sun. There were punnets of pansies to be planted. At the right time, in the right place, the world is beautiful.

He put the gun in his mouth and pulled the trigger.

There were jurisdictional issues for the police. This case was leaving bodies all over Sydney but it was Detective Senior Constable Dowse from Rose Bay who interviewed Patrick the next day, with Cooper sitting in. His holiday up the coast was over early. The world had ended, and resumed, before the third of January after all. Cooper looked irritated.

Dowse had Patrick recount the details of his meeting with the professor just before he had driven to Double Bay and murdered Finnearty. What had his mood been like? Had Patrick known that he had a gun? Had he made his intentions known? On and on.

Then it was Cooper's turn. New evidence suggested he had a murder to solve too. Had Finnearty ever confessed or implied that he had murdered Anne Benson? No, Patrick said; the opposite. What had he said about the nature of his relationship with her? On and on.

Patrick didn't tell them about the diaries. Dowse would have had his guts for garters. Cooper too. And what was the point now? He didn't want to jeopardise whatever good work Beth might quietly achieve with them.

'I'll need to interview Ben as well,' Cooper said, eventually, but his gaze was kind. Patrick nodded. He didn't know what new evidence Cooper had but it didn't seem to incriminate Ben. It seemed Finnearty was responsible after all.

For the first time since Patrick had answered that telephone call from Ben, way back when, he felt like this would soon be over.

Alice hadn't come to them yesterday after all. She had been there for Stephen, as she had said she would be. She was staying at a friend's house and two of her sisters had driven down from the Hunter Valley. She had gotten a message to Patrick, thanking him. He got the bare bones of what had happened. At least Alice had been spared the very worst of it.

Or was that yet to come?

Claire provided context to fellow ABC news journalists but kept her family out of it. A murder-suicide involving a prominent academic in the quiet news days after Christmas was briefly big news, but in the end, nothing could conquer the stun of summer, and the cricket. The days began to resume their old shape.

Patrick stayed in Balmain in the 'spa' bedroom, with daily trips back to Forest Lodge to feed Eve and water the garden. How long could this go on? He texted Helln and wondered if she still needed somewhere to stay. She could sleep with Eve, he offered. It turned out Helln was in Bellingen way up the north coast. It was too expensive in Sydney.

'Helln in Belln,' Ben declared.

'Hell's Bells,' Claire joined in. They laughed like a family in a sitcom. He played Helln's CD to teach them both a lesson and they all agreed it was good. Wispy guitar and lovelorn lyrics. Men are bastards. But not all men.

They took down the decorations and put the Christmas tree out the front, to wait for the green recycling collection. Patrick thought about that article he had written decades ago now.

Ben set himself the task of 'reading' both giant dictionaries. Was that good or bad, they wondered. Or mad? There were other mild signs of mania in Ben's behaviour. He did yoga endlessly on the lawn long after they both thought he should stop. Patrick interrupted under the pretence of wanting to learn some poses. He enjoyed what Ben showed him. He was a good teacher. Ben completed his Christmas colouring-in book within days and bought some more. He took daily swims down in the harbour pool, regardless of the weather. He insisted on some foods and refused others. 'Listen to my body,' he would say to them, as if they could hear it too. But the torment and mood swings so far remained at bay.

It was remarkable.

Philip arrived back from Hobart and Claire went out to meet him somewhere. She dressed up, Patrick noticed. There was no suggestion that he might visit Balmain. To collect his shit sandals and accounting magazines. Patrick knew the balance had tipped his way, with Ben at home and all of them together.

The old year pulsed, worn out but relentless, towards a new year. Fireworks off the Sydney Harbour Bridge and from a nearby Balmain barge. From everywhere. Sydney goes mad for its crackers. They went down to a pocket park where they used to go when Ben and his friends were boys and their families were easy friends. Sleepovers. Sport. Wine in back gardens. PlayStation. Claire had texted those families, wondering about New Year's Eve plans, and a few of them were in the park again, or still, with sons and daughters who were around. Ben loved it. They all did.

Days later, Ben was on his yoga mat on the lawn, finished at last, baggy shorts and no shirt, a little more buff already. He no longer looked like he would break if you hugged him. Patrick was on the terrace with a cup of coffee.

'Do you want a job?' he asked Ben.

'Not really,' Ben replied.

Patrick could hardly blame him. 'It wasn't an idle question. What if I got you a job with someone Annie was working with?'

Ben's arms were flung back on the lawn above his head, armpits of blond hair showing. He looked ten feet tall and flat like a piece of paper. 'How? That would be insane.'

'I know someone who was working on Annie's med mix for you. And for the guy before you.'

'Moon?'

'Yes! Moon. So, Annie talked with you about other... what were you?'

'I was her boyfriend, Dad. We fucked.' He paused. 'Often.'

'Glad to hear it.' He remembered what Evan had said. Maybe Ben had been in the universe long enough to be cured. It seemed so, so far. 'His name's Evan, by the way. Why were you Fish?'

Ben rolled over onto his front, propped himself on his elbows and looked at him. 'I wish I wish I was a fish. See it quiver. Yes. The river.' He smiled.

It was mad and beautiful. Patrick decided to accept it as delivered.

'So, her name's Beth. This person. She's lovely. Annie liked her. All you'd have to do is talk with her.'

'Is that a job?'

'Not really.'

Ben picked at the lawn. 'I admire you, Dad. I do.'

Side-swiped, Patrick's nerves tingled. 'Thanks, Ben.'

'It drives Mum crazy how lazy you are.'

Family wounds. 'Did she say that?'

Ben smiled again and shook his head. 'Not lately. She seems to like you again.'

'Are you trying to get us back together?'

'If I could, I would. Give me some tips,' he said keenly.

The world sped up, slowed down. Stopped. After everything. This. 'Ben, I cannot – cannot – tell you how much I love you.' Ben rolled over onto his back again and did some sort of arm dance at the sky. 'My tip is for you to be well and stay well and be you,' Patrick said. 'That's my tip. That'll work.'

A cruise ship blew its horn three times in the harbour, calling passengers back on board, out of the Sydney bars and brothels and galleries. Sailing to Vanuatu at 16.00.

THE BEGINNING. THE END.

Flowers were falling from the summer trees. The footpaths were covered with them.

Ben got the 'job'. Ludicrously, he was determined to wear a collar and tie to meet Beth. He came into the kitchen looking young and handsome. 'I borrowed one of your ties,' he said but Patrick didn't recognise it. It was one of Philip's. Modern life. He admitted to himself it was a good tie, especially on Ben.

'You look great!'

He dropped Ben off at a cafe near Central for a meeting with Beth in broad daylight, to see where things might lead. No cloak and dagger this time. They'd copied the diaries and Patrick had handed the origi-nals over to Beth, after a meeting where Semper and Hodge had agreed Beth would be retained as leader of "Plan A". Plan Anne.

Andre didn't talk to Patrick any more. He didn't really understand why. Probably because he didn't need to, and Patrick had kicked his arse on finding the diaries.

Beth was 'super excited' about the potential in Annie's research. She envisaged a new holistic approach to treating mental illness. There would be trials and drugs, of course, but conducted through H and S wellness centres and retreats, with dieticians, mentors, yogis and yogi-nis. They couldn't go where Annie had gone – the sex and soul that were part of her trials, the LSD, 'finding the centre' – but it was excit-ing. Ben was on the books as a consultant.

Now Patrick was on his way to meet with Cooper. They met in the enclosed courtyard out the back of Sappho Books on Glebe Point Road. It was a weekday and they found a small table away from the rest, up against a wall of bold graffiti. Patrick grabbed a bottle of water and two tumblers. Soft jazz played from speakers in the trees. There were students leaning into one another, a brightly dressed older women read-ing a magazine, a man working on a laptop. Glebe in all its glory.

It was a hot morning and Cooper was in a short-sleeved shirt. Who loses weight over Christmas, Patrick wondered, but Cooper had.

'Thanks for coming,' Patrick said, pouring water. 'It's probably not worth asking, but how were your holidays?'

'Short.'

'And thanks for being kind with Ben, by the way. You're the best cop ever, apparently.'

Cooper smiled. 'He's a nice young man. We had enough evidence on Finnearty and it was good to put his mind at ease. We didn't need to hit him with a phone book.'

'Do you ever do that, by the way?'

'Only on TV.'

'I don't suppose you have phone books any more anyway.'

'Oh, I'm sure I could find one in a broken cupboard at the station if I had to.'

A young Asian waitress appeared with their coffees and smiled. 'Enjoy!' Cooper tore and stirred two bags of sugar into his.

Jazz. Warmth. 'So! Cases solved?' Patrick asked.

'Pretty much. Plenty of witnesses for the murder. The suicide solved itself, with very sad testimony from Alice. She didn't deserve any of this. None of them did.'

'Not Finnearty?' Patrick asked.

'Maybe him. Alice said the professor got a confession out of him before he shot him.'

'I suppose a gun's even better than a phone book when you're after a confession,' Patrick said.

'You ever thought of being a cop? You've got the gallows humour.'

'Now all I need is the training, the badge and the courage.'

Cooper grinned. 'You've done alright. We stuffed it up in the end.'

The 'we' was kind. 'I'm sorry. But I didn't *know* what I knew. I was making it up as I went.'

'All the more reason you should have told me! I don't make it up, Patrick, and I've done it before. I can go places and do things you wouldn't believe.' He sipped his coffee, as if to stop himself from saying more.

Patrick knew that he'd put Cooper in a world of professional pain. He accepted the rebuke, though he wanted to say that once things had started, they hadn't seemed to stop.

'And Annie?' Back to where it all began.

Cooper shook his head, some private regret, or anger. 'At least Finnearty had no chance to destroy evidence. The safe up in that room.' They looked at each other. 'There was a key to Forest Street...'

'He told me he didn't know where she lived!' Patrick said.

'Of course he did. The address was in the GPS in his car. He was there the night Annie died. With a key. We didn't need the pub CCTV in the end.'

Patrick was amazed. It all sounded so logical, when for so long it had seemed so hard and obscure. He assumed now that Annie hadn't given Finnearty the diaries after all. Why would she have? They'd been in the safe too, further evidence that he'd been to Forest Street at some stage to collect them. He'd offloaded them to Patrick with another lie. Maybe all those hints about the professor abusing Annie were lies too. All of it.

'What about the CCTV at his end?' Patrick asked.

'Yes. Annie came and went. Quite often. We also found her phone in the safe. As well as heroin with a batch match to the fatal dose in Annie's arm.'

'Fucking hell, he's a cool customer,' Patrick said, leaning back. 'I sat up there with him for an hour. He convinced me. I'm usually pretty good at reading people.'

Cooper shrugged his shoulders.

'And he *did* have a chance to destroy the evidence! He had weeks. Why would he keep all that stuff?'

'Trophies? There were sexual acts filmed on his phone.'

Say no more. Even so. It was stupid. Craven. 'Leave me alone,' Finnearty had demanded of Patrick. He had gotten his family Christmas, but not much more. Maybe he got what he deserved. But his family hadn't deserved it.

'What about that red dart?' Patrick asked.

'No idea. Red dart, red herring? Inserted post mortem, according to forensics. Maybe he thought we'd blame your son.'

It had almost worked. It had even had Patrick wondering. He tried to envisage what had happened in that room. That bed. His head reeled at the prospect of Finnearty beside the bed, supervising Annie's death and then waiting to mutilate her. A violent vigil while Ben slept.

'Ben had smoked dope that night,' Patrick said, still making excuses. Or maybe it was an apology.

Cooper nodded. 'And on who knows what mix of medications.'

Patrick knew. He poured more water. The coffee tasted too strong, even for him. 'It's mad. The whole thing.'

'It usually is,' Cooper said wearily. 'How was the professor's funeral?'

'Terrible. Not much of a turnout, even from the uni. It was at the same crematorium, though a different chapel. Poor Alice.'

'Yes. Finnearty wasn't meant to be there that day, by the way,' Cooper said. 'In the pharmacy. He was on leave until the new year but there'd been some mix-up on prescriptions and he went in to sort it out.'

Patrick shook his head.

'Indeed,' Cooper said. 'Those what-ifs attach themselves to every murder I've ever investigated.'

He thought about Professor Benson's 'dumb luck' in finding Annie; he had said someone had seen her walking into a house.

The courtyard was beginning to fill with an early lunchtime crowd. 'Do you want another coffee?' Patrick asked. 'Or one of those clever cocktails up on the blackboard?' Tequila Mockingbird.

Cooper looked at his watch. 'I better get back.' Their chairs scraped on the concrete. Cooper offered his hand. 'Thanks for your help.'

Patrick shook the strong grip. 'I'm sorry.'

'Sorry comes with the turf in this line of work. Happy new year.'

'You too.' He watched Cooper turn and leave.

He walked home via Forest Street. There was a FOR LEASE sign in the front yard of 102. That stopped him. He called Mick. *"The number you have called is not connected. Please check the number and try again."* He was gone, maybe all the way back to Ireland.

Miss the start, miss the end. Households and generations move through these old houses like a breeze at the end of a warm day. He stood in front of the real estate sign and the sad facade.

There was that brick in the front yard.

He stepped over the low wall and picked it up. Heavy and brown, it was warm now. The earth where it had been sitting was dead. He carried it back to his place. A mad burden. He put it on the small table out on his deck and looked at it. He couldn't figure out what it meant, but he knew it meant something. Somewhere? The past?

Maybe Ben could find the meaning in his dictionary.

He fed Eve. She was affectionate and sick of living alone. 'I agree,' he said to her. 'I'll have a talk about where we're all going to live.'

Then he drove back to Balmain.

YOGA BOYS

Alice was visiting Balmain at last. It was another warm day. Patrick and Ben were doing yoga down on the flat bit of the lawn by the swing. They were in shorts and shirtless. Patrick had a good body, but alongside Ben he looked old. Claire wished he would put a shirt on, especially in front of their guest.

'Ben's a beautiful boy,' Alice said after a while. Their wine glasses were on a wooden table between them.

'He is. Funny, that's just what we say about him too. Beautiful Ben Boy.'

'When he said Annie was like the sun...' She crumpled and looked away.

'It's OK.' They were up on the terrace, slumped in deck chairs. Claire's foot was near to Alice's foot and she nudged it gently.

'I'm glad he was with her,' Alice said.

When she died. 'We're glad too. She saved him. It's amazing and revolutionary. Incredible.'

'That's what she called herself. A revolutionary.'

'She was right.'

'When will that *Four Corners* episode go to air?'

'It'll be a couple of months yet. I'll show you the rough cut. Thanks again for agreeing to be interviewed.'

'Well, I'm proud of her,' Alice said, looking at Claire. 'That's about all I've got left.'

'It might sound trite but you've got us too.' She nodded down the lawn. 'This Ben is Annie's gift to us. To you, as well.'

Eve appeared from the house and walked slowly down the lawn to join the yoga boys. She rolled onto her back, legs akimbo, black against the green, an upward cat to their downward dogs.

IN THE END. ANNIE.

S he'd said she wanted to stop. Yet again.
    He thought about it. So did he, this time. He would make that happen, and clean up the mess she'd made in his life. It would be an 'accident' – like her meeting him in the street that time when his life was coiled around him like a python.

He knew where she lived. He'd followed and found her other life months ago. He had copied a front-door key from her bag, just in case. She had waltzed into his world, and now he could waltz into hers. He'd spent a couple of nights watching her with her fuck-up boyfriend, skinny as a rake. These were the people she was saving, apparently.

He wasn't jealous. It had been fun having sex with someone who was saving the world.

He parked in her street. Late, but not too late. He wasn't fixed on how all this would go. He'd planned it, but it didn't have to happen tonight. The prospect of being free of her thrilled him. She had said she had other plans now but he couldn't trust her. Or himself.

He knew she travelled lightly, and was a mad mess. He guessed her diaries were in that front room somewhere with all her earthly possessions, including her skinny boyfriend.

He grabbed his night goggles and the small diabetic care kit he'd repurposed: a loaded disposable syringe, face mask, gloves, chloroform just in case. He wriggled his fingers into latex gloves and pulled up his black hoodie. There was a pub down on the corner and there might be CCTV.

He wondered what Annie was on, what her home habits were. If she had Valium in her, it would help his cause.

He stepped over the low wall and paused by the front door. Silence from inside. No TV or music. No footsteps or pillow talk. A house asleep now. He inserted the key into the lock and let the door inch open. Waited a full minute. He could smell dope. That would help too. He started to believe tonight was the night.

He stepped inside. Listened. He put on a surgical face mask and his night vision goggles. The place suddenly appeared like a dark cave. He opened the door to the bedroom. Two bodies in the bed, green line drawings. Annie on the side nearest to him, on her back, her arms and breasts exposed. Those dark nipples. Boyfriend on his side, facing the wall. Snoring. Everything and everyone still.

He looked around and approached the bookcase. Her diaries were right there, stacked on top of each other, too easy.

He listened to the house. Snoring. He could hear the pub down on the corner. And his own breathing. He felt nervous as he knelt by the bed. The kit. The syringe. Annie lay ready, like she was waiting for him to fill her one last time, like he was doing her a favour, her arm right there. He delivered a subcutaneous injection to minimise whatever rush she might experience. She didn't flinch. Her breathing slowed. He waited. The boyfriend snored.

He saw a dart stored carefully beside her pillow, just so. She took a dart to bed! Why would she do that? A weapon against her boyfriend? A defence for when he got weird?

Her breathing was slowing now. Sometimes she didn't breathe at all. He waited. This was going to work. She wasn't breathing.

He put the syringe into her right hand and fingered the fix he'd already delivered. He dropped the syringe into the folds of the sheet. His head ached, suddenly and severely. Maybe it was the night goggles. He looked at the curve of her boyfriend, asleep against the wall. What did he know about life? Fuck all.

He picked up the dart and put it in her other hand and used her fingers to press it into the bullseye of his injection. Let it be weird, then. This was your life. Now leave me alone.

He stood up and collected his kit. His headache was intense but he made it to the door and made it outside. Sweet fresh air! A new world. He was tingling.

He'd be home soon with the family he now loved, and wanted.

ROBERT EDSALL

. . . .

Don't miss out!

Visit the website below and you can sign up to receive emails whenever Robert Edsall publishes a new book. There's no charge and no obligation.

https://books2read.com/r/B-A-ZEOV-BRKCC

BOOKS 2 READ

Connecting independent readers to independent writers.

About the Author

Robert Edsall has been a newspaper columnist, government censor, freelance writer, and frequent wage slave so he can pay the bills. This is his first novel. He lives in Sydney with a person named Robinson and a cat named Nina.

Ingram Content Group UK Ltd.
Milton Keynes UK
UKHW042206080323
418239UK00001B/164